The Silver Lining

By: L. Concepcion

Chapter 1

CASSIUS

No no, wait...please. Stop! Mom...MOM!
"Baby be strong, stay strong for momma."
"Mom, no they're going to kill you"
"My son, I love you, please look away. Be strong for momma."

No, what did they do to my mom? I looked away from her like she told me to, but I could still hear it. Within the cramped room we were in that I was sure was the back of a butcher shop, I could hear her screams echo. The sounds of them cutting her open in repeated torture using tools that were meant for cows and pigs. The cracking of her bones was barely audible as mom screamed even louder. Blood splashed onto the dirty white tiled floor as her life spilled.

Mama's voice was deafening, so loud I couldn't hear my thoughts. I couldn't look nor did I want to. To have to witness my mother in such agony was not how I wanted to remember her, but I was already traumatized. The fear of what I might see held me back from witnessing what they were doing because by the sounds of it, it was a fate worse than death.

With my eyes firmly shut, I rocked myself holding onto my knees. For as long as I can remember, which wasn't even that long since I was only eight years old, I would rock myself and hum to deal with anxiety. There were times before when I would have nightmares when I used to live with my father, and I would hear noises that terrified me at night. Since he rarely answered when I called out to him, I rocked myself to self-soothe. Mother calling out my name brought me out of the thoughts I distracted myself with and back into the horror we were living. Then the words of a song my mom used to sing floated into my mind.

No, something was weird. It was her actual voice that somehow flowed into my thoughts. As if she was telepathic and talking to me in secret. Mom sang to me my favorite song. So, I hummed to the words flowing through my mind in tears because it felt like a goodbye. I wasn't sure how I knew that. It could have been the sadness in her words despite it being a joyful song.

While it made me feel a bit better, her voice became weak and then it stopped. Within the silence that filled both my mind and the cold room, one message was clear, she was gone. I no longer had a mother that could sing to me. Or a mother that could make me dinner and laugh at the silly jokes I made in between bites. The quiet that filled the rancid air was louder than the sound of the boots approaching me.

I opened my eyes and looked over my shoulder holding my breath due to the putrid smell that encased the man. But what I saw left me wanting to throw up my innards as I gagged at the sight of his bloody mess. His clothes were a mix of old and new blood with what I was sure were pieces of bone. My mother's life was displayed on his clothes as if it were just another day at a slaughterhouse. A blood-stained hand that gripped my shoulder and...

"MOM!" I woke up in sweat to yet another nightmare. My hands trembled and the tears that burned my eyes fell freely to the wet pillow beneath me. It had already been over a decade and my memories of that day continued to haunt me. I relived it in my mind like a permanent resident too stubborn to leave me in peace. Too stubborn to let me heal. The details of what they did to my mother along with the smell of blood, ingrained themselves too deep to forget. The scars carved themselves into my bones unwilling to heal no matter how much time had passed.

Then like clockwork, they festered every time my dreams took hold and imprisoned me within the confines of my mind. If I could release myself from the nightmares I would but there were times I thought that this was the only way to keep my mother close. Her smiling face was becoming harder to recall, as her smile was replaced with each agonizing nightmare.

With the sheet I slept on, I wiped the sweat from my face and clicked my tongue at my shirt which clung to my body. "It's hot in here," I mumbled but that was not true. It was my body that was overheating. The nightmare must have given me a low-grade fever from the distress. I knew this all too well. A growl erupted in my chest at not being able to get my mother's pained face out of my mind. Instead, it lingered like a burned afterimage that wouldn't go away. I hated that it was the last thing I saw before she died.

Thinking back to just before our fate took a turn, it was just past breakfast, and mom was walking with me in the woods to pick some wildflowers. At eight years old they all looked the same, so I grabbed a bunch that I thought were pretty. Little did I know that they were mainly weeds but the yellows, whites, and blues mixed so well together. Who knew weeds could be pretty too? All I wanted to do was make mom happy by giving her something colorful to set on the table at home.

Mom laughed when I handed the bouquet of weeds, I had so neatly wrapped in an old newspaper for her. She patted my head and did a small courtesy which made me giggle when the sound of a branch breaking caught our ears. Mom knew the immediate danger we were in while I simply followed her lead. We dropped everything and ran but the men behind us ran faster.

Eventually I had then woken up to the torture from the men that caught us. My mother screamed when she saw the abuse that the men relished in providing me. But it was nothing compared to how my mother drowned in her own hell as well. Every day they made me watch what they did to her. They traded off in doing sexual things and painful agonizing things. Despite their efforts to force me to watch, I closed my eyes almost through all of it. I refused to watch my mother suffer and prayed for my father to save us, but he was nowhere to be seen.

We had to endure for two weeks before they had the nerve to kill her. At such a young age my mind simply broke under the gravity of it all. While at first, I was confused as to why it suddenly became quiet, I quickly realized with the blood on his hands that I no longer could call out for momma.

I waited like an empty shell for them to unchain me from the silver that had held me down. I knew it was my turn since they had only focused on momma for their cruel pleasure. One of them placed me back in my cell while the one that killed momma washed up. However, the one that placed me in the cell didn't leave. Instead, he eyed me with a hunger so vile, his face contorted and then he touched me.

His rough calloused hands ran over my clothes until he reached my private parts. I wanted to throw up when I realized he was about to do to me what he did to momma. I couldn't think straight with fear but the moment he ripped my shirt open a thought became clear. No matter what, I had to survive. Unlike momma, my hands were left untied and that was mistake number one. Mistake number two was the dirty weapon the pedophile in front of me had unsecured on his hip.

I feigned compliance to allow the man to get closer to me and like the pervert that he was, he enjoyed how easy it was. It wasn't until I heard the shower of the other man turn off that I put my escape into action. The second the monster leaned into me to place his dirty lips to my neck, I grabbed the knife from the pedophile's holster and attacked him. With screams of rage and anguish, I didn't stop until he ceased moving.

I had never felt so much anger inside of me, so much so that I would lose control like I did. This was the first time that I even held a knife as a weapon and the revenge I sought, the defense I held, left me feeling worse. Looking at the corpse in front of me I panicked despite how he was deserving of his fate for what he did. I stared at the crimson that bathed me, but I didn't feel better. The pain in my chest and the longing I had to see momma one more time lingered even more.

So, I ran. I ran away and hid in the woods. I ran so that I could find a way to live no matter the cost. It was the only thing I could do since I had nowhere to go. Horrible unspeakable things still bled in my memory of my mother. If I knew then what I knew now as an adult, I would have tried to finish off the other man that was in the shower. Then again, that easily could have meant the end of my own life. Thinking back, I got lucky with being able to escape the man that molested me.

My young naive mind didn't even know that those men and the ones around today were of the same kind. They were all hunters. Nasty, vile hunters that liked to kill our kind out of ignorance and pure enjoyment. They treated my kind like a game during hunting season to fulfill some sick ego trip. I never understood how people could hunt as a sport. Too many wolves have been killed because of this. If our kind wasn't hidden well, we sometimes went a long period of time without shifting out of fear of being shot for sport.

I climbed out of the bed and dragged my tired body to the bathroom to shower away the sweat that dried onto my skin. It was thirteen years ago today and it still felt like yesterday. Like clockwork, my body remembered and into the pit of despair I walked until my sorrows retreated, only to return the following year. My sweet mother didn't deserve the death that she got nor did my father deserve her kindness.

The hot water pelted against my skin in rhythmic patterns, massaging away my tension ridden shoulders. It was the best feeling to stand under the scorching water so it could knead out the remnants of my nightmare. I lathered my body and cleansed the stench I developed from sweating through my fever. Ever since moving into this packhouse, I could no longer see myself bathing in the river like I did before. Then again, at that time I didn't have a choice.

After surviving in the woods for a year as a kid, sleeping by a large rock in my makeshift canopy, I came to live here. The Alpha at the time, Jude, blessed me with this home and a new family. Everyone was kind and loving even though we didn't share any kind of kinship. I was a stranger to them, but I was sure they took pity due to how malnourished I was when they found me. Yet as if it were nothing, they offered me my space and a place to call home. In return, I eventually told them my story since they truly were good-hearted people. And because of it, growing up, I never felt like I was anything else but their own.

It wasn't until my 10th birthday that they decided to take the chance and told me how they found me and how special we all were. They told me how I was actually a werewolf, and it was my unique smell as a wolf that alerted them of my presence during one of their runs. They explained that I was living in a packhouse and that every member of the family was also a wolf. It was like something out of a novel, but it made sense the more I thought about it.

Small things that I overlooked made sense if we were indeed wolves. I never knew I was anything special growing up and never suspected it either because of how distant my father and family were with me and my mom. When my mother was alive, she and I would sleep away from everyone. Our cottage was very much out of the way while everyone else lived close to one another. So, the knowledge of who I was, never occurred to me and mother never shifted in front of me either.

Kristofer, the current Alpha, and son of the Alpha that saved me, never failed to mention that the smell of my wolf was peculiar. The night I was found, everyone was caught off guard. Everyone expected a great and mighty wolf, only to find me sleeping in a fetal position from the cold. While all wolves had distinctive smells, he said mine was more distinguished than others and slightly intimidating, but he couldn't place why. Quite frankly as long as I didn't stink, it didn't faze me one way or the other.

Growing up and even now as an adult, Kristofer was almost like an older brother to me. He could be dry at times and wasn't a touchy-feely kind of wolf but he was always there when anyone needed him. I admired his strength and how everyone looked up to him because of it. He made living in an unfamiliar house fun because he always made sure I was involved in everything. While of course it wasn't always rainbows and butterflies since we did squabble at times, I wouldn't trade it for the world.

On the night of my birthday, when my wolf revealed himself under the full moon for the first time, the rest was history. My life took on a whole new meaning and I felt empowered. I sighed at the distant childhood memory. I would love to see my mom again or at least tell her that I survived and lived well. Then again if everything I learned about wolves was true then she might already know. She was most likely looking over me if she hadn't already reincarnated. I'll never forget the feeling of finally thinking to myself that as a wolf I could finally do something about my mother's death. Yet, as time went on, I realized it was a foolish thought. The hunters that killed her were long gone and I had no other lead. If anything, it would just start a useless cycle of death between hunters and wolves.

I looked out of the bathroom window smiling at how well the pack took care of me. My life had been comfortable considering how I got here. The sun was barely up, and my mind was too alert to try and fall back asleep. While the shower did well to help me cleanse my body and my thoughts, going back to sleep was not an option. My wolf, who I named Wolfie, howled inside agreeing to me starting my day instead. It made me chuckle as I recalled my first shift as Wolfie. The first time I ran with my wolf, I felt something I never felt before, freedom. It was at that moment that I knew I would be okay.

I wrapped a towel around my waist and stepped into my room. It grew warmer and brighter by the rays of delight bouncing off my poster-covered walls. Celebrity posters graced my room along with a few rock bands I loved. Kristofer poked fun constantly because he said I shouldn't have a childish room at twenty-one, but I liked how it was. My room was my own little world. The gold sunlight filtered into the rest of the room, casting a shadow of the windowpane down my wall and onto the floor. "I should really clean this room up," I mumbled but my stomach complained and that was enough reason to change and get some breakfast, leaving the cleanup for later.

With my room on the first floor, it was easy to not wake anyone, or at least it usually was. It wouldn't surprise me in the least if my shouting myself awake from the nightmare this morning woke someone up. I tip-toed on the parts of the wooden floor I knew wouldn't creak and made my way to the kitchen. A small habit I had formed from the number of times that I snuck out of my room in the middle of the night. While I wasn't always sneaking out of the house, I did often sneak into the kitchen to eat leftovers of Cecile's cooking.

"What are you doing up so early?" A soft whisper spoke from the shadows of the kitchen. I froze mid step, caught trying to be quiet. With the kitchen on the opposite side of the house, the sun didn't brighten it up right away, which left me with but a shadow to talk to. I flicked on the switch and spotted Cecile in sheep pajamas standing against the counter with a steaming mug. The coffee she brewed filled the kitchen in richness and a hit of cinnamon.

Cecile was Kristofer's mother and the former Luna to the packhouse. Most of all, she was like my best friend. She took a sip and hummed as the hot liquid consumed her waiting for my answer.

"Jeez, Cecile you scared the hell outta me." I grabbed my chest and feigned myself dramatically dying in slow motion to my knees. She chuckled in her sweet soft voice and took a seat in the pulled-out chair by the breakfast table. Looking around the kitchen, almost half expecting for someone else to speak from the lessening shadows, I smirked at my foolish thought.

The kitchen itself was huge but still it was comfortable with a very country aesthetic. Everything was made of dark wood with antique hand crafted knobs. The stove was old and gas-powered with pots that hung above it and a vent that led into the wall and out the side of the house. A small spice rack lined the backsplash behind the stove and a small shelf above the sinks held a mug that used to belong to the late Alpha Jude. I poured myself a cup of the coffee Cecile made, added some oat milk and vanilla, and joined her at the table. It tasted delightful.

Cecile settled in as well and turned on the television that Kristofer recently installed in the corner of the kitchen, landing on the morning local news.

"That's it for this week's forecast. Now onto wolf matters. Yesterday, a protest broke out in front of the courthouse in downtown Ludwing. They peacefully rallied calling for action to protect the wolves and enforce severe penalties for those daring enough to hunt. An hour in, they were tear-gassed by the very hunters in question…"

Cecile lowered the volume, shook her head, and handed me a croissant from the center of the table. It was always the same thing when it came to the protest. For as much news coverage as there was about it, anyone would think that the hunters would start being held accountable for their actions. Truth of the matter was, no one cared. It wouldn't surprise me if the government allowed it to happen to control the population of wolves the same way they did everything else.

"I had that dream again," a sigh full of sleep escaped my coffee-stained lips. "I hate this time of year because of it." I raked my fingers through my long hair while shoving the buttery croissant she baked yesterday in my mouth. My fingers got stuck in a knot and worked my fingers carefully to let it out. My long hair was the one thing I couldn't part with. My mother had long hair and I refused to cut mine ever since she died.

"Are you going to be okay sweetie?" Cecile placed a hand on mine and gently rubbed it soothingly. She was the only one that I talked to about my recurring dreams. Worry filled the lines of her aging face. Her years were starting to show ever so slightly. At seventy-seven, she still looked like she was in her forties but only now were her wrinkles starting to show ever so slightly. They graced her deep green eyes as if they were darkening with age. Luckily for us, werewolves lived a longer lifespan than humans. That was why it made it hard to tell our age.

We were babies still, compared to the older generation and the elders. The elders were a small group of wolves that have lived incredibly long. They were well into the hundreds and encompassed wisdom from all generations passed. The path to becoming an elder was one of the more difficult paths for any wolf. It encompassed many years of training and apprenticeship.

I pouted in response to her question and Cecile stood up to wrap me in one of her wonderful warm hugs. All the tension seeped out of my body as she held me tight. She practically raised everyone that walked in through our door in need. She was the main reason I felt loved and gained the weight and muscle that I maintained. Every time my emotions swayed or faltered; she wrapped me with her warmth like a band aid over a wound. Without her, I might not have mentally survived. I loved her as much as I loved my mom.

Even with Kristofer being her only child, she always told people she had two sons and included me. When Kristofer and his dad found me, he was eighteen. But even with our age gap, Kristofer was a cool big brother. Eventually, Alpha Jude stepped down, giving the title to Kristofer at 20 after the pack agreed to elect him in. Little did everyone know; Jude would only die a year later. Now he ran things smoothly, with his mother still helping as a guide when she was needed since Kristofer had yet to find his mate.

"Yea, I'll be fine. I think I'm gonna go for a run. Might do my head some good." I gave her a smile and Cecile placed a kiss on my head before ruffling my hair. I loved her ruffles but sometimes she did it when I had my hair tied and would mess it up. It always made me feel like a kid, but I hated having to redo my hair afterward. Savoring the last sip of my coffee, I placed the mug in the sink, trying to drown out the news that was now having an open debate over wolves' rights within the human world. If only humans weren't so willfully ignorant. It didn't matter how much we explained that we were once human as well, they simply glossed right over it. As I walked out of the kitchen, Cecile stopped me with increasing worry behind her eyes.

"Cassius, please be careful of who sees your wolf. Why don't you go with Alex? These hunters have been ballsy lately, we already lost three wolves in the last 3 months and that's in this side of town alone," she pleaded.

With my wolf being so different from everyone else, she feared a hunter would spot me and put a price on my head. It was a legitimate fear considering the spike in hunter activity in our area. I'll never forget when Kristofer brought home Mrs. Miner, dead in his arms while in her wolf form. All because a hunter felt like it.

"I'll be careful, don't worry. I just want to be alone for a bit." I smiled at her until I saw her shoulders relax but the worry never left her face. It was risky but I felt uneasy, as if I needed to go out. Something inside me stirred and Wolfie felt it too.

I stepped out into the golden sky and inhaled the cool crisp air. October weather was always the best for runs and clearing anyone's mind. The winter chill and the dry air allowed for the freshest scents to pick up in the breeze. My favorite was the smell of pine that lingered heavy in the air with the morning dew. My wolf inside yipped eagerly for the morning run. Wolfie was everything to me. He was my partner in crime. Ever since he revealed himself when I was a kid, he had been a true mentor through thick and thin.

Wolfie explained the relationship between the human host and the wolves and what that meant. The harmony behind it and how the wolves themselves live many lives by constantly being reborn. Because of that they didn't always get along with their host and sometimes only ever came out during the full moon or if forced to shift due to danger. That's why my relationship with Wolfie was special to me. We had constant conversations together and I would give him his own personal time in his form to stretch his legs and run.

We wolves were basically two in one. We carried our own human soul along with the soul of the wolf. The magic that was once considered a curse was now considered a blessing that made way to allow our physical transformation. The wolf souls reincarnated generation after generation as each werewolf bloodline was born. However, there was more to the story that Wolfie wouldn't tell me. Since it was basically a history lesson, and I hated history, I never pressured him into revealing the secrecy either. It most likely wasn't pleasant and I had my fill of unsavory things in my life. Eager for my run, I stripped and left my clothes by my open bedroom window on the side of the house and shifted into Wolfie.

***

My paws hit the floor in a soft thud as I dug them into the earth reconnecting to my roots. The ground broke up beneath my paws and spread around my extended claws leaving a perfect print. The scent of dewy grass clenched my nose, invigorating my soul and thus began my sprint. *Man, I needed this*, I thought to myself. At full speed, I charged towards the line of the woods. *Freedom.* Even though the last time I shifted was just a couple days ago, there was something different about today. It was like an itch that I needed to scratch.

Dodging between the trees, a small yip escaped between my teeth. I was the fastest wolf in the pack and while others attributed it to my wolf being so different, I said it was because I shifted much more compared to others. But deep down, I knew it was because I was different. Satisfaction consumed me with the wind blowing through my fur. The cool air combed over my body greeting my wolf form in gentle hellos. When I reincarnated inside of Cassius, he gifted me with the most freedom in my form. All my other human hosts suppressed me.

Left to right, I zigzagged between trees and jumped over rocks. I didn't mind, per say, sitting in the back seat and witnessing the world through Cassius' eyes, but I was so grateful when he proposed having personal time. There was no better feeling than being in control.

I trotted to my favorite spot and almost howled at the excitement. My muscles warmed up from the run and a bit of my tired mind began to show through. A cliff that overlooked the nearby riverbank deep in the woods came into view. Scents here and there filled my snout with other animals that came to this spot. Harmless small critters like rabbits and squirrels often scurried around leaving their scent behind. I plopped on the ground and let out a soft rumble, soaking up the morning sun. *Feels nice,* I mentally whispered to Cassius. Bits of dandelion fluttered around me making me sneeze in response. I sniffled and lazed my eyes at the ants crawling over the edge of the cliff carrying a variety of things I could only assume was food for the winter. *How nice and carefree they are,* I thought as I drifted to sleep.

Chapter 2

WOLFIE

I inhaled the morning warmth covering my fur. The invigorating nap filled me up with the calm I needed to help my human with his emotions on the anniversary of his mother's death. I could feel Cassius resting deep in the depths of my mind just like the small, orphaned child I first got to know. In the dark trenches of my mind was his favorite hiding spot and in times like these he slept peacefully. In a moment, similar to this one, it dawned on me after I had my first shift, why Cassius' mother and him were captured. They were simply caught because we were wolves and to the hunters, we were nothing but a mounted taxidermized head on a wall. Yet, I knew there was another reason that I never told Cassius, and I hoped he never had to find out.

I nuzzled my face into the grass and closed my eyes. There was nothing I wouldn't do to protect my precious human. Listening to the sounds around me I refocused my thoughts. The day was still young, and I had to push out the negativity and zone in on the birds that chirped their song, the water that rushed beneath me, and the howl of a crying wolf. *That's nice. Wait, what? That's not, right?*

My eyes shot open and my ears perked. It wasn't one of my pack family. I tried to listen carefully as my ears twitched in the direction of the tortured sound. Again, an agonizing howl pierced right through my eardrums, filled with torment. Without a moment to spare, I ran. My legs dashed toward the wolf's sounds of distress. Howls of pain echoed between the trees before me, ricocheting against one another. Flashes of Cassius's memory invaded my own. His mother flooded through me, her struggle, her own screams, her pain but I had to focus. The wasn't room for a mistake

My paws gripped the ground as I sped through the trees. I hit the ground faster, picking up traction to gain speed and I could smell it, *hunters*!

With long deep breaths, I slowed down to not give away my presence by getting too close. The scent of the wolf and hunter told me they were just several feet ahead of me, but I had to lay low first. Making sure to stay out of sight, I lowered myself to the ground and scanned the area. The quiet between the hurting wolf's cries was almost scarier than the cries themselves. At least her cries told me she was still alive. Birds no longer sang, squirrels scurried away, and a single vulture circled in the sky above to what it thought was its next meal.

A hunter came into view from behind one of the trees and laughed at his morbid version of victory. The camouflage he so proudly wore hung heavy with his overstuffed pockets. His matching shirt flapped in the wind, revealing how it was a size too big for the man.

He was a ghastly sight and one I did not care for. On the ground, however, was the poor female wolf with her back paw in a bear trap. With how mangled it looked; I was sure her bone was broken. Blood stained her brown fur into a mix of dark red hues. I could only imagine the pain she experienced when it first clamped down. The man in camo approached her with a machete ready to finish his kill. Without a second thought, I took a step forward cracking a branch beneath my paw.

The hunter jerked his head in my direction, but I froze low to the ground. It was a rookie mistake to make but the hunter disregarded the sound rather quickly. A rookie mistake made on his part as well. One wrong move could get us both killed but luck must have been on my side. Sniffing the air, I studied the scents around me and listened. *He's alone*, I confirmed to Cassius who was listening and alert. Thank the goddess. I steadied my footing and made my way around the hunter. The man laughed while taunting her with the machete. He raised his rusty blade in the air and my body moved on instinct.

All the training and discipline the pack taught me over the years brought me to this moment. In swift careful movements, I pounced on him and bit his neck. My jaw clenched in a tight hold as I dug my teeth in. While I held tight to catch my breath as he lost his, I assessed that no one else was coming. The hunter gurgled his blood, forcing some to ooze into my mouth and at that point I knew he was done for. The warm metallic tasting liquid pooled under my tongue, pressuring me to hold back the gag it provoked. But it didn't matter. I let go with satisfaction so I could watch his life fade from his eyes. *Another scum is gone*, Cassius echoed in the back of my mind, and I grunted in agreement.

While it didn't feel good to take a life, it was a relief to know the packhouse was safe and that this poor wolf had a fighting chance. I turned around to the poor wolf who was unconscious and bleeding. With my snout, I nudged her, but it did little to wake her. She remained unresponsive to my attempts and whimpers. Having no other choice, I shifted back to my human form so I could help carry her to safety.

***

I pried the trap open, careful not to hurt my fingers. With my bare foot, I held one side of the trap down as best I could and removed her leg with my free hand. The trap snapped closed again, jostling in the air before it settled on the ground next to my foot. The poor wolf who seemed lifeless in my arms with how limp she was, seemed young. She looked close to my age. Her fur brushed against my bare skin, tickling me and only then I realized how soft she felt despite the blood drying up on her injured leg.

The wind blew against us, sending a good whiff of her fur up my nose. With my eyes closed, I inhaled deeply smelling roses possibly from a garden, ashes from a fire pit, freshwater from the river, and something soothing. *Lavender maybe?* My mind picked at the idea of lavender, but that scent in particular was faint. It was a scent that had long been able to comfort me. The memory of the lavender fields that used to sway behind my childhood home came to mind. It was exactly what I needed on a day like today.

I shifted her weight in my arms and carried her, following the scent that now formed a map in my mind. The scent locked into my nose to track the direction she most likely came from. My day was only just beginning, and it was already eventful. I noticed something else on her that was just as lovely. It mixed subtly underneath the scents of her fur, but I couldn't seem to pinpoint what it was.

All I knew was that I was close to her territory or at least to the source of the soothing faint smell in her fur. It wasn't perfume either from what I could tell. Maybe another wolf she was close to rubbed off on her. It was so inviting that I felt something bubble inside me. My mind shook off the thought as I could see the tree line. I placed her down spotting a packhouse just ahead in the distance.

What is that scent, it's strong here? I took a deep breath. *Lavender and oak. Oak! That's the other scent I got off her. It's amazing.* The alluring scent I previously got from her fur filled my lungs full force, but it came from a different direction that wasn't the packhouse. I struggled to focus but I needed to call out for someone to help the injured wolf. I shifted back to Wolfie to howl loud and clear.

***

With a strong loud howl, I called out in distress towards the packhouse. My call rang out across the way, and I spotted some movement in the house stir in response. Despite the strong scent that Cassius first picked up caressing my senses, I didn't see anyone around which made me feel disappointed for some reason. As much as I wanted to track the source of the smell, this was not a time for distractions.

From the corner of my eye, I caught a quick glimpse as a head popped up and spotted me. *It's you I smell!* The pull it had on me intensified but I dashed immediately away. I only wanted to help the wolf, but I couldn't risk being seen and Cassius was panicking in the back of my mind. I couldn't risk being caught in someone else's territory either. From a young age, Cassius was reminded that territories were to be respected, and trespassing could cause tension between packs. I agreed that it had always been that way and ingrained that idea into my human.

I slowed down and smiled inside because for the first time in a long time I helped Cassius help someone in danger. We saved her from the same fate my human's mother couldn't survive. Ever since our kind became common knowledge, the problem of hunters has arisen at an exponential rate. I guess it's no different than humans murdering their own, but hunters didn't treat us like anything other than mindless animals. I shifted back into my human form and grabbed my folded clothes from my window.

***

Another shower was in order to help rid me of the lingering scent of blood on my skin. Yet the man's scent remained trapped in my mind. It was exciting to realize it was coming from him. It could only mean one thing but was that something I was ready for. With my hands tracing my body to wash away the soap, my lower half reacted to the idea of maybe meeting that person again.

I finished bathing and slipped on my pants. Nothing about the girl's scent was threatening. Nor was the scent from the man that pierced my senses. Maybe her pack was kind, unlike some other ones I had the privilege of knowing. There were many times I joined the Alpha in meetings or trades with other packs and the families weren't exactly welcoming. Just strictly business. A tingly sensation ran through me at the thought that it wouldn't be that way with his pack.

Someone's there! Wolfie whispered in my mind. I turned towards my window, but no one was there. It was odd for me not to notice if someone was there since my senses were usually sharp. Although a strong scent of lavender and oak filled my room. Maybe he followed me to see where I lived. Or I could be imagining things.

My stomach growled from hunger with the adrenaline dissipating from me. It was going to be a good day even though it started out rough. I walked into the kitchen ready to destroy a giant bowl of cereal while I thought about what I wanted to eat.

"Alex you're up!" I walked to the cupboard and pulled out a large polka-dot bowl.

"Yea, I was hungry," he smiled. He was the youngest wolf living in the main packhouse after me. The families with younger pups were all in their own homes while the main family, Alex, and I stayed here in the packhouse. I guess that could be why we got along great. I was only older than him by three years. His green and hazel eyes focused on his sandwich as he took another bite.

"Yea, me too," I sat down across from him and enjoyed the comfortable silence. Every now and then I could feel his glances, but I ignored them and continued with my massive bowl of kernel pop cereal. He thought I never noticed but ever since his fifteenth birthday he has had a crush on me. I've turned him down already a couple times, but his eyes never stopped giving him away although lately, I did see his eyes wander to someone else. Again, I acted oblivious and carried on.

"Morning, Cass," Kristofer walked shirtless scratching his chest with a loud yawn. His large frame made him a bit intimidating, but in reality, he was a teddy bear inside. He must have had a late night for him to wake up late in the morning.

"Morning Alpha", I nodded towards him.

"Alex," Kristofer looked at the trembling pup.

"M-Morning Alpha," Alex barely managed to say above a whisper. He was in trouble for not training with the pack the last two times we held sessions. Even though we no longer fought between packs, we still trained to stay fit and be prepared for the worst. We feared with the increase in attacks by hunters that there would be an uprising of sorts. But after the lecture Alex received from Alpha and Cecile, he was a nervous wreck whenever Kristofer came around.

"Alright, I'm going to head out and finish chopping the firewood. Feels like winter will be here soon." I gave them both a nerdy thumbs up in both their directions and left after placing my bowl in the sink.

Asshole. Alex mind-linked with me. I chuckled.

Stop being such a pup and grow a pair. I replied knowing he was probably fidgeting in his seat at being left alone with Kristofer.

With the cold crisp in the air, I grabbed my jacket to head to the barn outback. I quickly cut through the living room for the front door but found Cecile with a few teens giving her usual lessons in wolf anatomy.

"Okay, so what have we learned so far?" Cecile asked the four pups sitting with her.

"When you find your mate, you can recognize it's them by their smell. Your mate's smell will appeal to something you like." A skinny redhead about fifteen years old answered. Her freckled cheeks reddened when she spotted me standing there.

"That's right. Anyone else?"

"At eighteen you can start to recognize who your mate is, and your hormones go crazy and all you want is to do bow-chicka-wow-wow." The tall boy joked prompting a laugh from the others while he gyrated his hips in a suggestive manner.

"Although true, I need you to use proper language." Cecile scolded the boy prompting more laughter from the other three and me included. I remembered this conversation clearly when I first had it with Cecile, and I think I was just as much of a clown as this kid. Smiling, I let them be and continued outside.

A pile of wood stacked neatly sat waiting for me to split. I perched one on the stump, swung the ax, and split the wood to toss into the done pile. This had been one workout I never thought I would enjoy but the arms I developed from it was well worth it.

The sun rose a bit higher in the morning sky reflecting off the sweat from my face. Time eluded me but the soreness in my arms told me I needed a break. The amount of wood I chopped was decent enough for a while and the rest could be done another day. I slumped my shoulders in exhaustion until my ears twitched. Someone was approaching.

Turning my head towards the sound of footsteps, I swung my ax into the log on the ground and focused my hearing on the intruders. The scent wasn't from a wolf. *Hunters,* I grimaced. Those awful humans smelled like old blood whether from unclean knives, boots, or clothing. It was that rotting smell on their clothes that made it easy to identify them. They hunted so much that even if their clothes were washed, the stench of death lingered in the threads of their camouflage.

Quickly, I sent a mind-link to my Alpha to alert him of my location and the situation on hand. I rolled up my sleeves just as the hunters approached the area of the barn. The steps were heavy in my ears, but I crouched down listening to which direction they were coming from as I faked tying my shoes. My ears strained to confirm how many were approaching but the scent of my Alpha having shifted and circling us calmed my nerves.

There's two of them, I told Zeus, Kristofers wolf, through our mind-link.

Yea, they are approaching to your right. Be careful. I'll circle around. Zeus quickly moved through the trees.

My heart was steady. One of the men dressed in dirty brown jeans, unwashed hiking boots, and a camo jacket appeared before me. I stood up slowly as a shotgun followed my body's ascent. **Zeus… he has a shotgun pointed at me. Be careful with the other one.**

"Are you a werewolf?" The man held a shotgun pointed at my head. His finger twitched on the trigger. It was obvious he had every intent on shooting if I didn't provide an answer he liked. The scent of the man I killed hit me like a ton of bricks. *Shit, they were together,* I mentally whispered to Wolfie.

The Silver Lining

"No, I'm not and you're on private property. I suggest you leave. We don't need cops getting involved now." I snapped, gritting my teeth. This was getting out of hand. Now it seemed they were willing to kill my kind whether we were shifted or not. The second hunter that was hiding appeared next to him. The stench on him was worse. He wore a full outfit of camo foliage stained in red.

"How do I know you're not lying?" The man replied with an evil grin suggesting my answer didn't matter. "I know there's a wolf nearby. He killed my partner this morning." The second man raised his rifle.

"Well, you'll have to take my word for it," I smirked knowing I was getting under his skin with my calm facade. All I needed was to stall long enough for one of them to let their guard down for Kristofer to attack if they didn't leave peacefully.

"Bobby, go see if he reacts to silver. I got your six."

This so-called Bobby nodded his head and pulled out a silver knife. He cautiously approached me, wary of my movements but my eyes never left his. With my rolled-up sleeves he had perfect access to my exposed skin. My heart raced but I couldn't let on how nervous I was. I trusted that Zeus would jump in if needed be. This would be the moment we fought. I would shed blood, be it mine or theirs. **Kristofer, hur-!** I tried to yell mentally before looking down at the knife touching my skin.

Cass, what's happening, Zeus popped back into my mind.

I'm not burning. The silver did nothing.
...?

"What's happening Bobby, did you, do it?" The hunter with the shotgun called out. Bobby stepped aside to show the other hunter the blade flat on my skin.

"He's human, John," Bobby removed the blade and walked back to where John stood.

The hunter lowered the rifle. "My apologies sir, you can just never be too sure these days. I suggest you be careful out here. Those animals are ruthless savages. Killed my friend for no reason."

"I appreciate the concern, now if you don't mind leaving my property. Your weapons aren't welcomed here." I stood my ground in false confidence. What just happened didn't make sense.

Bobby and John man tilted their hats in a slight nod and walked away.

In the house now! Zeus' voice sounded scared but so was I.

The silver was supposed to burn so why was I okay? I walked in through the back door and removed my boots with Kristofer right behind me putting his clothes back on.

"Let me see your arm." I lifted it towards him, and he ran a finger down the length of my forearm.

"There's really nothing there, no burns. Are you sure it was silver?" His eyes darted up to mine in disbelief. It had to have been. I couldn't imagine a hunter having fake silver on him.

I shrugged my shoulders unsure, "the last time I was touched with silver was when I was kidnapped as a child. I remember it burning... I think. Maybe?!" I paused with the realization that I truly didn't remember it burning and looked around for something silver. "Do we have silver in the basement?"

Kristofer understood where I was going with it and ran downstairs. He came back wearing gloves and holding a silver shackle we had taken from one of the hunters a while back. I closed my eyes waiting for a burn that never came. When I peeked, Kristofer was wide-eyed staring at me. He had the shackle firmly pressed against my skin with no reaction. "I'm immune?"

"This stays between us. You tell no one. This can put you at risk and make you a greater target even. " Kristofer grabbed my shoulder and gave it a gentle squeeze. "Ever since I first saw you, I knew you were special.… but mostly weird."

"Ew, leave that kinda talk for your mate," I acted like his words gave me the shivers and prompted a laugh out of him as I exaggerated a shake further.

"Shut up and learn to take a compliment. Besides, I've given up hope. I'm a 30-year-old wolf and no mate," Kristofer's voice trailed off.

"Don't give up, she will come." I patted him on the back, but he didn't seem too sure. Usually, you found your mate in your early to mid-twenties but for Kristofer, it had yet to happen. It weighed on him. Especially when others around him were finding their significant others. He knew what a bond with your mate could do. He had seen it with his parents and other couples in the pack all the time and he yearned for it.

Not every wolf wanted to have the mate bond though. Others simply dated casually and let things go with the flow while others remained celibate. One thing I did come to learn was that finding someone you could rely on and love for life was something I craved but for some reason it also scared me. I didn't want to end up like my parents. Then again, growing up in such a positive family I grew to understand that happy endings did exist.

I also had the security of knowing that I could find my soulmate if the mate bond wasn't meant for me. While it did the same thing in matching you with your fated partner, the way you found out was slightly different and less intense. Yet even in that respect, Kristofer didn't find a soulmate either.

Mate bonds were a force of nature that rendered you unable to control yourself around your mate. You found them through scent but for it to work completely, you must accept them, or the bond would weaken and die off. As for soulmates, you find them through a spark in a way. The attraction would be strong but to find that person was close to impossible unless they were within your area or if you traveled. However, when you find them, the attraction was strong, but the spark didn't occur until both parties accepted each other. Only then could a spark ignite between the two and form a soul bond. Which in turn would behave similar to the mate bond.

Unlike the mate bond, the soul bond doesn't lift any veil between you and your partner which enables you to be more in tune with the other. Being honest or communicating would be a challenge if the other wasn't willing to do so of their own accord. Just like any other normal human relationship. At twenty-one, I was hoping that one or the other would happen. Ready or not, I didn't want to end up alone like Kristofer either. So, I sat between a rock and a hard place. I left Kristofer to his thoughts and went up to my room.

Throwing myself in my bed, I fell asleep with the face I had seen earlier and the lovely scent that followed floating in my mind.

Chapter 3

ATLAS

The smell of the morning dew filled my nose, waking me up from a heavy sleep. My body ached from the training I did with my pack yesterday. It was a very much-needed session since it had been a few weeks since the last training session. My Beta, Mavis, had just found his mate and left for their honeymoon. Nothing could pry that man off his mate but who could blame him? The bond was all he ever talked about, even as a kid. So, to end up finding his mate, dating for a year, and finally tying the knot, we skipped the training for the month and helped him with the wedding.

The bond that was physically created between mates was like no other. It was a gift and the way the bond amplified the qualities of one another was unexplainable. Something I longed for. The moon goddess took her time to make sure her children were matched with the perfect person. Well, perfect in the eyes of the beholder at least. If the couple chose to not stay together and break the bond, that was fine but then it left them searching for a soulmate which was difficult to do. They could still find happiness by simply dating like humans do but it wouldn't be the same as the bond or a soul mate. I was happy for Mavis and Dona. They were wonderful together.

I kicked off my blanket that had wrapped around my legs and jumped in the shower to start my day. The hot water melted away the soreness in my muscles. *I definitely overdid it,* I thought. The last punch I threw hurt a bit in my shoulder. Might have pulled something and now my arm felt stiff as I tried to rotate my shoulder under the scorching water. *Man, this shower is amazing.* Definitely, grateful to Mavis for installing an updated bathroom. He was not just my Beta but the handyman in the packhouse. That wolf could build anything. I owed a lot of our renovations to him.

The shower's heat seeped into my bones temporarily filling me with a warmth I longed for. With that thought, I got out of the shower and put on some clothes. With a good swipe on the mirror, I stared at my damp hair that was stuck to my forehead. With minimal hair mousse, I let it air dry in soft waves while I skipped down the steps and into the kitchen. The house was quiet with soft sounds of birds chirping accompanied the silence. The morning was beautiful.

I loved my home in the mornings because of the stillness it evoked. However, the kitchen was my favorite room in the house. After my father died, I took to cooking as a way to heal. I poured my emotions, my thoughts, and my sorrows into my cooking. After many trials and errors, I became decent in the kitchen. It was my solace, but it did make me gain weight which I was finally able to work off.

However now with the holidays approaching, I had to be careful not to get it back.

After all the time it took for me to find my healing through cooking, my mom had become restless and eventually left to travel, which made me fall deeper into a cooking frenzy. She never said why she left though, but I did sense that she left in a rush. A year came and went, and I missed her terribly. There were times when I needed her advice or help with the pack, and she was the first person I wanted to turn to. Then I sat realizing I was alone. If only I could see my father again, but nothing could bring him back from the dead. I missed his stupid dad jokes or how he used to make crazy cookouts for the pack in the summer by the lake.

The sound of coffee brewing pulled me from my thoughts. I added a dash of cinnamon, some oat milk, and a teaspoon of sugar. The morning air greeted me with a cool crisp through the kitchen window, perfect for reading outside. I needed to clear my head. Rick was up to no good again and I've had to keep an eye on him lately. He was the lone wolf I wished would disappear. Nothing good ever came of his presence.

I put on a hoodie I kept by the door on a hook, grabbed my book from the stand next to the door, and carried my mug with me. I walked a bit away from the house and sat in the tall grass under the giant oak tree. The canopy swayed above me in a light rustle with the gentle breeze of the morning. Small sips of hot coffee filled my cheeks with the sweetness of the milk and spice of the cinnamon. Sitting my coffee on the small table I installed specifically for my morning reads, I opened my book to where I last left off and tucked the bookmark in the back of the book.

Murder mystery was my favorite go-to. The words on the page would transport me to the scene of a crime in the late nineteen-thirties in the streets of London. My eyes no longer registered the words but instead picked off the images of the story. On a dark starry night, streetlamps flickered down a wet cobblestone street. The sidewalk was void of people and in the alley between a residential home and a shop was a dead body. Bloody, mutilated, and hidden behind the dumpster with nothing but a foot poking out for passersby to witness. It was the last murder before the killer was almost caught.

As I read, the pages thickened in my left hand, alerting me that I was near the end of the book. This would be the fifth time I finished this book. It was my fallback for times that I was in thought. The spine of the book was already creased with signs of wear. The corners of the pages were stressed from the number of times I've folded them as place markers until Mavis got tired of me torturing the pages and bought me a bookmark. One page, in particular, had a coffee stain on the bottom from tripping as I walked with the book, coffee in hand. He would have had a heart attack if he knew.

The glaring sun melted the chill off my cheeks and fingertips as it peaked just above the top of my book, catching me in my eyes. I flinched at the assault and laid down on the grass to continue reading, using the book as a shield of sorts. I liked the peace around me and the breeze that chilled me every so often. It almost felt as if I were the only one in the world as I read.

The sound of twigs breaking and rusting by the trees broke me out of my book. I was only a few pages to the end but the suspense of someone behind me was too great to ignore. I stayed still listening to the sounds carried in the air. My mind was still buzzing from the book, but I focused on any signs of danger. My ears twitched while they strained.

I kept low in the tall grass to hide from whoever was approaching and waited to see if they posed a threat. The wind shifted bringing with it all the smells from the tree line. A divine scent wafted up my nostrils, encasing every bit of sensory my nose had to offer. It smelled like winter crisp snow and a touch of cinnamon. But then my nose crinkled at the faint smell of blood which distorted the moment of bliss I had found myself in. A distressed howl pulled me from my slight euphoria, and I propped up to look at the wolf. Iris was on the floor bloody in front of the most majestic wolf I had ever seen.

His scent hit me again with another gust of wind but the moment our eyes met he bolted at amazing speed. His sudden escape act had me reeling back to reality quickly. My sister was injured and here I was in a trance. I got up and ran over to Iris, **hey, sis...can you hear me?** Nothing. The mind-link brought back nothing but silence. I could feel her breathing, but she was unconscious. My wolf inside whimpered wanting to follow the scent, but my sister was the priority. Family would always be a priority. I lifted her up and rushed her into the house taking note of the wonderful faint scent coming off her fur. For a brief moment, as I rushed inside, I enjoyed the cinnamon and snow that lingered on her fur.

Annoyed by how that scent affected me, I gently laid her down on the sofa and called over our pack healer. She was a genius when it came to medicinal herbs and with her nursing background, she was able to perform more than just a mean stitch or two. Sylvie entered and ushered out everyone else that kept trickling into the living room.

"Alpha, what happened?" She pulled out a needle and filled it with a dark liquid that was usually used to counteract poisoned blood.

"I don't know. Some wolf brought her home and howled to get our attention, but he ran before I could question him."

A hand grabbed my shoulder. The shaking in my hand stopped as I balled them closed. Finn stood beside me with pain all over his worried face. I didn't care much for him, but I couldn't deny how much he cared for my sister. Finn was a wolf my parents found as a baby abandoned by the lake. With him only a few months younger than Iris, they grew up together almost at the hip. But he eventually developed feelings for her as a teen. After noticing his feelings, she maintained a distance ever since, but he couldn't take no for an answer.

" I don't think he was the one that did it though," I reassured everyone but mostly myself.

Sylvie administered the injection which forced Iris to shift back into her human form as it worked through her blood allowing her to heal. I immediately grabbed the throw from the side of the sofa and covered her naked body.

"I need to set her bone and clean the wound. I think she is just in shock and exhausted from trying to heal unsuccessfully." Sylvie grabbed some smelling salt and placed it under her nose. Iris jolted and screamed from the pain in her leg. "It's okay, your home now. Let me give you something for the pain but first bite this stick while I set your leg." Sylvie handed her a bite stick and counted to three. On two, Sylvie pulled on Iris' ankle setting the bone. My poor sister screamed, biting down aggressively on the stick. Sweat beaded down her face from the slight fever developing but at least she was safe.

"Why isn't she healing faster? Her wolf should be helping her." My voice trembled at the sight of Iris in pain. It was rare the times I saw her like this. Growing up she always laughed at the silliest things, always with a smile, always happy but this past year had been tough and her smiles, although present, were slowly fading. It was hard to see. Yet, even so, this type of pain stricken over her face was new and it terrified me.

"The trap was laced with silver and it's in her system. I got some of it flushed out by cleaning the wound but until it leaves her bloodstream, her wolf will have a hard time healing." Sylvie packed up her things. "Take this and make her a tea with these herbs to help her speed up the process. Anything else Alpha?" Sylvie handed me a small bag.

"No, Sylvie. Thank you. "

She nodded with a smile and left the room. Finn rushed to Iris' side and picked her up like the bride he wished she was. He had been in love with her for so long despite not being mates, that he ignored everyone but her. He worshipped the ground she walked on. She told him to stop because it wouldn't be fair to their mates if they had feelings for each other. In all honesty, it was her way of turning him down gently. She only saw him as a friend. Maybe even a little brother. Always had and always would.

Now that my adrenaline faded my mind went back to that scent. My body hummed at the thought of it. I knew I loved the winter, but I never thought it would be the scent I was attracted to along with cinnamon. A shiver ran through my body, *I need a run.* With that thought, I darted out of the house and removed my clothes as I went, so I could shift into my wolf, Leo. Traces of cinnamon barely remained in the spot where he stood but it gripped my focus.

***

My paws hit the dirt as I ran trying to find any trace of that wonderful smell. Nothing but faint hints here and there whispered to me. I couldn't find a strong enough scent that I could follow. Then again, it could just be Atlas affecting me. He was worked up a bit over his sister's injuries and the worry that lately the hunters had been using sprays to mask themselves. Whatever they were using altered their scent and weakened any trail left behind. I wasn't sure if this was a tactic to disorient us while they hunted but it was definitely inconvenient.

I ended up at a cliff I had not noticed before and sat looking over the edge. The view was beautiful, and the scent seemed to be stronger here than anywhere else so far. This could very well be a spot he visited often. The river rushed beneath me with its sounds calming the eager human inside me. I took a deep breath and picked up more of that crisp winter scent before I laid down on my paws allowing the wind to lull me asleep. *He was here for sure.*

Chatter started to echo in the woods. My sleep filled eyes opened to find the direction of the voices. I rolled in the grass and dirt to mask my scent by covering my fur. Fortunately, I wasn't spotted sleeping, or I would have been vulnerable to anyone. Slowly, I crept at a distance and followed the echoes. *Hunters! What are they doing here?* I mentally whispered to Atlas who was just as alert as I was.

Two hunters were whispering and holding weapons. They had to have been the ones to hurt Iris. I watched them with slow steady movements for several minutes and stopped when they approached a barn. This could be the perfect opportunity to teach them a lesson for hunting my kin, but it then hit me, winter snow and cinnamon.

The wonderful smell that invaded every inch of my fur was close and these men were going straight towards him. If I acted now, then I could risk putting him in danger but if I didn't, I wasn't sure if he would be safe. This was maddening and Atlas was restless in the depths of my mind but assured me to stay close. My eyes darted back to the hunters as they talked among themselves. Chopping sounds of some sort filtered through the sounds of the woods and then it stopped. They must have approached him, or the wolf noticed their presence.

I watched from a distance as another wolf snuck up behind the hunters waiting for an opening. It put me and Atlas at ease knowing they had a handle on the situation. He looked strong and the way he carefully placed each step definitely made him the Alpha. His moves were calculating and patient. Tactile in a sense. With everyone so far away, I couldn't hear anything else that was going on but no screaming or howling was a good sign. A few moments go by, and the men leave. The hidden alpha wolf waited for it to clear but turned in my direction looking around. *Did he sense me?* He looked directly towards me, and I lowered to the ground before he ran towards the barn.

Curiosity was getting the best of me, and Atlas wanted me to follow to see if I could catch a glimpse of the magnificent silver wolf. I waited a bit considering I was already trespassing on their grounds and the Alpha was wary of me. *Fuck it, I'll just be careful.* I suppressed my scent as much as I could and made my way up to the house. The hints of cinnamon invaded me, almost making me lose my composure and led me to a window.

The strong scent invaded me almost to the point of me wanting to howl. I slowly peeked inside by standing on my hind legs. *Oh, my goddess, he is gorgeous,* Atlas echoed in my mind. A tall tanned skinned man with long waist length black hair removed his clothes. Atlas stirred inside me as he witnessed the man before him through my eyes. His muscles contracted across his back as his arms moved in a sexy manner. He did nothing out of the ordinary but made it all seem so sensual. The man definitely had good taste with the posters gracing his wall. *I wonder how old he is.* Atlas asked me but I truly couldn't say. While Atlas was distracted by the human, I was distracted by the scent of the wolf inside him. The form he had was breathtaking and one I hadn't seen in centuries.

The scent was so much stronger now that he was naked and it was dizzying, to say the least. *It's definitely him. He is my mate,* Atlas called into mind. With that sudden realization, I slipped with my vision blurring slightly. The sound must have caught my mate's attention. He turned around with all his muscular glory, and I ducked just as quickly. If he saw me then I'd have no choice but to face him, which I wanted, but before I could give him the chance to approach the window, Atlas had me on the run.

I sprinted away like never before because Atlas went into full panic in my mind. My sore muscles pushed themselves to work faster. *I can't get caught. I'm not ready. Not now.* Atlas kept repeating the words in my mind. Tears streamed down my face as pain jolted through my body. My legs were giving out, but I couldn't stop. Every fiber of my being raged on fire. I was at my limit, but I needed to get home for my humans' sake. The house came into view, and I slowed down to catch my breath. My shift was almost involuntary at that point and with unsteady numb feet, I went straight to my room.

***

Holy shit, I found my mate, I thought to myself. My mind swirled with that revelation, and I threw myself on my bed and closed my eyes. Tears burned their way through my closed lids, and I cried harder than I ever had in a long time. My dirty hands wiped them away leaving streaks on my face. I thought I would have been happy if I found him, but I couldn't breathe. My chest felt tight, and I wanted to claw at myself just to get a full breath into my lungs. With my pillow I covered my face and cried into the soft plush. *I want to be happy, but I'm scared. Who will ever love a broken person like me? No one wants a person with baggage.*

I took a deep breath and blocked Leo from my thoughts. Everyone knew that the last thing anyone wanted in a relationship was someone damaged and violated. My mate would turn me down at the drop of a hat if he ever found out. I dragged myself to the bathroom to fill the tub with steaming water to soak myself and soothe my aching heart. *I'm not ready. I'm not ready for someone to know how broken I am. No one can know I was...* My mind pounded with a headache too loud to hear my thoughts anymore, which was a blessing in disguise. Tears threatened my eyes again and I let them fall freely to salt the water I sat in. Sobbing quietly into my rough hands, soft echoes of my whimpers surrounded me in company

Chapter 4

A week went by since the incident by his window. I couldn't bring myself to go back to him, not even to apologize because it would make it harder to stay away from him if I did. I knew I would lose myself in the moment if I were to go near him again. My body ached with the want to allow the mate bond to bring us closer. This alone confused me. From everything that I had learned about bonds, we were supposed to have an option. An option to stay away or say no but for this was nothing like that.

Everything in me wanted to run to him and claim him as mine. But my mind wasn't ready to accept someone in such an intimate way. Not yet and the only way I knew to keep myself from caving in was by keeping my distance.

Even my wolf kept telling me to go find him and introduce us all but the fear of him learning my secret scared me. What if our bond solidified and he was later disgusted. If I told everyone that I was gay and that I knew who my mate was, everything would unfold. Everything would unravel and Rick would make sure of it. That vile man didn't deserve to walk this earth and yet he had been my shackle since my father's death.

Rick was supposed to be my father's best friend. Yet he waited for my father to die to show his true colors. Then threatened me if I were ever to rat him out, but how could I ever do that? I could never admit to anyone what happened to me because it would mean something worse happening. How could I ever look at my loved ones as Alpha and admit that I was a victim of rape and by one of our own, no less. It would make me a sham of a leader for allowing the perpetrator to still live among us. But I had a good reason.

The only thing worse than that truth was the threat of him doing the same to Iris if I ever revealed what he did to me. It has haunted me to this very day. Because of him I have had to act as if it was nothing just to maintain a safe pack. Coming out wasn't even the issue but risking my secret being exposed terrified me. The fact that I might put others in danger and then lose my title was something I wasn't willing to accept.

If I could come out without the worry that Rick would tear my pack apart then I would, but his threats were nothing to laugh at. I've already kept this secret for nine years and each year it weighed heavier than the last. Rick was my dad's best friend or at least I thought he was until my father died. My view of him changed that one night behind my barn.

I cried quietly with a half empty bottle of rum out of grief for my father's death. I had shredded a bit of wolfdrink in with the rum so I could get drunk. Since it is harder to get drunk as a wolf, we have to add something to our drinks to feel the same effects humans did. So, I sat there drinking away my pain in hopes that I would black out and wake up to find that my dad had never died.

Rick had stumbled his way over to where I was, downing in his own bottle of whiskey. He slurred his way to me and got comfortable against the barn crying over the loss of his best friend, my father. I laid back against the wall and cursed the world for giving me a fate without my father. I was lost without him. Rick threw his now empty bottle of whiskey before pulling out another bottle from his inside jacket pocket.

Through both of our drunken stupors, I foolishly admitted to him what I was afraid to tell my father. I thought I could trust the only other father figure I had in my life. Thinking it was okay, I admitted to him the weight I carried in my heart with tears of sadness. At sixteen, I confessed out loud my sexuality for the first time. For a brief moment in time, I felt light. I was able to breathe better than I had in the last sixteen years. But only for a moment.

As a teenager, Rick was like a second father to me. He taught me a lot of what I knew when it came to hunting and fighting. He was there as I grew into the teen boy I had become. Even the hunter knife that I carried was hand carved by him and gifted to me when I was thirteen. After heartbroken tears and a nearly empty bottle of rum, an unthinkable nightmare began to unfold between the man I had looked up to and me. Rick began to whisper inappropriate things and repeated how much I looked like my father. He moved closer to me with what was a grin full of lust and need. At the time, I didn't even understand what his intentions were.

All I knew was that the look on his face changed the moment I revealed my secret. It was almost like he took it as an invitation to fulfill a fantasy that he dared not share with anyone else. He then pinned me down and had his way with me. His stench of whiskey rolled over my skin and ravaged my body along with his rough calloused hands. Every inch of my skin started to burn with the traces of his fingers and untrimmed nails. I cried out into the trees that spanned behind the barn. His breath was heavy and licked away at my skin, filled my lungs, and snuffed out my voice. I couldn't move.

How could a person think that because someone was gay, that it would be okay? It wasn't. It never was or would be. Aside from the fact that I looked up to him, I was a minor. Where was the respect for the other person involved? I struggled against him, but he was so strong that it was impossible to escape his grip. Tears burned my eyes as I thought about how my father was looking down at that moment. Disappointed. Ashamed.

The rum in my body weighed down my efforts further. Had I not drank so much then fighting could have worked to some extent. But I wasn't fooling myself. Even in a sober state, I was not a match for Rick's size. My chest tightened. The only sound I could hear were the grunts of the whiskey filled bastard hovering over me with his flaccid penis in his hand. Although it wasn't long before he grew into his own hand, and it touched me. His pants hugged his ankles while mine were pulled down just enough to expose me.

I cried for him to stop but my own voice betrayed me. A mere whine escaped my lips as my voice gave out. My dehydrated body struggled to function. Struggled to provide the force needed to push him off. No one was even around or close enough to be able to hear the struggle. They were all far off by the river lighting the pyre for my father. The grief that filled the air provided the perfect cover for this treacherous and horrid act.

The vile man, if he could be considered as much, flipped me around and laid his chest on my back. His weight made it difficult to breathe. My lungs struggled to expand between the ground and his weight. Then he positioned himself. With a dry, dirty, and unprotected, unwanted hardened flesh, he forced his way into my small body. I was no longer a virgin; my innocence was stripped away in the most violent way possible.

Pain slammed into my body in the form of hot burning sensations and jolts or fire that radiated from my anus. My body tore apart in a way I could never describe because nothing could ever match the intensity with which I fell apart. Blood trickled beneath me from the invasion of his sin, and I knew the damage was far greater than I thought. This wasn't how it should have been. Rick was supposed to be the person that helped me through this difficult time, not the one to drag me down a deeper hole.

I was robbed. In more ways than one, I was robbed. My dignity, my virginity, my body was gone. All my hope, trust, and dependence, gone. Everything I ever thought was good, my faith, my chance for a mate, all gone. I was stripped clean of everything and all I could do was cry hoping it would end soon. When he was done, he sat up proudly and called me a gay-whore-bastard, even though he just took my virginity and enjoyed it. At sixteen my world was ripped from me, twice.

Rick, as if to give a final blow to insult then threatened to do the same to my sister. He would tell everyone in the pack how I moaned beneath him if I ever tried to do something about it. Of course, I did no such thing but at sixteen with newfound trauma, I sat there shaking and scared. I was to do or say nothing. It was the only way I could protect Iris. There was no way I would let Iris go through the same experience.

So, I stayed away from him, remained silent, as he drank himself to a stupor every day. The only time I could breathe peacefully was when he disappeared with his friends. They would go out on a binge and disappear for days at a time. It was the only time peace fell upon the house. Looking back at it all, I couldn't believe how I managed to tolerate him for so long still being in our pack.

The more I thought about how he acted after my father's death and his sudden fall into alcoholism, I had a very unreal realization. My mind swirled as I snapped back into reality. There was almost no doubt in my mind that Rick must have had something to do with my father's death. I couldn't understand why but something told me that it was a possibility. *If he truly hurt as a friend, then why do what he did to me?* It was a question that constantly plagued my mind.

While a person could change when they experienced a tremendous amount of grief, Rick's change was too volatile. What if it was out of hatred or revenge for something that I wasn't privy to? It had to be why he would mention how much I looked like my father over and over. After what he did to me, I wouldn't be surprised if he liked my father in a romantic way. The thought crossed my mind a few times, but I never had any other proof that he did. So many tears fell for a long time after that, feeling defeated and scared, unable to tell a soul.

Yet now, now could be the time to say something but it still terrified me. My eyes dropped with the weight of my pain, closing briefly as the pangs of my past rang behind them. I needed to know the full story or if my hunches were right. My mother never clarified it with me about how my father died, no matter how many times I asked. Nor did she ever tell me anything that happened between Rick and my father. The secrecy between the two and then what he did to me made my imagination run wild with certainty that something else happened.

All my mother would say was that my father died and that was that. I was never to question it and so I never did. Circling the barn behind my home, I paced over a patch of hay that was spread across the floor. A weird feeling churned in the pit of my stomach. It matched the sad hollow walls that closed in on me the more I paced. My hair stood on end from a chill that seeped into my bones. Nothing good ever came from a feeling like this. My heart thumped against my chest, almost hurting my ribs in the erratic act. Something didn't add up.

"Hey, what you doing?" My Beta, Mavis, peeked into the shed. I jumped, lost in my nightmare of thoughts, to the point that his presence never registered. Had it been anyone else then I would have been dead. His tall lean tattooed stature didn't help either. It made him seem intimidating when he didn't crack a smile. The only thing that softened his appearance was the messy man bun he liked to wear that sometimes stuck out funny because of his straight hair.

"Just finishing up here," I stepped out of the barn and clapped my hands together shaking off dirt from the lawnmower I was initially fixing.

"Okay, are you gonna join us? We're going to hang out by the lake. Iris is able to walk well now so she wanted to get out of the house for a bit." Mavis smiled and grabbed my shoulder. "Come on, you're always working, relax a little. Besides, you're getting lost in that head of yours again. You haven't been yourself lately and I'm worried."

I reluctantly agreed. He was too perceptive for his own good. Maybe spending some time with everyone was what I needed. The distraction from the mindless torture I gave myself was very much needed. Although, not mindless at all since it was a pain that would never go away. An unfortunate memory that was forever ingrained in the very trenches of my faded soul. I slumped my shoulders, *let's stay out of my head for a while and join the others.* Leo agreed that maybe a break was in order and nudged me to go.

I went inside the house for a quick change of clothes and joined my pack out front. Everyone was laughing and in high spirits dressed in warm clothes and scarves that hung a bit too long. This was what I lived to protect. This was the fruit of my sacrifice, and it was worth the years keeping quiet. How could I not want to protect the peacefulness we found in these woods?

The weather was perfect for a bonfire and a cold beer. Iris laughed at something Mavis had said while Dona pouted. It must have been something that teased Dona, but it was wonderful to hear such a hearty laugh come from my sister. She stood there dressed in a warm wool lined jacket and a beanie carrying a picnic basket while Dona wore a long coat unbuttoned and fingerless gloves with a bundle of blankets in her hands. Dona was the sweetest person and the perfect match for Mavis' more reserved demeanor. She was very petite with short fiery red hair and freckles galore. She and Iris were very close since they had a lot of similar interests. They were practically like sisters. I could always count on her to be with Iris when I was not around.

As we made our way to the lake, the sounds of everyone laughing and telling stories was music to my ears. Mavis nudged my arm laughing at something his wife said about Iris and I laughed with him out of need to seem okay. But I heard nothing of what was said or what was going on. Even as I joined my family in person, I was still mentally far and detached. As reserved as Mavis could be, he was always a clown around me and Iris and now his new wife, Dona. Mavis and I grew up together and he knew me better than I knew myself. It was always why he could read me so well without having to use the mindlink or smell my pheromones.

We arrived at the lake and settled down by a few tables that had been left there and the dry bonfire that we had used last time. Music played softly from someone's phone connected to a speaker and the girls gathered on the oversized blanket they laid out chatting away with wine in one hand. One of the ladies kept looking at me, making eyes and smiling whenever I spotted her. She had been trying to get me to bed for a while, but she didn't do it for me.

Of course, she didn't know why either and watching her try was painful to witness. But I brushed it off as not wanting to do anything unless it was my mate. I thought she understood so I didn't approach her again over it but evidently, she wasn't. She fixed her overly styled hair with her pink manicured nails and tucked a curl behind her naked ear before winking at me. I gagged but I didn't bother to hide it from her. The look on her face was priceless and maybe she finally got the message.

I chuckled and looked away to avoid her glare. The guys managed to rekindle the fire pit and clinked their beer bottles in cheer. It was interesting watching how carefree everyone seemed when just moments ago I was having a mental breakdown. *I needed this*, I sighed and sat under a tree that was close to the lake. The literal tension in my body loosened within my stiff muscles. A small shiver crawled up my back as I laid against the cold tree. Spending time with everyone in my pack and feeling their happiness eased my body into comfort. This was how a family should be. Happy and enjoying each other's presence without fear of what the other person might do.

The sun began to set, and the crowd gathered by the fire to roast marshmallows along with various other food items. Some had hotdogs, others had fruit, and some had shrimp for some reason. That was probably Jimmy since he was obsessed with seafood. Jimmy was hilarious but a kind fourteen-year-old. His twin brother was identical in looks but different in all else, like how very book smart he was and how he detested seafood. The selection of food was an off mix for sure but to each their own. A strange knot formed in the pit of my stomach again. The calm I briefly enjoyed didn't last long. It never did and it was always for the same reason.

I looked around and there he was staggering drunk, making his way to the roaring fire. The reason for my unease, Rick, stumbled and from this distance, I could clearly see the nasty grin plastered on his face. He grabbed Iris on the shoulder to stabilize himself, almost faltering in his step. *This asshole needs to stop touching her*, I thought with a rage so fierce, I almost marched over. She laughed it off and helped him steady before brushing off his hand as he regained his stance.

He must think he was bulletproof knowing I had kept quiet all this time. His careless hands and eyes were all over Iris. Every time he touched her I felt like I felt it on my own skin. The only thing keeping him here was my fear of him but having to watch him do the sly stunts he pulled pushed me closer to the edge. I watched him like a hawk to make sure he didn't hurt anyone else, and I stepped in if I needed to when he got too hammered. Despite our inability to get drunk easily, he kept himself in a constant state of influence with wolfdrink mixed into his alcohol. To this day, I had no idea what was in that concoction, but it was the only way wolves could drink.

Keeping an eye on him was all I could do to make sure everyone was safe, but things needed to change. *What if I said something?* We were grown now and could handle our own. As the Alpha, surely Mavis would have my back and I could hide Iris until I knew she was safe. *But if Mavis didn't back me…* My hands trembled at the thought of the what-ifs. They truly were what bound me along with the very vivid memories that imprison my mind. Through shaky eyes I spotted Rick approaching Iris again.

"You look beautiful today", Rick slurred into her ear, but I barely managed to hear. He had to know I was watching. He knew how to test how much he could get away with.

"Thank you," Iris smiled and walked away. *Good girl,* I thought to myself and watched her stand next to Mavis and Dona to grab some marshmallows from the bag Dona was claiming for herself. I let out a breath, but my nerves still rattled.

Rick looked my way and grinned with so much evil intent evident in the wrinkles of his old face. At eight-five he was showing the signs of age but still looking only half of it. It annoyed me the way his handlebar mustache curled up at the end of his lips. The way his eyes hooded from the stupor he was in, ominous and unsettling. The face of a murderer emerged from the mole of his left cheek to the short stubby lashes that did little to hide his true intentions.

Murderer? Did I really think he would have gone that far? With how much he loved my father, I doubted he would have killed him. That knot in my stomach formed again but it paralyzed me this time. Fear, disgust, humiliation, and bile all rose within me working together to destroy me from the inside out. My throat almost closed as if choking. His stare nailed my body against the tree, crucifying me with his cruel intentions. Mavis looked my way. The sheer panic in his eyes helped me shift my focus.

Atlas? His voice tried to pierce my mind, but I fought it. I tried to block him out, but I felt myself breaking. My thoughts, anxiety, the stress of suffocating under Rick's malicious glare were all seeping out of me. **Atlas, are you okay? What's wrong? What am I feeling from you right now?**

I locked my mind again, blocking everyone out but Mavis. Rick stumbled over to Iris whispering something, and she walked away with him looking concerned. The bile rose quicker up my throat. I wanted to throw up. But moreover, I needed to get to Iris, yet I couldn't move. I...

Mavis, keep an eye on Rick and Iris but act naturally. I struggled to tell Mavis with my throat closed, I couldn't breathe. It hurt. Desperately, I clawed my chest.

Is everything okay? You look sick. Mavis started toward me, but I held out my hand to stop him.

I don't know, please just watch her. Mavis felt my panic intensifying and jerked his head my way. I let too much slip earlier. Gripping my chest while taking deep breaths to calm myself, my vision blurred. The bile made it the rest of the way up and I was ready to hurl. I got up and ran to the other side of the tree and vomited all my anxiety. **I feel like shit, Mavis.** I spat that taste out of my mouth and walked over to the blanket the girls laid out to grab water from the cooler. I swished a bit in my mouth and spat it out, repeating the process a few times. My nerves settled, but the feeling was still there. So, I chugged half the bottle of the water and took my seat back by the tree. The night was no longer relaxing and the last thing I wanted was to be around everyone.

The night went on and thankfully Rick didn't do anything but talk with Iris. I kept swallowing the bile that wanted to break free from my body every time I saw him make passes on her. I didn't know if he was alert enough to feel the extra eyes on him or if he noticed how my Beta's wife kept pulling Iris away to dance or do other things. All I knew was that I was grateful.

Mavis kept linking with me to give updates on what he overheard them talking about, which helped keep me calm. I just wished he didn't talk to her at all. By the time Iris was alone and Rick left to bother someone else, I was too wound up. It was mentally too much to take in at the moment. What started off as a relaxing retreat had me through a rollercoaster of turmoil.

With the little bit of strength I had left, I walked over to Mavis and told him I was leaving. I couldn't handle the stress and I was better off staying on my own at home than witnessing Rick being the arse that he was. Then again, I wouldn't have been able to watch over my sister if I was home.

Despite being outside and sitting so far from him, I was on pins and needles around that bastard. Mavis assured me that he would continue to watch over my sister, which allowed me the freedom to wallow in my self-hate, alone, so that was exactly what I did.

My feet dragged me away from the life of the party and into the dark cold night. The moon was high in the sky suggesting it must have been very close to midnight. Times like these I wondered what my mother was doing and if she was looking at the moon at the same time as me. I chugged the last bit of the water I had left in the bottle. It was refreshing or maybe it just felt that way because my nerves were finally at ease again.

The chill of the night was cool but very much welcomed against my heated skin and current state of mind. The way I was spiraling earlier slowly dissipated into a calm nothingness the further I walked away from the lake. A heavy sigh filled my chest and left my lips. The way the situation weighed on me and dragged me down, as a leader, was not Ideal. I could handle anything else that came my way without a second thought but the moment it concerned my own troubles, I broke down inside. Inside I hosted a wolf with a body made of broken tainted pieces only held together by the skin and a fragile heart. I was a few anise cocktails and a therapy session away from a trainwreck.

I sat under the oak tree that had been growing in front of my home for generations, my mute therapist, when I needed a moment to speak my thoughts. The clear sky expanded above me like a navy blanket. The moon was almost full, glowing bright and magnificent between the twinkling stars. I took a deep breath closing my eyes, *winter snow and cinnamon.* My eyes shot open, darting around in the dark. The smell was real and not my wishful thinking. Too many times I had lingered on the memory of seeing that man through his window and thought I could smell him. But this time however, it was real. He had to be nearby.

I squinted towards the tree line trying to decipher what were the different shadows that I had seen and from behind a tree, out emerged a beautiful enormous silver like wolf. With the shift of the clouds, the moonlight kissed his fur and reflected glimmering silver streaks across his body. He glistened and it was the first time I had seen any wolf as magnificent as him.

The Silver Lining

Our eyes met and lingered upon one another. He held my gaze and took a step forward. *How is it that his scent can pull me out of my darkness so easily?* Each step thumped with the beat of my heart. Forgetting the last bit of anxiety from just moments ago, I shifted into my wolf, Leo, never looking away. My clothes shredded and fell on my feet as I shifted. Silly of me to forget something like removing my clothes but I couldn't help how enthralled I was.

***

The scent of cinnamon wafted up my snout and I growled deep in my chest with pleasure. A rumble so deep within me, triggered by the intoxication of his scent. It pulled me to him like a red string of destiny had us tethered, shortening its leash between us. But if he was my destiny then I'd gladly accept getting to know what that future looked like. I walked towards him slowly with careful steps so I wouldn't startle him. The thought of scaring him off wasn't something I wanted to entertain.

His paws gracefully made their way towards me. Even the way he walked demanded attention with his larger than normal size emphasizing his grace. My body trembled in delight as he neared. I wanted to touch him and feel his fur against mine. Out of all my years of being able to reincarnate, I had never had the pleasure of meeting a wolf like him. His silver eyes gleamed against the moon, searching deep within my eyes, recognizing the connection between us. He was close enough that I could hear if his heart was beating as fast as mine. And it did. My bond called for him and he called for me in return. A mutual yearning, that although was triggered by our bond, I wouldn't dare ignore the feeling.

I trusted the goddess to mate me with someone I could fall in love with, but this felt different. It felt familiar. An adrenaline that I had long forgotten and was just reminded of. Atlas hid within me, still not ready to meet his human mate but I was ready for mine. To meet him again. My forever wolf. He whimpered softly at me, and a flood of butterflies raced from my ears down to my tail. *My goddess, this is killing me.* My silver wolf stopped a foot away from me. His scent devoured me, sending my heart to the brink of cardiac arrest. *My mate.* I shouted in my mind with excitement.

Rustling leaves and laughter caught my ear from behind me. It broke the moment that held me in a state of suspense. I turned quickly to see my pack arriving and snapped back towards my mate. *He's gone.* I searched everywhere knowing my wolf vision at night was much better than my human one. *Nothing.* It was like I had seen a ghost. Only his scent lingered gently, and a sense of clarity washed over me and assured me he was real. *My silver ghost.* The way this encounter gave me strength and yet it took it all away just the same, was curious.

My vision adjusted, sharpening itself further to look between the trees, but still, my silver ghost was long gone. I slumped knowing Mavis was going to interrogate Atlas tonight and anxiety began to nudge Atlas but with the calm that being near my mate provided, Atlas shrugged it off and snuggled within the peace it offered. Maybe I could finally convince Atlas to open up to our Beta. It would be a good start. Then he could ask for help like he did earlier. He could help keep Iris safer if he had more watchful eyes on her. While I knew Atlas didn't want anyone to know his secret, if it meant keeping Iris safe and ridding the pack of *him*, then he needed to consider it.

"Leo, what are you doing over there?" Mavis called out to me. "And why are your clothes torn up?" Mavis continued shouting. I turned around and ran towards the house to help Atlas face the music. It was now or never.

Nothing to worry about. I'm gonna go get clothes on. I mind-linked with Mavis and ran into the house, making a dash upstairs before shifting back in my room.

***

By the time I came back downstairs, mostly everyone was in the living room chatting and laughing over their own silliness. They were happy with the fun they had by the bonfire and cracking jokes over misshapes that had occurred. Within my family infested living room, I found a small space at the edge of the sofa and parked myself in it. Too soon did my Beta spot me and made his way like a bee line express. I grabbed the beer that he passed my way with a half-smile after he pressed the cold bottle to my cheek.

"You good bro?" Mavis took a swig of his beer and sat on the arm of the sofa which was practically also my shoulder.

"I'm fine," I popped the lid and gulped half the bottle. It was a new flavor of IPA that Mavis had found in our local store. He was always on the lookout for the fruity ones. This one was blueberry.

"Don't look it, to me," Mavis snapped, tired of my half attempt at avoiding an honest answer.

"Drop it!" I peeled myself from the small space I sat in and walked over to the kitchen window. I had a feeling I wasn't going to be able to avoid the topic anymore. Not if Mavis had anything to do with it. Especially not with Leo nagging me inside as well to open up to Mavis. But I wasn't sure if I could do so without breaking down.

Mavis stood up and handed me another beer, "no, I won't drop it. In fact, the way you were panicking earlier had me worried. Why was I babysitting your sister? Who is a grown woman by the way," Mavis furrowed his brows and motioned for me to follow after I ignored his question.

I sighed and quietly followed him to have the inevitable conversation. *You can do this Atlas. You got this. He's your bro*, Leo encouraged me in the back of my mind. He was my personal cheerleader minus the pom poms. I bumped into something hard before realizing it was Mavis' back. We had reached the back porch outside and he stood there staring at the mess that another pack mate left behind.

"Sorry," I mumbled.

Mavis raised an eyebrow, taking a seat in one of the chairs. "Okay lay it on me. Why have you been acting weird?" Mavis downed the rest of his beer and placed it on the table along with the other empty bottles and cans.

"Okay before I start, I just want to say that all this stays between us. Not just as Alpha and Beta but as my best friend." Mavis nodded with worry, and I continued. "I'm telling you this not because I have to but because I feel I should in order for you and only you to understand the gravity of the situation." My lips quivered a bit. I could already feel the tightening in my chest. The way it gripped my heart and squeezed it.

I took a seat in the chair next to his and sat there quietly for a moment contemplating my words. My leg bounced almost uncontrollably while my thoughts jumbled, trying to form a coherent story in my mind. There really wasn't a way to tell my story without falling apart, exposing myself, and revealing my wounds.

"I need to say some part with the link, just in case of prying ears." I whispered and Mavis slowly agreed with a nod of his head.

So, when my dad passed away, I was a mess. We all were but…. one night I was crying behind the barn drinking rum. Rick found me and joined me with his stupid whiskey habit.

My heart started beating frantically against my chest as the words spilled out of my mind and into Mavis'. My vision blurred but I tossed my head back in a childish attempt to stop the tears from falling. **After we talked and cried about my father, I ended up… I told him….**

My hands calmed up with sweat. *Shit, I can't do this Leo. I can't breathe, help me!* I wasn't strong enough to say the words. They couldn't form in my mind just as much as they refused to leave my lips. My eyes squeezed as my breath became shallow, leaving my chest in short burst. The tears I tried so hard to hold back finally broke free and streamed down my face and into my ears.

"Hey…hey take your time. You don't have to tell me now if you're not ready. I didn't know it was this deep." Mavis moved his chair closer to me and rubbed my shoulder in an attempt to comfort me.

"No...no... It's cool. It's not how I thought I would tell you but it's part of the story so…." I took a deep breath and finished off my beer.

Okay... so I told Rick that I'm gay. I looked at Mavis and he just nodded for me to continue. I could see the shock, but he remained silent. **Once I told him that, he took it as an invitation and...** I gagged as the memory of Rick's whiskey breath came back. Mavis rubbed my back in circular motions. He clearly knew where I was going with this. Either that or he was showing sympathy and pity for the state I was in. His warmth spread through my chest.

Just breathe Atlas. Breathe. Mavis' words echoed in my mind. He wasn't turning away from me. He was still here, listening, and patiently waiting for me. It was a relief. I stood up and took the deepest breath I could manage.

I wanted to hide in a hole. I wanted to sit in a ditch licking my wounds. Anything was better than having to tell this story.

"Buddy, it's okay. Don't finish the story. Take your time and maybe tomorrow or another day we can continue."

"NO!" I snapped. "If I don't say something now, I never will. Just don't hate me, please. I don't want to lose you as my best friend. Mavis, don't..." I clawed at my chest trying to grasp my breath. The anxiety kept slamming into me in waves.

"Atlas please, breathe." Mavis stood up and pulled me into his chest. "Follow my breathing, nice and slow." In slow long inhales, I followed his rhythm. I followed his breathing, crying, and panting all at once. "That's it. Nice and slow, just breathe the way I do." My chest loosened up.

He... he raped me. The words finally fell out of my mind and into his in a mental vomit I couldn't contain.

Mavis froze. I cried harder having finally said those words to another person. Mavis hugged me tighter as I let it all out. With each silent cry Mavis tightened his grip around me as if to suffocate my pain away.

When he was done, he threatened to do the same to Iris and tell everyone how I liked it if I ever said anything.

Mavis handed me what I hoped was a clean tissue from his pocket to dry the free-falling tears.

"Jesus, why did you wait so long to say something?" Mavis looked mortified but mostly concerned about my mental state. I didn't know why I thought he would shun me if I told him the truth. He wasn't that kind of man. But the fear I carried made me a bit irrational.

"Because I'm scared. I don't want him hurting Iris. I'm her older brother and with my father gone, I am to protect her and everyone here." I turned around trying to avoid him seeing the tears threatening my eyes again.

"So why tell me now?"

I found my mate. I half turned back and smiled as Mavis' eyes grew wide. "He is beautiful," I fully turned to Mavis, "I want to be happy, but I can't do that with you-know-who threatening to destroy my happiness and family. I also think there is something more to that person. He is hiding something, and I need to find out what, before he decides to strike." Mavis nodded and we both sat in

silence thinking about what came next. But the tears kept
on coming.

Chapter 5

CASSIUS

The scent that seemed to linger in my senses refused to let go of me. To be attracted towards the combination of lavender and oak was sort of surprising to me but here I was wanting to smell it again. The very thought of that combination sent my hormones into overdrive. *I wonder what his wolf looks like.* A smile formed on the corners of my mouth. A week already went by since I last saw him, and curiosity was finally getting the best of me. Even Wolfie inside kept annoyingly asking when I was going to approve him again.

I could honestly say I was happy with my mate turning out to be a man. And a delicious one at that. A woman didn't cut for me, not even if I tried. Women never seemed to provoke any arousals in me. I had tried once and simply couldn't get it up no matter what she did, until her brother showed up of course. The girl I had convinced myself to date was sweet and patient with me. She was beautiful and had curves any straight man would die for.

All I wanted was to fit in and that meant not being gay according to society and the media. I had been hard bent on the idea that if I dated a girl long enough that I could come to love her. And if I could love her then I could eventually learn to have sex with her like any other man but that wasn't what happened. After we dated for a few months, it was finally time to get intimate. The mood was right, and we had an intense make-out session in her room. Kissing for some reason was no problem for me. Then again with my eyes closed, I could easily disregard her sex.

She pulled all the stops for me and wore sexy lingerie and the sweet perfume I liked so much. She even tied up her hair in a messy bun which I thought looked wonderful with her freckles and high cheekbones. I could fully appreciate her beauty but that was where it stopped for me. Her beauty did nothing for my libido. She worked to seduce me using her lips to make her way down my body, but I felt myself getting tense because of it. I tried to relax but the moment her lips touched my flaccid member, I felt like it shriveled up further.

Every ounce I had mustered to try and make it work vanished and the hurt on her face made it worse, but as she decided to try again, her brother walked in with his sexy shirtless body. Her brother was shaped like a god among men. His intense stare over my half-naked body alone gave me a raging boner in an instant. Of course, he took note of the splendid growth I presented while I stared at his chest and smiled. But then kicked me out of the room for trying to sleep with his sister.

I couldn't deny it at that point. It could only be a man, especially if he looked like the furious specimen that walked me out of the house. But just before he could push me out of the front door, I turned to him to say something but in the most aggressive way, he pulled me in for a heated kiss which forced my erection to knock against his thigh. I had only pulled up my pants but had left them unbuttoned. He grunted and bit my bottom lip before he whispered in my ear that I should have gone for him instead of his sister. The whisper in my ear with his warm breath sent a shiver of excitement down my body. He must have noticed as he chuckled and nibbled my earlobe. I blushed only to have him admire the spectacle that I was and then slammed the door in my face. I was only seventeen.

No matter what I did after that, I had to accept the fact that I was gay and that was that. After coming out to the pack at eighteen I did everything to hook up with men but within a year or so, I stopped. The sex experience I gained made it all worth it but every time they walked away; I stayed a bit emptier inside. It was all just meaningless fun, and I grew curious to feel the bond that everyone talked about. A bead of sweat trickled from my brow to my temple.

The room felt oddly hot, and the heater wasn't even on. I opened my eyes to find my curtain ablaze.

"What the hell?" I sprung out of the bed to put it out with my blanket, slapping it repeatedly but then the flames went out on their own just as I thought they should extinguish. In a wide stance holding up the blanket towards my window, I stared at the black burns that decorated the new set of curtains Cecile had just bought. Oddly enough, weird things tended to happen in my room. Cecile had a theory that there was a spirit playing tricks on me, but I didn't know if I believed that's what it was. Then again, I didn't know what to believe at all.

First of the crazy occurrences were my socks levitating for no reason, crazy, but not crazier than being a wolf or a vampire or even an elf in this world. Then there was a time where I thought about turning on the light to read my book and it turned on without me flipping the switch. The more things happened the more I started to feel like I was the one causing all of the incidents. Yet when I intentionally tried to make something happen, nothing ever did.

Another time, while sleeping, I kicked off the covers feeling hot and then a cool breeze swept over my skin, sending chills down my body. The window was always closed, and the ceiling fan didn't work at the time. But it was the most comfortable sleep I had ever had. Now, I could add combustible curtains to my list of weird things. All of which was within the past several months, since my twenty-first birthday to be exact.

I grabbed my jacket and left the room, closing the door behind me. The last thing I needed was Cecile down my neck about the curtains. I left the house for a walk in thought about how crazy the last week had been. I finally found my mate and it had my head spinning in a swirl of emotions. It was the only way to explain why he smelled so lovely to me. I couldn't help but remember how much Cecile jumped for joy when she smelled Jude after they were apart for a bit. It was her happy place, and I wanted that too. I needed to confirm it despite it scaring me a little as well. I knew that if I were to confirm he was my mate, I would want to accept it right then and there. But would he? What if he didn't want me and turned me down, essentially weakening the bond?

My feet carried for a while through the expanse of the trees behind the house and somehow guided me back to where I took the she-wolf. Lavender and oak invaded my senses. *He's here.* I was scared to meet him in person out of fear of rejection but in my wolf form, I could run quickly if something were to happen. So, I shifted into Wolfie and slowly approached the end of the tree line in wait.

***

In the distance, I saw a man looking around squinting in my direction. *My mate is beautiful,* I whispered to Cassius, and he hummed within me. While I could appreciate his human form, I wanted to see his wolf. Even in the moonlight, I could acknowledge how handsome he was. I stepped out into view and our eyes locked. The way he stared, taking in my appearance, felt like I was being devoured. As the only wolf around here with my size and silver fur, I was unique and always turning the heads of fellow wolves. But the one before me was the only attention I wanted.

My fur, which tended to glimmer under direct moonlight, gave me a more ethereal look. At least, that was what Alex told me and at this moment I was beginning to think he was right. No one in my pack could explain it but they accepted me all the same. I just prayed my mate did as well and at the very least, my mate seemed curious.

I took slow steps forward and my mate shifted before me. What a wonder to behold. His thick brown fur covered his body with hints of gray and his eyes reflected the fire I felt growing within me. The moment intensified as he approached me slowly until we were a foot away from one another. I could happily drown in his scent. It's intoxicating. He was definitely my mate and one that seemed familiar. I whimpered wanting to touch him, but Cassius was terrified. Although the want was great, I was scared to have it.

Noises of people laughing appeared in the distance and robbed our attention. But in that moment that my mate turned to look at them, I panicked and ran. I hid behind one of the trees and shifted to better blend into the night. My bare skin scratched against the jagged tree trunk, but I was finally regaining my wits.

****

I watched my mate turn around looking for me frantically until someone called him back. *Coward,* Wolfie insulted me for not staying there but I ignored him. Yes, I had heard the stories and yes, I knew how it should all go once I found my mate but all I could think about was how different I was compared to the other wolves. *What if he or his pack doesn't accept me?*

I wanted to claim him as my own but not at this moment. My mate ran off to the people that called him, lessening the hold his fading scent had on me. So, I began my walk back home with my tail tucked between my legs, so to speak. *Well at least I have a name now. They called his wolf Leo.* Wolfie happily yipped in my mind which brought a smile to my face.

It was mind blowing how alluring my mate was. His brown fur complimented him so well. I wanted to speak with him and hear his voice. I was curious to know his human name and every little detail that made him perfect for me. The smile that crossed my face was genuine but with my mind lost in thought, I failed to notice the hunter right in front of me. It was the man from before with his shotgun pointing right at my chest. His barrel held steady, but his chest was heaving in fear. I could smell it.

"I don't know how you managed to prove that you aren't a wolf, but I don't believe it for a second. My instincts are never wrong." The hunter laughed at his own words. I never understood how humanity could turn to kill so quickly.

As a wolf, I knew firsthand about death, but it only ever came to us when we were protecting ourselves. We didn't kill for sport, we didn't hunt humans, and we didn't go around harassing others for pleasure. Maybe once, when we were savages and territorial, we fought but that was because the times called for it and it was only amongst each other. In this day and age, we were all civilized and wanted peace. Yet this man thought he was above us despite his lack of intelligence.

"I have no idea what you're going on about. Where's your little boyfriend Bobby?" I was sure it wasn't a smart thing to say at the moment, but my goddess was ruining my night.

"Shut the fuck up, I ain't no faggot. Unlike you, walking around with your big dick all out on display." He spat at me, disgusted because I stood naked and proud. My clothes ripped earlier when I shifted so, here I was in all my glory.

"What I do on my property is none of your business. Besides, me being naked doesn't make me gay, it makes me a nudist. However, the man that has been taking glances at my 'big' dick, well that's another story." I chuckled at my emphasis.

"I SAID SHUT THE FUCK UP!" He waved the gun at me in an attempt to intimidate me. Which was working. This man seemed like a firecracker compared to Bobby.

"Why do you feel it's okay to trespass? Do I need to actually call the cops on you?" I choose my words carefully at this point. His breathing had steadied, and I could feel his determination to kill me on the spot. He only hesitated because he didn't have definitive proof that I was a wolf and because of that, I couldn't afford to shift involuntarily. I had the bad habit of shifting when my anger and anxiety got the best of me, and I could already feel my nose twitching.

"I don't give a shit about trespassing. I hunt wherever the fuck I want. You think I care about laws. Besides, unless you got a phone up your ass, you're not calling anyone for help. So, it's like I was never here." He stepped closer to me with his gun, but I didn't move. I held my ground which made the hunter take further caution. Unfortunately for him, he was way too cocky and that was his mistake. He continued to take steady steps forward and brought his barrel a few inches from my face. *Shit, I pressed him too much.*

I could almost see in slow motion his finger pressing the trigger. "You know what, wolf, today yo-" I quickly shifted and tackled him as his gun fired upwards.

***

The gun shot into the air, missing me completely. Pinning him down, I put all my weight onto his chest. His ribs simultaneously cracked beneath me as I pounced. Fear overran his face. His eyes lost all hope of life, and his breath began to struggle in and out of his most likely punctured lungs. A slow gurgle began with blood pooling in his mouth. I definitely punctured something.

A gun rang out in the distance and hit my leg. It pierced me with vengeance. I quickly bit the neck of the gargling hunter under me for good measure and dashed in the opposite direction. Pain traveled through every inch of my body as my foot hit the ground running. The bullet didn't go in too deep, meaning the shooter was far enough away but it also meant that it could be lodged in my bone.

Blood dripped down my leg, but I needed to find safety. *Shit, I think the bullet is laced with something,* I warned Cassius who was doing his best to stay calm inside. My vision blurred but I made it to a cave. I collapsed in its darkness unsure of where I was. This was all the strength I had left in me. *This is it. I'm gonna die. I just found Leo and I'm gonna die.* My eyes closed and darkness wrapped me cold.

***

I woke up to someone manhandling my body. I was being hog tied by none other than Bobby. That bastard must have been hiding, keeping watch, the same way he did the first time we met and shot me the moment he could. Pain shot through me again. The bullet was still in my leg preventing me from healing properly.

"Well, look who is awake. Explain to me how a filthy animal like you doesn't react to silver?" Bobby took his knife and touched my face with it. Nothing happened and Bobby was tickled pink by it. Giggling at his discovery.

"I don't know either, I found out the same time you did." I gave him the deadliest stare I could muster but I was tired. My body was running on fumes at this point.

"Interesting. I'm sure your head will go for a pretty penny in the black market. Unfortunately, someone else wants that pretty head of yours and after seeing that beautiful silver coat, I am doubling your bounty. So how about you stay right there while I go get my truck. Yeah? Make yourself at home," Bobby laughed and walked out of the cave.

The cave I was in was small and it didn't seem there was another way out. It was rather small and not as dark as I remembered seeing it when Wolfie fell unconscious. The moonlight was enough to fill the cave. My eyes grew heavy and whatever was on the bullet was spreading through me. I slipped back into darkness once more, unable to scream.

My eyes fluttered again. The brick walls were painted a rustic orange with a dark red trim. The ceiling was covered with soundproofing and a single set of iron bars draped to the floor. I was in a basement, locked in a makeshift cell. Thankfully I was no longer hog tied but instead wrapped in a rather warm blanket. A bit of moonlight showed on the wall opposite me. It highlighted the stairs leading most likely to the house.

The window was small but the air flowing through it was fresh and smelled of a nearby body of water. I removed the blanket to check my leg and for some reason, it was bandaged. The bandaging was done well and only someone with medical experience could do such a fine job. At least I thought so. I doubted Bobby was the one responsible since he would never have bothered to bandage the wound. In fact, I couldn't feel the bullet anymore.

Could it be this buyer he mentioned? My senses recovered just enough that I could smell wolves upstairs. A lot of them, actually. *Are there other wolves trapped?*

My eyes darted to the door that was opening slowly and I shuffled back on the stiff bed I sat on. A burst of lavender invaded my senses. *My mate. Boy you better talk to him this time,* Wolfie snapped inside but I ignored him as I inhaled the wonderful scent. I sent a prayer to the moon goddess, hoping that this man wasn't the buyer Bobby referred to.

"I knew it was you the moment they brought you in", a tall man stepped into the room. His dark brown hair fell in waves to one side of his face just about level to his eyes. His eyes were the color of honey almost gold, framed by perfectly groomed brows. His body, even under his clothes, had well defined lines from his muscles that showed through. He was strong and delicious for the taking with a heavenly voice to boot. This man was already the death of me, but I blinked my way from his chest to his toes, taking in all of what he was.

At this point, I had no idea if it was really me lusting over this man or if it was the mate bond that pulled me from all reason and let me see him without constriction.

"Why am I here?" Of course, that wasn't the first thing I wanted to say but I honestly just wanted him to let me out so I could touch him. *Wait, touch him? What if he is the buyer?*

"My Beta found you in a cave tied up. We heard some gunshots and figured hunters were out again. I set out to get them for having hurt my sister but instead, they found you." He walked over to me, pulling out a set of keys. A sigh of relief left my lips as my heart skipped. *He isn't the buyer. Accept him already, I want to connect with my wolf mate,* Wolfie continued to badger me.

"Your sister?" I asked, watching his beautiful fingers fumble through the keys while I ignored my annoying inner wolf.

"Yes, thank you for saving Iris. She told me everything she remembered, and I knew it was you that saved her from your scent."

"You're welcome," I blushed, and silence filled the room followed by the clank of the iron bars unlocking. The tension made it hard to breathe. Then again it could also be his scent that was filling every inch of my lungs. Yes, it was his scent. Lavender and Oak choked me to no end which made my skin tingle with the desire to please my wolf and accept the bond.

"You're my mate, aren't you? ...I'm Atlas." He opened the door and stepped in. I sat frozen on the bed, but my wolf was running in circles inside as Atlas approached me. I stared at him and gulped in sheer panic but not Wolfie. He yipped inside me anxiously. *Please calm down Wolfie. You're making me more nervous.... shut up and go to him already you idiot.* My wolf snapped back impatiently. Atlas stopped before me. Just inches away. His perfectly sculpted body towered over me, smiling gently waiting for me to respond. Waiting for me to react.

"I guess, I am," I tried my best to sound cool, but my voice came out cracked which made my tanned skin redder than an apple. "I'm Cassius by the way." I stood up, thinking it would keep me from making a fool of myself but now I was only a couple inches from him. I was slightly taller which boosted my self-confidence but not enough to keep me from thinking straight.

"May I touch you?" Atlas' eyes looked up at me just as scared as I felt but excited all the same. If we touched with intention, it was like accepting that we were each other's mates. My heart was beating loudly within my ears and my eyes flickered between his. I wanted this and it didn't seem like he would reject me. This could be my happy beginning.

"Yes, you may," I barely managed. Breathy and shaky, my voice was a whisper. I finally got to meet my mate and the moon goddess gave me a perfect specimen of a wolf, I was beside myself.

Atlas raised his hand and placed it on my chest. It was only then that I realized I was completely, and utterly… naked. The blanket must have fallen when I stood up. Warmth spread within me like wildfire. My wolf howled inside with pleasure and there it was. I could hear his wolf howling back to mine. It was beautiful and I closed my eyes enjoying the strange sensation of our bodies recognizing and accepting each other.

An aura of sorts formed around us, connecting us and fortifying our bond. I heard something like this doesn't always happen instantly. The bond only ever fully recognized the other when both parties truly wanted it. If that occurred, then the mate bond would instantly strengthen, seal, and enhance everything between the two. Their passion, lust, abilities, and communication included.

For those that were more reluctant at first, the connection and the solidification of the bond occurred much slower. A low growl bubbled in my chest, and I opened my eyes to meet his. I was positive that my irises were silver now because of the heat building in my body.

I raised my hand and placed it on his chest as well. It felt like literal sparks flew between my hand and his body. Acceptance from both our wolves. A surge of what felt like electricity coursed between us. It was a feeling so intense that we both briefly got weak in the knees because of it. We caught each other and placed our foreheads against one another in a soft chuckle and a bit out of breath. The feeling that engulfed me was something I never wanted to let go of. It was addicting.

My mate, Atlas whispered into my mind, and I smiled at his words. **And your mine**, I mentally whispered back. As fast as it all was moving, it felt more than just familiar. It felt like home. Although I was worried at first that I might not be ready, the reality of it was, I wanted an intimate connection for a long time. Our wolves howled in unison filling the hole that plagued my lonely heart.

My mate felt slightly tense, and I couldn't tell if it was due to how fast it was all happening or if he suddenly regretted accepting the bond. But I ran my hand across his chest and down his arm. Little goosebumps reacted to my touch. It was a cute reaction and one I did not expect to arouse me.

Chapter 6

CASSIUS

Atlas wrapped the warm maroon blanket that covered me earlier around my shoulders and turned around avoiding eye contact. It was a sweet gesture, but it only made me more painfully aware of nakedness. He led me out of the basement and through the stillness of the home. It was quiet and seemed desolate but could only be the result of everyone sleeping. Or at least I assumed that was the reason why. For all I knew, Atlas lived alone with his sister.

I stayed close behind him, taking the exact steps he took to avoid the possibility of making noise. If his floor was anything like mine, then I was sure a loud creak would ring out if I didn't tread carefully. We passed the front door in the foyer, and I almost stopped confused as to where we were going. When Atlas led me out of the basement, I was sure that he was guiding me out of the house so I could go home. Didn't seem like that was the case since Atlas kept going towards the stairwell.

As we went up the stairs they creaked gently as each wooden plank gave way under our weight. The dark rug that lined the stair neatly and tucked, tickled my bare feet. It felt fluffy like the way rugs tended to puff up after they were vacuumed. It felt nice not having to continue on a cold floor. My eyes danced with the sway of Atlas' behind and the thought of us possibly going to his room both excited and terrified me. It was the only reason I could think of that would require us going to the second floor. Either that or he was ready to push me out of a window, which I doubted was the case.

The hall on the second floor was dark with only the light from his room peeking through from underneath his closed door. My vision adjusted enough to make sure I didn't bump into anything like the tall white vase against the wall that had long stalks of dried wheat for decoration, and it brought me back to when I was a teenager.

I was very familiar with having to navigate through dark halls if I wanted to avoid Cecile's wrath or waking Lenny. Whenever I snuck out for one of my rendezvous, be it with friends or just wanting to be alone, I always made sure to remember which plank didn't creak on the floor. If I wasn't careful then Cecile would make sure she punished me for it. But if I was trying to get something to eat, I was more terrified of waking up Lenny on nights he visited since he had the bad habit of eating the kitchen clean.

I followed Atlas into a massive suite, and I was taken aback by the strong scent in his room. It only made sense, but it was still like an embrace I wasn't expecting. He pointed at the door wondering if I was okay if he closed it, which I didn't mind. The room was filled with neutral tones which were very befitting to the colors of Leo's fur. Even the soft yellow light from his bedside lamp was dim which gave a warm glow against his fitted sheets. A king-size bed sat in the middle of the room with a chaise at the foot of it, adorned with a throw.

To the left of the room was a mahogany desk situated neatly in the corner surrounded by books and papers on top. I was almost surprised it wasn't made of oak. On the wall beside it there seemed to be a walk-in closet which was suggested by the opened door. Next to that I presumed was a bathroom, but it could very well be another closet. Another wave of his scent filled me with a sense of tranquility. It was like having a personal walking aromatherapy stick as a mate if this was how he affected me.

Atlas walked over with a set of clothes and smiled. "Here. You can change into these for now."

I reached out for the clothes and grazed his fingers. That simple gesture sent a bolt of tingles straight to my member, making it twitch with excitement. Just like earlier, the slightest whisper of his skin against mine, lit me up inside like the fourth of July.

"Thank you," my voice quivered. Already embarrassed by how I sounded like I hit puberty, I walked over to the bed and dropped my blanket to change. I did my best to ignore the possibility of him looking at my body. While it was completely natural for our kind to see each other naked due to our shifting nature, this was different. It made me nervous knowing that the person watching me was my mate, but I guess I could have easily told him to turn around. Yet, I didn't.

"Oh. My. God," Atlas' voice dipped as he covered his mouth. I turned to him slightly to see a blush spreading across his face as his eyes took in all of me. *I guess he didn't get a good look at me when we were in the basement*, I thought. From a place unknown, a sense of bravado surged from the smirk on my lips to the half turn of my body on display. I would hate to be the only one reacting to his presence, so it was only fair if I teased him a little. Slowly, with my growing semi-erection I turned more towards Atlas providing a view of my excitement.

"What's wrong?" I asked with my front in full display. This was where I put all my playboy skills to good use. Atlas' eyes widened and I could only hope it was with eyes of hunger. But he never answered me, instead he watched me as I reached for the shirt first and tossed it on. My mate burned my skin with a gaze that sparked my growth further between my legs.

"N-nothing," Atlas' finally answered with a face turned 30 shades of red. He turned away from me to face the bedroom door and moved his hands in front of himself. He seemed so innocent in his reaction, and it made me wonder how innocent he might be. His chest pumped as his breathing quickened and I could smell his arousal. This mate bond really did a number on our hormones because I was beginning to feel just more flustered than he was. We were reacting to one another, bouncing off the other's pheromones. The air smelled different as well. The lavender scent was potent, and the lust was thick as it mixed with my own.

I stilled my mind with a deep breath in hopes that I could contain my carnal desires. Having him stand there blushing as he turned away from me was too enticing. I didn't want to do something I would regret by acting too hastily. Quickly, I slipped on the sweats he gave me and walked over to him. "So, can I ask you something?"

Atlas turned back to me and nodded. He looked almost relieved that I was fully clothed.

"Do you really accept me as your mate?" I questioned as I closed in on him just enough to feel his warmth.

His eyes flicked between mine as if searching for his answer within them. It wasn't too obvious, but I could sense the mental struggle he was having, and it pained my wolf. Even though our bond solidified instantly which told me he was all in, there was something else there that I felt. Something that he struggled with and prevented him from accepting us openly.

After a brief moment he closed his eyes, "yes..." Atlas bit his lower lip pensively. The word really weighed on his lips.

"Why do I feel there is a 'but' coming?" I cupped his face into my hands so he could look up at me. His eyes almost glowed in the dimly lit room. "I want to try this with you. My wolf wants this too. Even though we just met, I am ready to get to know you and be your mate." I nuzzled my nose on his and closed my eyes taking a deep breath of his lavender and oak. It would be impossible to let go after experiencing this, but I would if he asked me too.

"I want this too, it's just…I need to take care of something first." A tear rolled down his cheek and I quickly wiped it away with my thumb.

"Okay, then, let me help you." I gently pressed my lips to his nose. "Please don't be sad." A soft sigh left his lips and brushed against mine. His heart raced with how close we were to one another, and my heart responded in kind. Atlas wrapped his arms around me and tugged me gently closer to him.

"Is it okay to kiss you?" My lips feathered his skin as I whispered against his cheek. It was the best I could do without stealing the kiss before he could answer.

Atlas looked up at me with a smile and kissed me. Our lips touched and locked together to play a symphony that was made just for us. Light spread through me as the scent of lavender and oak covered my body in swirls. The sweet tender kiss finished lighting the ember that was growing within me. His hand blindly found the hem of my shirt invading my skin underneath with his fingertips. My eyes opened slightly at his touch, and I spotted a glow emanating from our bodies, like the aura from before. The glow surrounded us in soft hues of purple and gold mixed with silver and blue.

I gasped as his hands explored my body further, "fuck". A moan rippled out of me.

Atlas kissed me again just as the glow deepened. My tongue licked his bottom lip and gladly they parted for me. Our tongues fought one another for dominance, sending waves of excitement to shoot between our heaving breathing and panting. I could feel the glow seeping back into us. It had to be a reaction to our bond. Our wolves. We really were meant for one another, but I had never heard of a glowing aura before, and it was slightly distracting.

"Cassius", Atlas pulled my hair back and growled into my neck asserting his dominance. I whimpered in his hold. *Why didn't I realize sooner he's an Alpha?* His tongue trailed my neck finding my pulsating vein. My wolf howled wanting his mate to mark him, but Atlas hesitated, and I was glad that he did. It was too early for us to mark each other. We hadn't even had a chance to properly be with one another. I also wanted to respect his wish to finish whatever unfinished business he had. Instead, he brought me back to his lips and passion erupted again.

The chemistry between us was something I'd never seen before nor heard of with other couples. Even though I knew and understood I had only just met him, it felt like I already knew him my whole life. The familiarity within his touch assured me that he had always been mine, long before we met again in this lifetime.

We finally pulled ourselves off of each other. Neither of us was able to breathe. I had never kissed someone to the point of wanting to come. This was definitely the first, but I didn't want to soil his clothes. "Should I go?" I managed in a breathy whisper.

My eyes were firmly on his although they couldn't focus. It took every ounce of restraint to not continue on. It wasn't what I wanted; it was what I had to do. I knew he saw the silver in my eyes. The desire surging within them and how much I was struggling to hold back.

"Yes, that might be best", Atlas grabbed the collar of my shirt and pulled me down to him. His forehead touched mine and we stood there with our eyes closed, taking in as much of each other as we could. Our auras mixed once again in blues, silver, purple, and gold. This time Atlas noticed it too before looking back at me.

"Why are we glowing?" Atlas whispered.

"I really don't know." I wiped some of Atlas' hair back. He smiled and my heart melted at the sight. "When can I see you again?" I placed my hand on his chest, feeling his heart beating fast against my fingers.

He finally looked away from the aura, "you know that small cliff looking over the river? Meet me there at dusk the day after tomorrow." He kissed me gently this time and my wolf howled in excitement. I sighed into the kiss. It was heaven on my lips. There was no lie when everyone told me that finding your mate made you lose all control. Because here I was, wanting to strip the man before me.

"Okay," I agreed and went to his window. I peeked down and the distance wasn't too bad for a jump. I'd rather exit this way than walk back through the house.

I turned back to Atlas to take in the handsome specimen that he was before opening the window and jumping out of the second floor. The land was steady and soft on my feet. It was better than I expected, and into the woods I dashed away. The run felt refreshing, but my feet felt heavy. It bothered me that there was something that Atlas was struggling with, and I prayed it wasn't something within his own home. An odd feeling that someone was watching pricked my skin as I ran through trees, but I didn't care. If it was a hunter watching, he wouldn't shoot me without confirming if I was a wolf first. I ignored it along with the truth that I was going to get reamed by Cecile when I got back.

The high I was on from the strength of our bond had me more elevated than cloud nine. With the stories I heard I thought it was a steady build up, but I was incredibly mistaken. We must be one of the few that fell hard and fast with a bond that was solid from the beginning. I was beyond happy that I found my mate and he accepted me so quickly. The feeling of being able to belong in someone's heart. Someone to call my home. As I ran further away and slowed down my steps, the pull from our bond lost its grip. While I still felt deeply for him, I had a better hold of my wits.

We wolves would be in great trouble if we had no control because of our bonds. I would hate it if I didn't have the choice to walk away. Even now with how strongly our bond solidified, if I went back and turned him down, our bond could still break. There was also the option of just never seeing him again and that would cause the bond to wither slowly. A pain no wolf should ever go through. All I could do was hope that Atlas didn't change his mind because of whatever troubled him.

I made it back to the house and tried my best to sneak in through the back door. Unfortunately, Kristofer was on the porch with a few bottles of beer looking angry as all hell. There was no doubt in my mind that I was part of the reason for his anger.

"Where the fuck have you been?" His Alpha tone was strong, trying to put pressure on me the same way a mother's tone does to a child. An Alpha tone, when used, had the ability to bring anyone down to submit onto one knee should they choose to do so once they felt the force. For some wolves that were extremely weak, it almost felt as if they had no choice, but that wasn't as common. You had to have a real constitution for that to be the case. While this was something mostly used in past times, it was only used to lower the heads of those targeted. Still the person had a choice, they would accept and lower themselves as a sign of respect or stand tall and show defiance. However, I was a bit different.

"I was attacked by hunters, the same ones from before," Kristofer jumped out of his chair looking more concerned than angry.

"What? Why didn't you mind-link me?" He gave me the once over taking notice of my clothes and his nostrils flared.

"It all happened too fast and next thing I know I blacked out." My hands were shaking. He was close enough to smell Atlas on me and with how his nose flared I was positive he had a good whiff already. He wasn't even my dad and yet I wanted to run to my room. The look on his face was scarier to me than his tone. He knew it didn't affect me like it did everyone else but whenever he was incredibly serious without room for humor or gentleness that was when he used his Alpha tone.

"Are you lying to me boy, you know I can smell it," Kristofer sneered at me. Beer was on blast on his breath, yet he was as sober as could be. Wolves didn't get drunk with just a couple beers and from the looks of it, he only had three.

I huffed out an annoyed breath, "I'm not lying. The wolf you smell, was the one that saved me". I looked him in his eyes not even so much as flinching as he released his pheromones to put pressure on me. It was smelly and annoying, but it was an effective way to get a wolf to admit to a lie. Typically, the intense use of the pheromone was so nauseating that anyone would rather admit to the lie than keep up the ruse.

Kristofer knew well that there was more to the story and was trying to be his usual big brother dick head self to get his answer. With his Alpha pheromones as strong as his tone, he could easily get a confession. Luckily for me, I was not like the rest, and it could take a lot to get me to comply and Kristofer hated it.

These days, Alphas don't actually need to rely on tones or pheromones since the structure of a pack changed over time. Back then those tools were used to keep a pack in line. Although there were some Alphas who were strong and notorious in our history. They would sometimes use their ability to force their pack into submission or force a false confession from someone by continuously exposing them to pheromones. Sometimes it was even used to challenge another wolf for Alpha status. Thankfully as times changed and wolves became more organized and acclimated to society among humans, the structures of how we chose our pack leaders and established rules changed as well.

With more modern times, an election of sorts was held for our leaders and if the pack was a well-established one, we would sometimes train the next successor from birth. As for tones or pheromones, an Alpha would only ever use them to demand attention or silence in serious matters the same way a mother gives her child "the look". Or if done correctly, it could be used to get a person to tell the truth if a lie was suspected. A good leader would never abuse their abilities. Kristopher never did.

Since none of it truly worked on me from day one, I would do my best most of the time to fake it, so he didn't seem like anything less than the strong leader he was. Kristofer even called me out on it once and I explained how I was immune to the tone of Alphas but that pheromones only bothered me but nothing else. I realized it when former Alpha Jude tried to punish me as a kid for sneaking out of the house and it didn't work. He was using his tone, but I felt nothing and when the pheromones poured out, I only found it smelly or stuffy.

"Who was it and what happened to the hunters?" Kristofer stopped releasing his pheromones and backed up, realizing his attempt was futile, yet again.

"Well, they are dead, but I don't know where the bodies are or how they were dealt with. The wolf that saved me...." I could feel my heart race at the thought of my mate. *Should I tell him?*

"Speak", Kristofer gritted his teeth and I flinched.

Weary of what Atlas told me I used my mind-link with Kristofer instead.

He is my mate. I finally found my mate but please don't say anything.

Your mate? The shock in his words was clear as day in my mind. **Who is it?** His face softened at the news. It was a soft spot for him.

Atlas, but I don't know his last name. He's the Alpha of the pack one territory over. I smiled brightly just by saying his name.

Hmmm that name rings a bell. Why is it a secret though? Kristofer's brows furrowed with his question. This was something everyone wanted to scream from the rooftops but instead, I asked for silence. I wanted to scream it too but respecting my mate's decision was just as important.

Something is going on and he isn't ready to announce it, so I agreed to silence for now.

Kristofer let out a sigh and squeezed my shoulder in comfort. I hugged him instead, but he pushed me off quickly.

"Stop it," Kristofer punched my arm. He didn't like hugs unless it was from his mom. There was a reason for it though, but I couldn't remember why. He had always been like that. Maybe not finding a mate made him a grumpy old man inside. He relaxed and gave me a congratulatory smile instead.

"You know mother is going to kill you right," Kristofer whispered as we walked into the house.

"Kill me, why?"

He turned around in disbelief. "You've been missing for over 24 hours. No one could reach you and now you turn up smelling like another wolf. So, yea, you're dead," he laughed at his words and froze right alongside me.

"Cecile, w-what you doing up so late?" I stammered my words while shooting a pleading stare at Kristofer who was trying to sneak out of the situation.

"You better explain what the hell is going on right this minute. Both of you, office, now!"

"Yes ma'am," Kristofer and I said in unison. Kristofers Alpha tone may not work on me, but I was terrified of her motherly one. I followed with my tail between my legs or at least it would be if I was still in wolf form. Kristofer, however, stomped his way there like a bratty child. I was almost positive that he was wondering why he was in trouble too and snickered at him prompting a slap on the head by Cecile.

"Ha, ha," Kristofer mocked before Cecile slapped him as well. "Hey!"

I stuck out my tongue while he rubbed his head muttering something about being a grown man.

"Okay, speak and don't leave anything out." Cecile sat down in Kristofer's chair as we took the other two seats in front of her.

I told her everything that I told Kristofer, careful not to mention how hot and heavy me and Atlas got. She didn't need to know the intimate details.

"So, we need to put out some warriors on guard and alert the other homes in the surrounding areas. These hunters are working with someone which explains why their activity has increased," Cecile looked at her son.

"Yes, I'll get a meeting going in the morning and I'll make a few calls to the neighboring territories." Kristofer nodded.

"So, you found your mate then. That's great news at least," Cecile turned back to me.

"Yea, I'm a little scared though. Is it all supposed to hit you so hard and fast? How do I know what I'm feeling is real and not what the bond wants me to feel?" I blabbed on without even realizing. Deep down, maybe I needed to know if it was indeed real.

"Cass, the bond doesn't make anyone FEEL anything. It only enhances what is already there. For example, if you meet someone that matches your chemistry then the moon goddess makes it, so you notice them faster and feel that connection deeper. If you are already inclined to like them then the bond will pull that emotion out quicker as well. It helps drop the wall that we put up around our heart so we can accept the other person easier, but we still have a choice. We can still say no or slow down and take our time."

I looked at her already knowing all of this but still just as scared, "so my attraction to him is genuine then?"

"Yes, very much so. Does he like you back?" Cecile smiled excitedly. The stern look she had a few minutes ago faded into that of a loving mother.

"Yes, we apparently are so attracted to each other that something interesting happened. Our bond solidified instantly but what was unusual was the aura. I've never heard of seeing a physical aura during a bond before." I mentally slapped myself for telling her more than I should have but at this point the cat was already out of the bag. Or is it a wolf out of the bag?

"Oh, now that is very interesting but there is actually a reason for that." Cecile stood up and walked around the desk and over to me. Her delicate fingers combed my hair and then she hugged me tightly. "That means, he isn't just your mate but your soulmate as well. So, if both of you feel strongly for the other too quickly, it's normal, if not, expected."

"Wait, whaaaat? How?!"

Cecile chuckled, "There are different ways that wolves can bond with one another. We have the mate bond, which is the more common way, soul mate bond which is when two past soul lovers reunite, and the twin flame bond which is when a human soul and a wolf soul split as usual in death but are reborn with their mates soul, only to find each other again. Although the last one is rare, it does happen." Cecile laughed as she saw the wheels turning in my head.

"Wait, say that again," I scratched my head.

"This is a lot. So basically, you're saying that at one point, Wolfie used to be with Atlas' soul and Atlas' wolf used to be with Cass's human soul. When they reincarnated, they ended up with each other's wolves, making them a twin flame?" Kristofer asked.

"No, that's the twin flame. What Cass has is a soul mate. Wolfie and Atlas' wolf used to be mates in a past life and now they are reunited within Cass and Atlas," Cecile corrected, while I was still too stunned to speak. "The both of you will be inseparable." Cecile walked towards the door. "Go get some rest, we can talk more later."

"Well then, that's great. Guess you're gonna act like a horny teenager now that you found your mate slash soul mate slash whatever. Please try and keep your shit together. I'm off to bed." Kristofer mocked sarcastically and left as well while I sat soaking in what I just learned.

***

I finally got myself in bed and closed my eyes. The evening had been long and draining. My muscles relaxed against the softness of my bed, taking in his scent that still lingered on his clothes. It was like a diffuser for me, so I pulled the shirt up to my face and inhaled deeply the calming notes. *Why does he have to smell this good?* I thought. His scent was like a switch in my mind that only went two ways, relaxed or horny. It easily could turn into an aphrodisiac that I couldn't escape if my mind went there in any way. *Maybe that's what Cecile meant about soulmates, my soul remembers him and now that we reunited, it yearns for him.*

My sweatpants began to tent as memories of the kiss we had had earlier raced in my mind. The arousal was uncontrollably fast and almost violent in nature. I reached down and released my throbbing manhood from its prison. My wolf howled inside calling out for his mate in a plea that echoed my own. The heat that built in my chest was intense and the only way to cool the fire burning inside was to release it.

Like an adolescent that just discovered what it meant to feel hot and bothered, I tossed in my bed. Kristofer was right. I was going to be a horny mess if I wasn't already. Heat surged through me with just the image of Atlas behind my eyes and his soft skin against mine. The memory of how we kissed tingled softly against my lips. I wanted him. And with that thought I started stroking myself in slow pumps, taking in the lavender and oak from his clothes with his shirt still over my nose.

My eyes rolled back as I sped up my hand, thrusting against the stiffness within my hand. The build-up from before, when we kissed in his room, quickly returned. I wanted to feel him again. Kiss him again. *Atlas.* His name came out like a whisper in my mind. How I wished he were next to me, helping me cool this heat within me. I whimpered into his shirt going faster with my erection. **Atlas!** I called out in my mind with a desperate need to hear his voice.

Yes?

My eyes shot open. **Did he just hear me?** Tingles from hearing his voice created a bigger hard-on, almost painfully so. I throbbed, aching to be released by just the sound of his voice.

I did. What are you doing?

His voice was edging me to my climax.

I don't think you want to know. I smiled hoping he still wanted to know.

Does it have anything to do with me feeling so aroused?

My face cracked a bigger smile hearing those words. It was too late to stop what I was doing and hearing him so clearly in my mind didn't help my cause. It was surprising to hear him say he was aroused. I didn't know mates could feel each other's arousal through the bond. When I was learning about mates, I only thought they could only sense danger and fear. It made sense if they also felt other intense feelings or emotions.

Maybe. I responded a bit too cheeky. A long pause lingered after my response, and I almost feared he shied away or was upset about what I was doing in his name. But then he whispered in my mind.

So, are you gonna cum for me?

Fuck! My mind went blank as hot streams pumped out of me. Unfortunately for my shirt, all of it landed on top.

I guess that's a yes. A giggle echoed in my mind. It was too sexy for words.

Goodnight my mate. I whispered in my thoughts. Content.

Goodnight Cassius.

I opened my eyes wondering how in the world his voice affected me like it did. My name had never sounded so seductive before and yet he accomplished it with just one try. It was odd how it had me in a haze. Even the room seemed to glow as if the sun was beginning to rise through my window. *Wait, what?* Blue flames engulfed my body. I jumped out of the bed afraid to have another curtain scenario, but it vanished. *What the hell?*

Nothing looked burnt and I didn't feel any heat like a fire would provide. The oddities that occurred in my room were getting worse with this being the worst.

"Maybe I should call a witch over to inspect my room?" I changed my clothes and went to sleep after standing there for a few minutes. It didn't make sense as to why I was covered in flames or why they were blue, but something had to be going on. But what?

Chapter 7

CASSIUS

The morning sun woke me up from the deepest sleep I ever had, feeling great. It might have had something to do with letting off a load last night which I hoped no one noticed. Although I wasn't loud since my conversation with Atlas was mental, I grunted when I came and then went into the bathroom. Anyone would know what that meant. With a good stretch, I strolled to the bathroom humming to myself a joyful tune.

Undressing, the bandage on my leg from the gunshot wound fell off to the side reminding me of my injury. The sleep must have undone it and the only thing that had held it together was the small piece of tape holding on for dear life. I ran my finger over the wound that should have healed completely but instead still seemed rather fresh.

With my immunity to silver, I thought I would have healed quickly but it didn't seem to be the case. Instead, it looked almost infected. In fact, the area looked worse than it should and was irritated with a bit of white and yellowish pus-like film covering over top. Whatever Atlas treated me with didn't completely do the trick. At least it didn't hurt, and the bleeding stopped. With a shrug, I entered the hot shower. The feelgood feeling of the scorching shower was short-lived. I hissed as the wound opened up and started to bleed again with the water having removed the film from my skin. I winced at the pain it caused. It worried me, to say the least.

Werewolves normally healed at an alarmingly fast rate but for whatever reason, this wound wasn't closing fast enough. *I wonder if the bullet was laced with something different.* Thought left my mind just as quickly as it came. It would be giving the hunters too much credit.

I jumped out of the shower and put on a hoodie with shorts. My mind was still trying to figure out why silver reacted differently to me compared to others. It was already bad enough that I looked so different that now I'd have to add this to the list of things. I did my best to dress in comfortable clothes, but the wound seemed more irritated than before. I rewrapped it in the bandaging to control the bleeding, but it did little for the increasing pain. With a separate wrap, I secured the bandage in place in hopes that Cecie would know what to do. I limped all the way to the kitchen to find Cecile with each step making the pain worse.

"Why are you limping, did the wound not heal?" I showed her my thigh. The bandage was soaked in blood and dark veins had formed in the short time it took to walk from my room to the kitchen. She agreed with how unusual it was and called the pack doctor to get his opinion.

***

"Good morning, Cecile, I hope all is well with you," he nodded in her direction and smiled at me.

"Yes, Michael but I do need your professional opinion on Cass." Cecile closed the front door behind him and walked over to the room, we turned into a clinic so I could show him my wound. It took a bit to explain how I got it and what I was experiencing since the pain was now becoming unbearable.

"Do you mind if I take a sample and run some tests? It'll hurt a bit, but I'll be quick." I looked at Cecile nervously, but she smiled and agreed.

"Okay," I grabbed the bite stick he offered me and bit down as hard as I could. Dr. Michael put on a pair of gloves and took out a swab from his bag before he peeled off the sanitary cover. My eyes followed his every move, and I flinched as he touched the wound. Michael retracted quickly with a stern look.

"You need to hold still."

My jaw clenched, while my fingers gripped the side of the desk as he dug in. A deep profound scream vibrated in my throat. A scream I was sure woke up the whole pack. Tears rolled out of one eye and Michael apologetically pulled out the swab full of blood and pus. Small bits of silver glistened as he showed it to the light. The stick in my mouth snapped in half cutting my tongue but I felt nothing against the throbbing in my thigh.

"I'm so sorry but I need you to breathe as best you can. Take deep long breaths." Cecile was immediately by my side, doing her best to calm me down. Her gentle hands ran up and down my back, with a slight hum reminding me of the lullaby she used to sing when I was little. But it hurt.

It felt like the swab was still in me digging to the depths of my bones.

CASSIUS! What's wrong? Atlas slipped into my mind. His voice numbed my pain ever so slightly.

I'm okay, it's my wound. It won't heal. It just hurts really bad, that's all. I was sweating and the room spun into oblivion.

Are you okay?

Atl- His name couldn't form in my mind. My heart pounded out of my chest in a race I wasn't winning. Everything was hot.

CASSIUS?! CASS- I barely heard him calling out for me. Michael and Cecile came into view just before it all went black.

***

Sounds around me faded into focus. Beeping sounds were steady, and a soft snoring sounded in between. There was enormous pressure on my stomach and my body felt stiff. I tried to pry my eyes open, but they were heavy as if I had taken a sedative. The light was bright in the room, violating my vision as it took every effort to free my lids further. After a few more attempts, I opened my eyes a bit more, slowly taking in my environment. The room was painted with white walls and fluorescent lights hung overhead. The air smelled clean, but it could be due to the tube in my nose. That and all the beeping machines told me one thing. *Am I in a hospital?*

I reached over to my face and pulled out the oxygen tube in my nose. Then it hit me. My senses were bombarded with lavender and oak. Unfortunately, I was also hit with disinfectant and hospital smells. I was no longer in the clinic at home, and I knew something serious must have happened to end up here. My head lifted slightly following the direction of the calming scent. It was the hardest thing to do at the moment from how weak my body seemed to be. A million pounds of dead weight held me down, but I tried regardless. Looking down at my body, my eyes couldn't believe who I saw.

"Atlas?" I whispered; my hoarse voice was sore. His beautiful face rested on my stomach while he held my hand. He slept like an angel with soft snores touching his lips. If he had been with me this whole time, he must have been exhausted. Bags cradled his eyes along with dark circles. As tired as he looked, he was still beautiful. It amazed me how the mate thing works, and I might not ever get over it. The bond with mates was like nothing I've ever experienced plus we had the gift of being soul mates and it only made me want to get to know him more.

With our bond there's this freedom you gain to love hard, fast, and strong because we loved each other just as much in a previous life. The best way for me to describe this feeling is to say it's like a magnet that became active when we met and accepted each other.

"Hey, wake up," I gave his hand a squeeze.

"Cassius! Thank goddess." He blinked a few times, the relief that flooded my mate's face tugged at my heartstrings.

"What happened?" I plopped my head back down on the pillow, unable to hold it up anymore.

"From what Cecile told me, you fainted when they took a sample from your wound. Dr. Michael thought you went into shock and that sampling the blood might have pushed whatever was in there further into your bloodstream. Looks like the bullet had splintered because he found a piece when they examined you after arriving." Atlas rubbed the top of my hand with his fingers. Little tingles sparked from the small gesture. "You could have died, Cass." His voice dripped in sadness.

"Shhhh, don't talk like that. I am here and I'm fine now." I wanted to hug him but there wasn't an ounce of strength in me at the moment.

"Okay." He choked on the word.

"You met Cecile?" My voice croaked, drying out the more I talked.

A giggle escaped his lips as he reached for the bed remote and adjusted my bed, so I was a bit more upright. *Man, I love his laugh.*

"Yea and I met Kristofer, your packs Alpha. We ended up discovering our fathers knew each other." Atlas moved closer up to me and caressed my face. "They told me they scolded you and you told them about me. Not that it matters, I understand you telling them at the very least... Cass, I ran here the second we lost communication, so I was ready to reveal us to them if it meant helping you. I knew something was wrong."

"I made sure to tell them to keep our secret. I trust them but if you were going to come running to me, I wouldn't have bothered." I laughed but it only hurt my throat further and now my head. A small headache formed behind my eye.

"Since we are keeping us a secret from everyone else for now, Kristofer made it, so no one is allowed to visit. Cecile showed me a way to sneak in through the back to avoid nosey bodies too." His eyes fell down to the bed in thought. "You have been here almost a week Cass."

My heart skipped a beat at my name on his lips, but my eyes grew wide as my mind registered his words.

"A week?" My head jerked to the door swinging open. Dr. Michael walked in with Cecile and Kristofer. I almost sucked my teeth at their timing, but I managed to stop myself. Atlas didn't budge from his spot either but instead he gripped my hand tighter.

"You're finally awake. How are you feeling?" Dr. Michael looked over my vitals.

"I feel heavy, slight headache, but fine," I reached for the water that Atlas handed me.

"I see. All normal considering what your body went through. Okay, I need to discuss some of the tests I ran. Is that okay?" He made a gesture towards Atlas.

"Yes, you can say whatever it is with him here." I squeezed his hand.

"So, I ran a test on the sample I took in addition to some blood I drew from you when you were admitted. It turns out that the sample had traces of mercury and leech secretion. Mercury works in a similar way to silver but more aggressively when introduced to the blood directly. The leech secretion acts as a blood thinner which prevents the wound from healing and helps the mercury course the blood circulatory system quicker. This combination could be basically lethal to our kind." Dr. Michael paused to see if anyone had questions.

"So how did these hunters know to use such methods?" Atlas raised a brow.

"Now that is the million-dollar question. My guess is that this was intentional." The doctor turned back to me with slightly parted lips and a raised brow.

"Spit it out," I sighed. "I can take it. I'm a big boy."

Atlas squeezed my hand as if agreeing with what I said. He should know with all he has seen. Although now wasn't the moment to be thinking of such things.

The doctor took a seat ignoring the little exchange between me and Atlas and placed his hands by his temples and massaged them. "Cassius, where are you from? Do you remember anything?" I shook my head unsure as to why he was asking out of the blue.

"All I can remember is the winter being really bad at times, but I was mostly kept locked up with my mother. I barely had interactions with anyone else." Atlas squeezed my hand again and I realized this was the first personal thing I shared with him.

"Okay, so when I ran your blood, I got a match in our database. Apparently, you come from a protected line of wolves. Your bloodline is from royal descent."

"Royal? Me? What?!" I looked at him like he was stupid.

"Yes, there is this long line of royal blood that has gone into hiding. They are believed to be the first shifters who were said to be originally Native Americans that were cursed by an elder shaman. In doing so werewolves were born. When the curse revealed itself to be shapeshifting, the elder shaman fell to his knees and worshiped them as spirit gods. The three tribes cursed were known to be really powerful because they possessed the ability to not just shapeshift, but they also had a tendency for magic. The magical part I'm not sure I believe though. It is said they had a connection to the spirit world that was beyond what any elder shaman had." Dr. Michael took a deep breath.

"The elder shaman then grew jealous, wanting to shift as well and gain power. So, he began killing off the shifters he created. He would drink their blood to try and gain their power and eventually succeeded once he combined it with ritual incantations he said to have dreamt. Many wolves ran away to survive, and some mated each other while others married humans from other tribes. From the ones that mated with each other they ended up giving birth to wolves born with powers like their parents." Micheal walked around the room seeming lost in thought.

"If I remember correctly, history says that one particular child grew up to be stronger than any other but, in that time, the elder shaman grew stronger as well and became mad with greed. Eventually, the shaman caught wind of the powerful wolf, and they fought. The elder shaman lost, and the wolf became the new shaman of his people." Michael wrote a few things down on the clipboard he had tucked in his armpit.

"So, you're saying that I am one of them? Is that why my wolf is so different from everyone else?" It was too much to take in. I couldn't accept that I came from such a strong background only to grow up the way that I did. Why wasn't I sought after or where was my father? Atlas squeezed my hand trying to comfort me as I trembled. But the thought weighed down heavier as the seconds rolled by.

"Yes. It is also why silver has no effect on you externally. However, it will still hurt you if ingested or introduced into your bloodstream the way mercury did. The only difference is that it will take an absurd amount to kill you as opposed to other wolves." Dr. Michael placed a hand on my shoulder.

"Cassius, you are special, and your secret is safe with me, don't worry. There aren't many of your kind that live outside of hiding." He gave me a smile and turned to walk out.

"Wait, so if all wolves are descendants of my bloodline, then why don't all of us have the same abilities?" I had many more questions. Too many to have him walk out of the room. The doctor turned back around.

"Well, remember how I said wolves mated with non-shifters and humans? This resulted in less tolerant versions of your wolf. Or rather the host became less capable of protecting the wolf. If the offspring continue to mate with others that aren't of wolf descent, eventually that gene with the tolerance to silver becomes dormant. If they mate with other wolves from their original line, then they can preserve the genome and remain pure for lack of a better word. Although the new less tolerant generations are still strong, even if they can't be compared to the original bloodline. Even your wolf is still considered weak compared to your ancestors, but you are more powerful than the rest of us. Okay, I need to check on another patient." Dr. Michael left the room.

"Holy shit," Kristofer exhaled and we all just nodded in unison.

"I think I should try and find my father." I looked at Cecile who furrowed her brows. Her eyes dropped to her hands making her small wrinkles more apparent.

"I don't think that's a good idea." Cecile fumbled with her fingers.

"Why?" Atlas demanded a bit too forcefully prompting a growl from Kristofer. Atlas didn't back down, but he did soften his face and cleared his throat.

Cecile placed her hand out in front of her son, and turned to Cassius, "he already knows that you're with us. He found you shortly after your wolf came out. Your father said he felt it and found you here. That bastard wanted you dead, but I couldn't let that happen and neither could Jude. So, we agreed to never let you know who your father was. We just thought he was an asshole, but I guess this was the real reason. Although I still think he is an asshole." Cecile teared up as she fell silent.

"Mom, how could you never say anything?" Kristofer turned to her with his hands in the air.

"Don't you dare speak to me as if you know what it was like. I love Cassius like my own, I didn't want him to hurt or feel unwanted. But I couldn't let Cassius suffer or die because of some unreasonable hatred that man had. I did what I thought was best to keep Cassius safe." Cecile sobbed into her hands mumbling incoherently.

There was too much to process but the only thing that my mind held onto was my father not wanting me. Not just that, he wanted me dead. *What could I have possibly done as a child to warrant my death? What kind of royalty was he?* My fingers trembled under the hand that desperately tried to comfort me. The one thing everyone feared was to not be wanted. The staggering feeling of walking invisibly through life because no one wished for your existence, and therefore erased you from their line of sight was daunting.

A soul could not continue in life if the body which it inhabited began to reject its very existence.

The cruelty of a father discarding their child scarred even the strongest hearts, whether a pure blood, goddess, or human. My chest struggled to fully fill my lungs. I panted rapidly to catch my breath.

"Cass, you're panicking, breathe," Atlas placed his forehead on mine. "Breathe!"

I blinked the tears away, but my breathing wouldn't settle. It was like I was trying to breathe underwater. It felt thick and murky making sure to prevent me from taking a full breath. Then, as if all the sounds in the room stopped, I felt light as a feather. I inhaled deeply, feeling the bond working between us. The suffocation was easing slowly. My anxiety was fading.

Our auras flowed out of one another and entwined around us. Like a string it looped around our bodies and held us in place. It was like the world was no longer around us. A sense of calm traveled beneath my skin and took hold of every fiber of my being. My mind went blank for a moment and slowly I filled with warmth. Lavender and oak invaded every pore, soothing me like a medicated bandage. I knew I still hurt. I knew the pain was there, but it was bearable and dull.

"Feel better?" Atlas whispered as our auras dissipated and released its hold on us. I smiled and placed my hand on top of his that still held the side of my face. *I could really get used to this.*

"How did you know to do that?" I asked while kissing the palm of his hand in gratitude.

"I don't know. It's like I reacted on instinct." Atlas shrugged.

"I'm so sorry my sweet baby boy. I didn't mean to hurt you in any way." Cecile looked more like my mother now than she ever had before this very moment. I couldn't have asked for a better woman to raise me. "With what I just saw, I'm glad that you found Atlas. I hope you find happiness in each other."

"Cecile, it's okay. I'm grateful to all of you for taking me in. You did nothing wrong and I'm grateful for having found Atlas as well." She looked at me with red eyes, but a smile curved the corner of her lips.

"Thank you," she managed.
We stayed in silence processing the mess that had just become my life.

"Are we really not going to talk about how freaky that shit just was?" Kristofer pointed at me and Atlas dumbstruck.

Chapter 8

CASSIUS

An eternity had passed or at least it felt that way. I was finally released from the hospital and resting at home. The last of the mercury left my system and my wound fully healed, which allowed Dr. Michael to clear me for discharge. While it was nice to leave behind the strong smells of disinfectant and the annoying sounds of machines, I still couldn't get the thought of my father wanting me dead. It circled in my head like a brightly lit merry-go-round, and I couldn't shake the feeling that maybe he was the one that sent the hunters after me and my mother. He could have even been the one that sent the ones now after giving it second thought and deciding to snuff me out. I fell asleep for the millionth time, tired from my endless thoughts.

For the last two days, I had been in and out of sleep processing everything I learned and reading up on werewolf history to answer the endless questions that crept up every time I learned something new. The main book I read was about the shaman which interested me the most. It depicted what he studied and how his fate had taken a turn. There was so much I still didn't know about how any of us magical creatures even came to be. We all lived among the human world but not all of us started out as them. The only other creatures I know started off as humans were witches and vampires. But the more I read, the more I wanted to scream for being so naïve. Elves fascinated me but nothing like the different kinds of shifters that existed.

I would love to talk to another shifter and learn about their origins and how much we may be similar. There were questions that I simply couldn't find answers to in the books. I wanted to learn about the true lineage of all of our kinds, including elves and witches but everything I found glossed over the important parts. But all I had was this book titled, "A Chance at History". One thing it did well to explain was the council and summits where all the representatives of each magical community gathered to maintain peace and order among us all.

My eyes drifted across the page as I broached the topic of dark elves. As fascinating as it was, I could no longer stay awake. I fell asleep with my nose in the book drifting into a fantastical dream.

***

The smell of food woke me up in time for dinner. Steak pulled me out of the weird dream I had about witches, elves, and goblins fighting wolves. It was total mayhem. The stretch I gave with my body cracked a few joints relieving some of the sleep that lingered. A knock echoed into my room. I could tell who it was by the way they rapped on the door.

"Come in dummy."

"Dinner is ready, so come eat loser," Alex popped his head in the door with a grin. A small blush formed in his cheeks with his eyes devouring my shirtless chest. His feelings lingered on my body as if committing me to memory as if he hadn't done so already so many times before.

"Okay, I'll be right there," I was not hungry, at least not for food. Instead, I craved the touch of my mate or rather the comfort his presence brought me. Wolfie stirred inside begging to go find Atlas, so he could feel Leo's presence as well. He wanted to snuggle with his mate just as much as I did.

Honestly, with the wealth of information that I ingested recently; my brain was overwhelmed. It left me feeling alone for some reason. For the first time in a long time, I felt like I didn't fit anywhere or with anyone. My mini mental spiral took a turn on 'don't-go-there-ville' before coming to a halt. Alex left the room and closed the door. I'm sure it was due to my lack of response after he asked another question I failed to answer. I pushed myself out of bed to put on a shirt for a dinner I didn't care to eat.

"Hey sleepy head, hungry?" Cecile passed me a warm smile. Her love for me shot across the room. Never faltering and reminding me that my place would always be here. Even when I came out of the closet to everyone, Cecile continued her kisses and hugs like nothing. Unwavering love for a son she never birthed.

"Not really but I know I gotta keep my strength up," I responded in kind.

Kristofer huffed in agreement, and I took my seat at the table. Since not many of us lived in the main packhouse anymore, the enormous table we had felt bigger than usual. Most of our pack lived in groups of three in other houses or with their own mates with this being the head house on the property. The land we owned was massive and it allowed us to stay together while still having our own space.

I picked on my food pushing it around on my plate, mindlessly listening to the conversation at the table. *I miss him*, I thought, pushing the peas around on my plate within the gravy that spilled from my mashed potatoes.

Cassius?

Yea, my heart jumped at the sound of his voice in my mind. I peeked up to see if anyone noticed when I flinched.

I want to see you now. Can you meet me?

Yes, meet me at the cliff. I replied and quickly inhaled my food.

"Whoa, what's the sudden rush?" Alex laughed and shoved a piece of steak in his mouth.

"I just remembered I had to do something." I threw a glance at Kristofer, and he rolled his eyes catching on quickly.

"How could you forget, go do what I asked," Kristofer huffed my way. **You're meeting him, aren't you?**

"Yes, right on it Alpha," I replied. **I owe you one.**

Damn right you do. Kristofer smiled and continued eating. He was such a softie when it came to mates. I could only hope that he would find his son. He needed to hug someone other than his pillow.

I walked as fast as I could towards the cliff. The chill in the air prevented me from sweating. Had it been any hotter, then I would have already had puddles in my shoes. Every inch of my skin screamed to feel his touch. Every step I took towards the cliff allowed our bond to grow stronger as they recognized each other. He was close. Just out in the clearing, Atlas appeared with his eyes already set on me. We ran to each other like teens sneaking out past curfew. The night was beautiful and yet Atlas stood out like a god. In my eyes, there was no other that stood out like he did in that moment.

"I've missed you," Atlas whispered into my ear, hugging me tightly. I understood exactly how he felt. It hadn't been too long since we last saw each other in the hospital.

"It's been torture not seeing you," I pulled away and cupped his face. We looked into each other's eyes taking in one another's presence. A low growl escaped from Atlas when he inhaled what I could only assume was my scent. That sound alone put a smile on my face as I slammed my lips into his.

He invaded my mouth with his tongue taking control. *Damn, he's such a good kisser.* The tightness I began to feel in my pants was becoming painful and I needed to calm down. **My Alpha**, I mentally noted or so I thought. It was becoming harder to control my thoughts around him. Instead, I was voicing my thoughts to him.

Atlas pulled away from me, reacting to my words. His eyes were glowing a golden amber but if I didn't know any better, I'd say a fire burned within them. He wanted me. Everything about him screamed desire. The ember in his eyes, the aggressive way he held me, and the twitch of his lip as he bit it. Atlas growled low and deep in his throat as if going into heat. The sound was erotic and further tightened the space in my pants. I reached down and grabbed his hardness admiring the length that I discovered.

Atlas threw his head back enjoying the sensation of my touch. I squeezed it slightly and he snapped back at me as if I ignited something within him. **If only his clothes weren't in the way.**

With speed that defined the Alpha that he was, he had me on my back on the ground before I could catch my breath. He straddled me and pressed his weight against my erection. With his weight against my pleasure and progressing its growth, his hands tugged at the hem of his shirt. He pulled it off revealing a magnificent view of his toned body rippling with his movement. My mouth almost drooled at how his muscles flexed. As he came back down to me, I thanked the goddess for matching me with the perfect specimen.

He cupped his hands behind my neck and kissed me once more while his thumbs caressed my cheeks. Warmth rushed over every fiber of my being from his lips. It was a feeling I began to get used to just by being near my mate. The warmth he filled me with was becoming my Achilles.

He ground down with his hips into me making my dick harder than I thought possible. "Fuck, babe," I moaned into his ear. He removed his weight from me and lifted my legs to rest on his thighs perfectly situating his eagerness against mine. Atlas slid his hands down my body and admired every inch he had access to. His fingertips recorded every inch of my skin as if it were a map he etched into his mind. The way he took control of my body reminded me very much of how he was the Alpha. The only dominance I would submit to. His lips returned to my neck, and he licked just below my ear sending shivers where his tongue had just been.

"Cass," Atlas groaned against my neck as he thrusted his erection against my ass. He gripped my thighs pulling me against him further, "I want you." He slid his hands under my shirt to pull it off, allowing the bite from the cold to harden my nipples. I returned my arms around his neck aching for more of his touch.

His hands worked on my belt, and I worked on his. Atlas nibbled on my collar bone and trailed his tongue up my neck kissing right below my ear again. A shiver emerged from where his lips parted. It was an erogenous zone I didn't know I had. I could feel my ass getting wet from it. The amount of precum dripping down my ass confessed Atlas' effect on me, and I was only half undressed.

I hadn't had sex for a long time, and I was nervous if this was going to be our first time together. My breath hitched when he licked my sweet spot just under my jawline, pleased to have found another spot that made me tick. I moaned loudly as he sucked my skin to encourage a hickey to form. Both our members were free from their material confinement and rubbed against one another. Atlas grabbed them in one hand and rocked his hips against mine. "Babe slow down," it was too fast. My release was rising quickly.

"Cum for me Cass. Cum all over me." His Alpha tone took over. Deep, seductively raspy, hot, and heavy. While he didn't know it had no effect on me, I could still identify when it was used, and that knowledge alone had me edging.

"Ah, Atlas."

"It's Alpha," he whispered against my lips. Atlas licked them waiting for my response.

"I'm gonna cum, Alpha. I'm gonna…." I pant into his breath as he quickened his strokes.

"Yes, give it to me." He bit my bottom lip and sucked it into his mouth.

"Fuck, ALPHA!" I released myself between us. Covering both our chests but he didn't stop.

"Cass, I'm-" Atlas threw his head back and shot a load far enough to hit my face. The look on his face was that of horror for shooting his ribbons of lust on my lips. I studied his reactions as they stirred when I stuck my tongue out and slowly licked it off his release off my lips. His eyes shot to mine and glinted its golden hunger for more. *Guess I hit a kink.*

"So, you're still a fucking fag huh?" A man shouted, slurring slightly.

Both our heads darted to the man approaching us with unsteady feet. We straightened ourselves out to face the encroaching wolf. *An actual drunk wolf?* I thought to myself as the sight wasn't as common among our kind.

"I thought after I fucked your tight ass that you straightened out." The man pointed a finger at Atlas. I turned to him in confusion.

"Rick, what are you doing here?" Atlas was in attack mode and held out his hand making sure I stayed behind him. His whole demeanor was tingling to fight.

"Is that really the question you should be asking?" The wolf called Rick leaned against a tree and smiled almost as if he sobered up.

"What the fuck does that mean?" Atlas growled ready to shift at any moment. Even my wolf whimpered at the immense power Atlas released. The pressure in the air around us was the perfect display of strength from Atlas as an Alpha.

"I saw him leave your window a couple weeks ago in the middle of the night," Rick threw a nod in my direction.

"That was you I felt watching me?" I mumbled to myself. Atlas flinched, catching my words but stayed quiet keeping his eyes on Rick.

"I saw you leave again so I stayed true to my promise," Rick laughed and gulped the last bit of his bottle of whiskey.

"You better not have touched my sister. I didn't tell anyone. We had a deal."

The sound of Atlas' heart rate increasing filtered into my ears. He was scared but I knew I couldn't step in. This was his fight as an Alpha.

"Oh, but you did. I know you told Mavis. Why else would he suddenly become so protective of her even though he has his own mate to attend to? You made it obvious that night by the bonfire." He pushed off the tree and walked closer to us. "Gotta say, your sister tasted so sweet."

Atlas snapped and shifted into his wolf, Leo. He lunged at Rick and they both fought when Rick shifted as well. I flinched when Leo knocked Rick's wolf against a rock. There was no room for me to intervene with how brutal their blows were to one another. My feet moved on their own wanting to step in, but I didn't have my place as his Luna yet. I couldn't help him unless he asked as an Alpha protecting his honor and pack. All I could do was trust he would win. As much as I wanted to help, all I would do was shame Atlas and disrespect his title.

"Leo, let me help!" I yelled out.

He turned to me and growled, making it clear to not move but he yelped and flew against a tree.

"Leo!" I called out but Rick was already by my mate's throat threatening to bite it off. *Fuck, I distracted him, fuck the damn pack rules!* I began the process of shifting when another wolf jumped out of nowhere and tackled Rick. Leo limped as he approached where Rick's wolf landed and pounced on his neck. Leo stood there breathing heavily before collapsing. I stopped the shift and ran over to him. "Leo, wake up," I called out and petted his fur, but he didn't open his eyes. The wound on his side had traces of silver.

"Shit," I turned around to the sound of a loud yelp and then a crack. The wolf that attacked Rick snapped the neck of Rick's wolf leaving it limp. He walked over to us and pushed his nose against Leo. "Who are you?" I asked.

The wolf took a step back and shifted into his human form but remained crouching on the floor. "I am his Beta, Mavis. I presume you are his mate?"

I nodded my head and showed him my fingers. "He has silver in his wounds, he needs help." Mavis looked at me a bit shocked since my skin wasn't reacting but then his eyes shot over to our Alpha and back to me.

The Silver Lining

"How the hell did he get silver on him?" Mavis got up to inspect the dead wolf behind him and noticed the burns on his paws from having the silver painted on his claws.

"That wolf was a psycho," I scoffed. There was no doubt in my mind if he went to that length.

"Grab him and follow me. I have a healer at the house." Mavis started walking and I followed with my mate tucked in my arms. My eyes quivered with tears, but I had to stay strong.

"Mavis?" I croaked, not realizing how my voice trembled. He turned to me.

"Rick said something about Iris. He told Atlas that he kept his promise. I think he did something to her." Mavis's face sunk in, understanding the weight of my words which I had hoped was an empty threat.

"Shit, that fucking asshole. Do you know the way to the house?" Mavis asked and I nodded. "Good, I'm going ahead first. I'll alert the healer of your arrival then I'll look for Iris." Mavis shifted back to his wolf and raced off.

Babe if you can hear me, I got you. Everything will be okay. Both you and Iris. I picked up my pace praying to the moon I would make it back in time.

stabilize. Leo's body was working hard already pushing out the silver. Luckily that meant the wound was shallow and not enough silver made it into his system to do significant harm. It was a relief.

"Bring him here." A soft voice filled with age and wisdom called out to me. A woman looking to be in her mid-thirties signaled to the door across from her.

"Okay." I nodded and rushed towards the room as best I could. A cracking sound pierced my ears, and I knew all too well what that sound meant. I barely made it halfway across the living room before Leo began to shift back into his human form. "Oh shit," I tried my best not to drop him as his body contorted in my hold. Never had I ever felt something as odd as a shift in my arms. Even though this was normal and something I experienced myself, it was the most disgusting thing I ever felt. The way the bones shifted and realigned and the transition of his fur to skin almost made me lose my stomach in the process.

His body twisted and writhed in pain. His bones continued to shift and reshape under his skin. I fumbled with his weight teetering from one side to the other as I did my best to not drop him. His center mass changed as he finally began to look more human than wolf. *Just a few more steps and I can put him down in the room.* My balance waned as his body completed the shift. I buckled and dropped onto my knees wincing in pain but never letting go of my beautiful naked mate. In fact, I held him closer to me in an attempt to cover his body from the gathering eyes.

Atlas melted into my arms as his eyes opened, taking comfort in seeing my face staring right back. His muscles relaxed against me, and all the tension left when he smiled.

"Hi," his voice was but a whisper.

"Hi," I replied, running my fingers down the side of his face. He leaned into them and kissed my palm.

We sat there lost within each other when someone suddenly cleared their throat to remind us that we were not alone. Atlas and I turned to find a bunch of faces staring at us wide-eyed at our affection towards one another. Some smiled while others gawked in shock. Looking around at the number of eyes wandering over my mate's body, I growled allowing my incisors to become prominent. *How dare they look at my mate's body.* He was mine and I had no intention of sharing, including his appearance. A chuckle pulled my attention to my mate.

"Cass, relax. It's fine." He turned to the audience around us. "Everyone, this is my mate and soon to be your new Luna. Please welcome him." Everyone's eyes darted to mine with newfound curiosity. I put away my teeth and relaxed into complete embarrassment. They all bow respectfully but I did catch a few giggles from somewhere. I just bared my teeth like a child and here he was introducing me as their future Luna.

The healer brought a blanket to cover Atlas and I lifted him up once more to carry him into the room, grateful to leave the curious eyes. I needed to get out of everyone's attention before they could see how red I was.

"Ouch. Cass my ribs." Atlas winced as I placed him on the bed a bit too hard.

"I'm sorry babe." I kissed his forehead and stepped back for the healer to examine him.

"Mavis went to find Iris," I muttered, but my hands were shaking. I couldn't help but feel like Rick had something to do with Atlas wanting to hide our relationship. It hurt all the scenarios I was coming up with, but it was not my place to ask. From what that bastard said, I hoped it wasn't what I feared most. I tugged at my torn shirt from my attempt to shift during the fight earlier.

"Shit, Iris. I need to find her." Atlas tried to push away the healer, but she quickly pressed into his ribs.

"You are going nowhere, Alpha Atlas. You are hurt and in no condition to track your sister." She grabbed a few ointments and placed butterfly stitches on his wound. "Drink this, it'll help your body get rid of any remaining silver quickly. Once it does, your ribs should heal in no time." The healer handed him a cocktail that I was sure contained selenium and then she turned to me.

"Don't let him leave and thank you for saving our Alpha." She smiled at me and patted my shoulder.

The quiet of the room lasted only a moment before the door flew open. Mavis was sweating and panting at the door. "Alpha, we can't find her. We looked all over our territory. I can't even find her scent. I think he suppressed her pheromones. I can't think of another way to hide her scent that well." Mavis was barely able to breathe, grabbing his knees bent over trying to take a deep breath.

"Kristofer!" I shouted to Mavis.

"Who?" Mavis breathed hard, confusion in his voice.

"Atlas said his father knew the father of my pack's Alpha. If that's the case, then wouldn't they have known Rick?" It's the only thing I could think of that might help. Now that Rick was dead, we needed to try everything and anything for a clue. We were too hasty in our decision to kill him.

"That's right, my father was friends with Jude, Kristofer's father. I vaguely remember Kristofer when I was little." Atlas beckoned Mavis to come closer. "Take Cassius with you and go to his pack. Tell them what's happening and find my sister, please." Tears stung his eyes as he fought to hold them back.

"Yes, Alpha." Mavis put a fist to his chest in salute. "Lead the way Luna," Mavis said as he gestured towards the door.

"W-Whoa, I-I'm not Luna yet. Cassius is fine." I fumbled my words prompting a giggle from my Alpha. If my face wasn't red already from the embarrassment earlier, then it definitely turned red now. How could Mavis already address me as his Luna so quickly even with us just having met. Either he had that much faith in his Alpha, or he respected Atlas enough to not question it. Either way, he didn't hesitate. I turned on my heel to lead Mavis and a few others back to my packhouse.

We all shifted in unison, shredding our clothes in the process. It was a quick run to my home but in the several minutes it took to get there, I got a glimpse of what it would be like to lead a pack. It was an interesting and exhilarating feeling. One I had only ever felt in a previous life, but Cassius enjoyed the adrenaline the feeling provided inside.

I mind-linked with Kristofer the moment we got close to the house and asked him to meet outside with Cecile. It was our only chance at finding where Iris could be. If there was anything Cassius and I picked up by listening to that Rick person, it was that Iris could be in danger and damage could already be done. My paws slowed down as I realized the amount of distance I had put between myself and the others. Trying to rush to save Iris, I forgot about my heightened speed abilities. The house came into view and Cecile was standing by Kristofer chatting until she spotted me and then everyone else. I shifted back into Cassius first just before the rest caught up.

"We need your help," I asked, turning around as the others shifted behind me. "My mate's sister is missing.

we killed the man that kidnapped her while fighting and now we can't find her."

"You killed a…" Kristofer sighed and gathered his thoughts. "So, what can I do? Need more men?" Kristofer questioned, unsure of what I was asking.

"Did your father know a man named Rick? He was also friends with Raven, Atlas's dad," Mavis ran his fingers through his hair anxious of the reply.

"You mean Rick fucking Ashwell? That son of a bitch is still alive?" Kristofer spat, as if the name was acid on his tongue. I turned to Mavis to see if that's the full name and it was.

"Was alive. He's dead now but kidnapped Iris just before. Do you know where he might have hidden her?" Mavis answered. Everyone remained silent watching Kristofer and Cecile think. The seconds it took for one of them to speak felt like hours that hung on our shoulders.

"I've always hated that prick. Once he-"

"The shack!" Cecile shouted, cutting off Kristofer mid-sentence. "We had a shack we hung out in a long time ago. It might still be there." Everyone looked around clueless as to what shack she was referring to.

"We?" Kristofer turned to his mother, raising a brow. It must have been news to him for his shock to drip so heavy in his words.

Cecile let out a deep sigh, "Might as well tell you all since Rick is finally dead. Me, Jude, Raven, and Martha…we were swingers. We all enjoyed each other's company, and we had a shack where we would… meet." Cecile took a deep breath but the weakness in her voice gave away her pain as she continued her story along with the gasp from everyone else.

"One day Rick followed us and saw Jude and Raven together being intimate and he lost it. In a fit of his jealous whiskey drunken rage, he attacked them both and staked them." Tears flooded Cecile's face.

"Martha ran home to make sure Atlas was safe but before I could do the same for Kris, he told me to keep my mouth shut or he would kill Martha and Atlas in their sleep." Cecile sobbed telling her story. "He was apparently in love with Raven and since I love Martha, I had to protect her and Atlas. The four of us loved each other dearly and equally. So, I stayed quiet to protect her and her son." Everyone stared in disbelief. *How does a story that big stay hidden for so long?*

"Cecile take us there," I broke the silence allowing her to let go of the breath she held. Tears continued to fall at the recollection of such a tragic memory, but she agreed to show us the way. She shifted and darted towards the river. We all followed suit and carefully jumped the rocks to get across the cold racing water. After a few minutes running between trees, rocks, bushes, and animals, the trees thinned out and a shack came into focus. We all picked up speed with the hope that Iris would be inside.

Kristofer's wolf, Zeus, and I arrived first and broke down the door. The shack was small but exactly what I pictured. There were two large beds, tall cabinets, and a small kitchen. Nothing else. Iris was on the floor naked and tied up against the cast iron fireplace. Zeus froze at the sight of her. He stood there staring while Iris' eyes began to water. Whether it was from embarrassment or relief, I couldn't tell. I shifted back to my human form and ran to undo the rope and remove the gag from her mouth.

"Iris, are you okay?" Her eyes finally broke away from Zeus to look at me. She seemed to be in a bit of a daze as if still under the effects of whatever Rick gave her but seemingly okay, nonetheless.

"That's twice now that you saved me. I vaguely remember the first time though." A tear broke free, and she turned back to Zeus who was still frozen in place.

"Can you shift?" I asked as I changed back into Wolfie.

She shrugged and tried to turn into her wolf, Nora. It took her a few attempts, but she finally shifted and yipped in success. We led her outside to where everyone was waiting. They howled in cheer when she emerged from the shack. It was beautiful to see how they rejoiced in her safety. Iris howled in return, and we made our way back home.

Wolfie, did you say that's your mate's sister? Zeus caught up to me on the run.

Yea, why? I responded as we approached the river.

I think I found my mate.

I turned to him in shock and tripped on a protruding tree root. Laughter erupted in my mind from both Zeus and Cassius. **Shut up. Is that why you were staring at each other like that? Thought you were a pervert.**

Hardy har har. Zeus laughed sarcastically.

I got up and continued running with Cassius excited over what we just learned. We crossed the river and split our separate ways with almost everyone taking Iris home and Cecile going back to hers.

Go to your mate. I'll sort myself out. After Iris gets rest, I'll go over. Kristofer nudged me with his snout, and I returned with Mavis and the other wolves to their packhouse while Kristofer followed his mother.

Chapter 10

CASSIUS

I returned with Iris along with everyone else and the healer gave her a once over. Everyone in the home cheered to see her unharmed just like the others did earlier. It was honestly sweet seeing how much everyone loved her. They were a family very much like my own. I breathed in a bit of relief knowing how nice everyone was because not all packs were this close. Some were even borderline cruel with how they led their family. Take my blood relative for example, I wasn't even wanted by my father.

Mavis came over to me and handed me a pair of sweats, so I wasn't the only one swinging around. I smiled my thanks and slipped them on feeling a bit more comfortable standing among unfamiliar faces. Iris smiled and did her best to answer everyone's questions but behind it all, I could see her pain. She was trying to be brave, and the constant bombardment of questions was most likely making her uncomfortable. Something happened that she still hadn't processed, and her body was screaming to be saved once more.

In all my half naked glory, I walked over to her and grabbed her hand, pulling her away from the others.

"Excuse me everyone, I need to borrow her for a second." I loosened my grip as she followed me out of the living room and into the kitchen.

"Is everything okay?" Iris asked in a shy voice as she traced the lines of my chest with her eyes.

"I never had the opportunity to introduce myself properly to you. So, hi. My name is Cassius Avelious and I am your brother's mate." I smiled brightly as it dawned on me that I now had a sister-in-law. Possibly. If Atlas and I worked out.

"Wait, really? Oh my god, is that why he's been all weird lately? This is so exciting." She hugged me before stepping back.

"Sorry, um, I'm Iris Ellwood, your residential damsel in distress." Iris bit her lip and picked at the skin from her elbow with one arm crossed.

I chortled, "silly, you're not a damsel in distress. You're now my sister and I am here for you whenever you need me, even if it's to beat up Atlas."

Iris laughed with a slight frown while taking a seat by the breakfast bar. She didn't seem as anxious anymore, but her mind wasn't present. It was slipping to whatever happened before we rescued her. "Thank you for that. I don't feel as overwhelmed, but I don't think I'm okay yet either."

"I would be shocked if you were." I took the seat next to her. "You don't need to be brave, Iris. If you're hurt, then cry. If you're sad, eat some ice cream until you get a brain freeze. It's okay to feel your emotions. Most importantly, you are not alone. I have had my fair share of traumatic experiences growing up. It's hard to cope when it's bottled up inside. If not anyone else, you can come to me, okay?" I gently placed my hand on her shoulder. I don't know where those words came from or why I was being so nice to her, but they needed to be said. She needed comfort from whatever she was fighting inside.

"Thank you. I think I'm gonna go sit under a hot shower for a bit. Oh, um, where's my brother?" Iris looked around realizing he wasn't around. Hurt overturned her face.

"He's getting some rest. When he found out what Rick did to you, they fought. That son of a bitch is dead but not before injuring Atlas in the process. He's fine though, just resting. That's why he wasn't there when we found you or else he would have been the first one to break down that shack."

"So, he's okay? He's alright? That vile wolf, he…he…" Iris shook a bit with panic.

"He is okay. Everything will be okay." I kept my voice as soothing as possible.

"Good riddance to that filth…. could you let me know when Atlas wakes up?"

I nodded at her. Iris' eyes looked glossy and on the verge of tears. She stood up and pushed in the barstool before pausing for a second, gripping the back of the stool. "Who was that wolf with you?"

"Who, Zeus? He is the wolf of my pack's Alpha, Kristofer." I know she caught on to who he might be to her but with her mind as it is, I'm sure it's the least of her worries.

"Okay." She sighed and walked out of the kitchen.

It wasn't the reaction a wolf normally had when finding out they met their mate but considering what she just went through and whatever else Rick did without us knowing, it was a reasonable reaction. She needed time to process and decide if she was even ready. If Rick really did to her what he suggested, she needed to heal before accepting any other man in her life.

The sigh that left my lips was heavy but all I could do was hope she and Kristofer would work out. At least she was safe and sound at home and that's what mattered most.

With a bit of pep in my step, I made my way to Atlas. The room was quiet, and my mate comfortably slept under a light cover. *How did I get so lucky to find someone this perfect?* I thought as Atlas whimpered softly in his sleep. A tear rolled out of one eye, and he tossed slightly on the covers, "mom," he whispered.

My heart broke. What could he possibly be dreaming of that was so heart wrenching. I wiped away his tears and whispered, "shh it's okay". His whimpers dulled and then stopped under my touch. I ran my finger over his lips, and he sighed against them, the last of his worries. **This man is pure torture.**

Atlas' eyes blinked open. **Am I now?** He replied to my thoughts. Or at least what was supposed to be a thought.

My cheeks blushed in an instant. "Why can't I control my thoughts around you?" I slapped him in the chest playfully forgetting about his healing ribs.

"Ow, I don't know... but I like what I hear". Atlas' eyes flared an intense gold to compliment his devilish grin.

"Calm down buddy, you're not healed. Oh, and Iris is safe. She's a bit shaken up but resting." I rubbed the spot I hit, guilty for hurting his ribs.

"Says who. I'm not even bruised anymore; besides I was just teasing." Atlas chuckled. "Thank goddess you guys found her though, I can smell her on you so I figured she was okay, or you wouldn't be this calm. I don't know what I would have done if she-" I covered his mouth, not letting him finish his thought. No need to conjure up the what if scenarios. He smiled against my fingers and lifted his shirt a bit, my eyes fluttered across his amazing abs. He truly is a pro at changing the subject or mood.

"Mmmmm", I ran my hand down his chest and traced his abs. Warmth spread through me. This man did something to me I could not explain even if I tried. His stomach quivered under my touch as my finger dipped and rose along the lines of his muscles.

"Cass", my mate's breath hitched as my fingers reached the button of his jeans. My eyes never left his. They were locked in the flame of his arousal. I didn't intend to come into the room for this. All I wanted was to make sure he was okay but one touch against his skin and my hormones forgot what it meant to regulate.

"Yes, babe?" I slid my hand over the tight bulge and grasped it firmly. He was thick and a size that was nothing to laugh at. Atlas gasped under my grip then growled as his pheromones engulfed me with his lavender scented arousal. It felt good knowing I was the cause. That I could sway him to react so strongly.

He sat up and cupped the back of my neck to slam his lips to mine. My hand never left his bulge, which became increasingly bigger and throbbed against my fingers. I grunted into his kiss, moving closer to him on the bed. This wasn't the time nor the place, I knew that, but it was carnal. The attraction, his touch, and the taste of his tongue against me, all of it drove me mad.

Atlas grabbed my waist and flipped me over onto the bed. He undid my pants and ripped them off as if they were made of Velcro. The hardness of my dick on clear display under my briefs grew under his stare. He bent over me and grazed my lips with his tongue. It was sensual and dirty all at once. I loved it. I met his tongue with my own before he sucked it into his mouth. "Mph," I moaned at the onslaught of him sucking on my tongue.

His hands roamed my body finding my already erect nipple. My mind spun from all the sensations I was swimming in. This is all too much and happening so quickly. The lust was so thick in the air that it almost made it hard to breathe. I barely know him despite everything we have experienced together already. I should stop this and slow down.

Another wave of pleasure slammed into me as he teased me with a pinch. His lips left mine bruised and swollen while he trailed his tongue along my jawline.

"Fuck," I breathed out. Atlas took that as a request and lingered on my sweet spot. *I can't breathe*, I thought to myself. Everything was intense. Every sensation heightened. Every touch, electrifying. I was too far gone to stop him. The way he worked my body stole my determination to leave.

Atlas' tongue found my nipple and flicked it repeatedly. His hot breath tickled my skin as he did, and I groaned because I wanted more. "Babe, plea- mmm," my voice let out a loud moan when Atlas thrusted his hips against mine. A sensation of urgency and lust jolted through my body. Even through his jeans I could feel how eager he was. His erection being stifled by his pants pressed hard against me.

Satisfied with my reaction, Atlas sat up and removed his jeans and boxers. His cock waved its thickness in front of me, already dripping in pre-cum. My eyes couldn't seem to register how such a massive thing was going to fit inside me but before I could say anything, Atlas removed my briefs. My legs spread for him, and he lowers his mouth onto my erection. His tongue danced around my crown and down my shaft.

"Fuck babe, right there," I gripped the sheets beside me. His tongue swirled around my crown again and flicked in between the slit. I twitched. He was testing my endurance and most definitely he was winning. How was he so good at this? How many people had he done this to in order to perfect the way he moves his tongue. But before I could get jealous, his mouth closed over me and took me into his warm mouth.

I rocked my hips until I felt my dick hit the back of Atlas' mouth, careful not to come. He moaned, sending vibrations through my throbbing cock. My toes curled and I knew I was close.

Wave after wave, raw intense pleasure coursed through me. Our desires bounced off one another in cascades of relentless pleasures.

"Look at me," Atlas mumbled with his mouth full of my aching cock. My eyes flicked down to meet him. The view of him between my legs spurred me on to no end. A smile formed at the corner of his mouth and just like that I knew that I lost to this man. If a blow job was this good, then what about sex.

Then I feel the sensation of a finger tracing towards my hole. Atlas was a devil in disguise with how he teased my arousal. He used the saliva that dripped down my erection as lubricant and slid a finger in. My back arched from the intrusion. How long had it been since my body last shook like this from pleasure? Too long, I guess.

Atlas returned his swollen lips to suck the tip of my throbbing dick. I gasped at the invasion inside me thrusting slowly against the suction from his mouth as I slid deeper into his throat. My back arched and a moan escaped my lips louder than I intended it too. There were too many people on the other side of the and I was positive they knew very well what was happening. But if they didn't, then they knew now.

Atlas released me from the clutches of his mouth and once again stopped my release from happening. He was bringing me to the edge of orgasm and back to the point where I no longer thought clearly. My mind was going blank as it craved to hum in the feel of an orgasm. Atlas leaned over me and dipped his face into the crook of my neck, inhaling my scent with a low growl. His weight pressed against his hand rocking his hips into me making his finger pump deeper within me.

Another finger slipped in, and his hips moved faster.

"Babe, I want to cum", I moaned deep within my chest and against his ear.

"Cum for me Cass." He commanded and the sound of my name on his tongue sent shivers to edge me further. Almost there.

A third finger slipped, and he hit my prostate. Over and over, he poked it and massaged it using the weight of his body to reach into my depths. Atlas grabbed my dick with his free hand and pumped because he felt how close I was. "Babe, I'm... cum-"

"Yes, Cass, Cum for your Alpha."

"Fuck, fuck, fuck."

A few more pumps and I released everything in ribbons between our chests. Atlas removed his fingers as he kissed my cheek. As his lips lingered against my skin, I could feel the smile that curved his lips before he stepped off the bed. My chest rose and fell rapidly with each breath that I chased. That was the single most erotic moment I have ever had. None of my partners made me feel as intense of an orgasm as the one I just had.

I laid there staring at his gorgeous body enjoying the hum that my body vibrated too as the remnants of the orgasm swirled within me. I watched with fascination as he put on a condom. My dick sprung to action again and for the first time I was scared to have someone as big as him in me.

He looked through the cabinet for goddess knows what and with a smile pulled out baby oil. The small clinic room had just about everything I thought as I trembled with anticipation under the knowledge of what was about to happen. Atlas climbed on the bed and flipped me over on all fours. He wrapped my long hair into his fist pulling my head back and teased my hole with the oil.

"Beg for it", Atlas used his Alpha tone and tightened his grip on me.

"No", I challenged playfully. The word barely left my lips. I didn't want to say no. I wanted to plead and grovel to have his dick thrust into me despite its obscene size. But I also wanted to prolong this moment. Enjoy this domineering version of my mate. Atlas' hand came down hard and slapped my ass. The sound echoed in the room, snuffing out my whimper.

"So, we aren't going to behave? You won't get a reward if you don't". He inserted his tip in me and flicked it out.

"Babe don't tease me," I pushed my hips back against him blindly looking for his cock.

"Then tell me you want my cock in your ass," I could hear the grin in his voice. He was enjoying the power move. He was definitely a Dom and I never thought I would be into such a thing. Atlas rubbed his sheathed tip against my anticipating hole. I was losing at my own game. This would be our first time going all the way and I couldn't take the wait anymore. If I wanted to feel him inside me, I also had to play dirty.

So, I bent down laying flat on my chest exposing my ass more to him. With my head turned to the side and looking back at him, I reached behind me and spread my cheeks apart.

"Please Alpha, put your cock in my ass." The amount of fire that ignited in his eyes was an understatement compared to how he slammed his cock into me. His full length filled every inch of me. *It hurts*, I thought, but I knew it was temporary. I tried to catch my breath.

"Good boy," Atlas whispered with a bit of strain in his voice. He looked at me waiting for my okay to continue. The feel of the burn inside me was already subsiding but the pulse from his cock only grew stronger against my walls. I nodded. Atlas rocked his hips, increasing his pace with each thrust. The more he moved, the easier it became to take in his length. "You feel so good Cass."

I moaned into the bed, and he was right. It does. My muscles finally relaxed enough that I began to feel the pleasure of his heat within me. *Slap… slap*

The sound of our bodies colliding echoed in the room. "Cass you're so tight." Atlas slapped my ass cheek again and then the other for good measure. I screamed into the bed. My orgasm was climbing with each pump of his body against mine. Atlas lifted me up and put me against the headboard. Again and again, he slammed into me. The sounds I'm making didn't sound like my own. It wasn't my voice. I couldn't recognize the animal he was turning me into.

"Harder", my voice barely came out between the moans that kept erupting out of me. Atlas reached for my neck with his right and steadied my hips with his left. Ramming his length into me, he developed a rhythm that made sure to hit my sweet spot every time. I moaned even louder into the room. "Yes!"

"Like that? Is that how you want my cock?" He thrust one more time pressing it hard within me and then ground against my ass as if to stir me inside. Churning my pleasures with my pending orgasm. His left hand slid from my hip around to my dripping cock and stroked me. "Cass, your body feels amazing. I need more," Atlas whispered into my ear.

His breath trailed my skin as he licked my ear and then my neck. "I want to mark you," Atlas kissed my neck over and over. He was talking crazy, but I knew it was from the high of the sex. But I must be just as crazy because I'm drunk off of him as well. I don't care anymore that we barely got to know each other. I knew I wanted him from the moment our auras danced around us. He was my mate. I didn't care if we were moving too fast because I was all in. I was going to give it my all to keep the mate that the goddess chose for me because I chose him too. "Do it, I'm yours." I whispered back drunk in sex.

As if Atlas wasn't already a beast, he thrusted into me at incredible speed banging the headboard against the wall for all to hear. He stroked my dick in rhythm, and I lost it. The last thread that held my sanity together snapped. I threw my head back in ecstasy while he held my neck to the side and sunk his teeth in.

My wolf howled in rejoice as it meant him and Leo becoming one as well. It was a bit painful at first, but it quickly turned into the most incredible orgasm. Pound after pound he filled me with his girth, and I screamed my rising orgasm to the world as it continued to crash and build in waves. Atlas licked my mark as we rode our climax together. A new symptom of being marked. Nothing could have prepared me for how intense everything would be or how I could also feel his orgasm within me.

"I'm...cumming again," I barely managed between breaths.

"FUCK, CASS!"

We both released our passion. Atlas turned my head for a kiss, and we stayed there, attached. Never had sex ever hit me like this but then again, I was never marked. There was nothing like it and I was officially addicted. I closed my eyes and caught my breath while Atlas wrapped his arms around me. We leaned back and with his member still semi hard inside me I sat back onto his lap. In a flurry of kisses Atlas stirred my already overactive senses.

"I think I want to go again," Atlas grew inside me before the words left his lips.

I smiled as he circled his tongue on the bite. "Only if we switch positions," I replied with a mischievous grin. He chuckled and tossed himself back so I could ride him in reverse cowboy. I'll get him next time.

Chapter 11

CASSIUS

The light filtered into my eyes, waking me along with some muttering. This sleep had me feeling a million bucks. It was the kind of sleep you get after being under the hot summer sun all day. **[So, that's what you like? Maybe I can try it next time]**. The voice in my head came into focus and I realized it was my wolf. I always thought if I was sleeping, then he was too but I guess not. **[Damn babe, that's hot]**. In a sudden realization that my wolf was talking about sex, I gasped.

Wolfie! Who the hell are you talking dirty to?

Oh! You're awake

Yes, you pervert I am.

I'm talking to my mate, Leo. Do you mind? I didn't call YOU a pervert when you were masturbating while moaning Atlas' name.

Shut up. Wait? You can talk to Atlas' wolf?

Yes, now that you guys finally mated. Leo and I are connected again.

You guys really are soulmates then?

Yes. This is the first time we have found each other in centuries.

Aw I'm glad. So, how can I shut you guys out? I don't want to hear it.

Don't worry I can block you out. When you're awake I'll keep our convos private.

Please do. Enjoy!

I opened my eyes and looked down at the amazing body lying half on mine. I couldn't get enough of looking at him. The goddess really knew what she was doing to make such a perfect man for me. His body was beautifully lean but defined with well-toned muscles. His nipples were a wonderful warm shade of a pinkish tan, and a beauty mark sat just beneath his left pec.

Atlas was sound asleep, softly breathing into the crook of my neck with his lips slightly touching my skin, tickling me with his breath. If I wasn't so sore, I'd jump him right now, but I didn't think my ass could handle a fourth round. *Knock knock*

"MOM, WAIT!" Atlas jumped from his sleep reaching out, almost hitting my jaw in the process.

"Alpha, are you and Luna up?" Mavis cleared his throat.

"We are now. What do you need?" Atlas answered rather annoyedly.

"Alpha Kristofer is here and is seeking your counsel."

We looked at each other and sighed knowing we couldn't continue to laze around in bed. "Okay give us a minute, send him to my office." Atlas snuggled into my neck and took in my scent.

"Babe, don't do that if you want to get out of this bed anytime soon." I squeezed my sexy sleepy mate, pressing our bodies impossibly closer.

"I'm sorry, I had a weird dream with my mom again. I don't want to get out of bed yet." Atlas pouted against my neck sending chills down my body.

"And you think I do? Trust me, I'd rather have you in me but seriously what kind of dream? What do you mean again?" I grabbed Atlas and placed him on top of me, straddling my hips.

Laughing he looked me up and down, "then how about you let me have you tonight?" Atlas ran a finger down my chest biting his lip in thought. My erection was almost instant. "...and don't worry about the dream. It was nothing. Just her getting attacked or missing. Things like that. I'm sure it's just because I miss her that I keep having those dreams." He shrugged it off as if it were nothing. But I didn't believe it. The way he whimpered in his sleep said otherwise.

I grabbed his hand and kissed his fingers.
"Okay but talk to me if something is bothering you." I smiled at my mate, but his eyes were now glowing their intoxicating golden amber. He was aroused. A growl escaped my throat in unison with his. I flipped Atlas on to his back and this time I straddled him.

"I was thinking maybe you will let me have you instead. I've never topped before, and you were supposed to let me do it yesterday." I rocked my hips against his, urging his erection further. Atlas looked up at me smiling and pressed himself up into me. His eyes ate my body as they trailed from my eyes to my lips, my chest, and then my manhood.

"Okay, I'll guide you then," Atlas' grin became naughty.

"Why thank you sir, I can't wait." I replied while grinding down into him.

"Mmmmmm. Now that's a good boy." Atlas grabbed my hips pressing back against me very slowly, teasing me before tossing me to the side. "Now let's go before I end up losing all my self-control."

The laughter that erupted out of me was hearty but the look of frustration on my mate's face was priceless. I really did turn him on and that thought alone was such a trigger for me. Maybe it was good that he stopped first because I didn't think I could control myself very well.

***

"Good morning, Alpha Kristofer." Atlas sat down behind his desk, and I took the seat next to Kristofer.

The office was about the size of a master bedroom. A large heavy desk sat in the middle with little to make it look polished. Instead, it seems like someone cut a large tree trunk, stripped it, and carved it to resemble a desk. The edges were rough, and the wood was well-aged. Pictures of Atlas and his parents dwelled at the corner of the desk next to a small ashtray with the word dad in the center. The ashtray looked like something Atlas must have made as a child. It was adorable really. On the other end of the desk was a small trophy that read 'World's Best Dad Wolf". It was small like those you found in dollar stores.

Everything in the room looked more like what Atlas' father would have decorated with instead of Atlas.

The walls were beige and bear with only a roman numeral clock and a few paintings of wolves I didn't recognize. One of them was definitely a family portrait of Atlas, Martha, Raven, and Iris in their wolf form since I was able to recognize Atlas and Iris.

The brown curtains draped down the windows with a white mesh to accent the walls. The same earth tones as his room. A large in-wall bookshelf framed one side of the room from ceiling to floor while the other side had a small coffee table and a couch for guests.

"Good morning, Alpha Atlas. Cassius." We smiled at one another in greeting. Kristofer looked at me though with a dirty smirk.

What? I asked Kristofer through the link.

You guys reek of sex.

Is that so? Jealous? I smirked.

Shut up, I bet you bottom.

I had no words. Kristofer burst out laughing at my silence and like an idiot I sat there. Atlas passed a glance between us and raised a brow. I sighed and shook my head at Atlas to not even bother asking.

"Okay. Well, I've wanted to thank you for helping find my sister. I owe you one," Atlas beamed brightly.

"Honestly, we owe it all to mom. If she didn't tell us about the shack our parents used, I wouldn't have known where to look."

"Shack?" Atlas' eyes fell into confusion. And rightfully so. I completely forgot to tell him. Kristofer turned to me as if saying 'how doesn't he know yet' and I was nothing but a deer in headlights.

"Right, so babe, about that." I began to choose my words and turned to Atlas. "Kristofer's parents and yours were…um…."

"Swingers," Kristofer finished my sentence.

I paused to let it sink in. Atlas' eyes were wide, but he stayed quiet, so I continued. "Cecile said that the four of them would meet in a shack they had across the river and have…fun. Eventually, they all fell for one another and kept their relationship secret. One day, Rick followed your father and caught him and Jude being intimate which resulted in him going into a jealous rage.

He killed them both. Your mom ran back home to protect you and Rick threatened Cecile to not say anything or he would kill Martha. Cecile loves her so much that she agreed. Rick basically did whatever he did to you and Iris because of the betrayal he felt from your father." I sat back in my chair watching Atlas fight back the tears that stung his eyes.

"Are you okay?" Kristofer leaned forward resting his elbows on his knees.

"What I don't understand is, how he managed to kill two Alphas?" Atlas snapped at me, but I shook my head in defeat.

"So, I asked my mother the same question. Apparently, our fathers were into bondage."

"Wait what?! My dad and…." Atlas sat back in his chair in disbelief.

"Yeah... I know. I couldn't believe it either. My father was apparently tied up when Rick attacked leaving him vulnerable. He ran into the shack and began arguing with your dad but when he let his guard down to calm Rick down, he killed your father using a silver laced dagger and then did the same to my father."

We all sat in silence with those words hanging in the air. So much has happened that no one knew about. Rick was a slimy rat for holding two people hostage with his threats, all because of his jealousy.

"So that son of a bitch literally killed our fathers because he couldn't get what he wanted. What kind of twisted person does that shit?" The tears finally fell down Atlas' cheeks. He finally got the answer to his father's death, but I wasn't sure if the truth hurt him more than the ignorance to it all. I was surprised Kristofer was as calm as he was as well. We always thought Jude was killed by a hunter and now we learned he died along with Raven by the hands of the same lunatic.

"Well, I guess that could be why Martha left. She was probably trying to get away from Rick. If so, we can call her to come back home." I rubbed my hands on my jeans trying to hide how clammy they were. This was nothing of what I expected to hear yet I still couldn't comprehend Kristofers cool demeanor.

"If he wasn't dead already, I'd kill him again", Atlas hit his desk. "All the shit I went through to hide my truth and protect Iris and yet he still managed to hurt her". The tears freely ran into a pitter patter on his desk and burned his cheeks in salted streaks. He swiped his desk in anger, throwing all his paperwork on the floor.

"Babe, it's okay now. We are all safe and he no longer is a threat. I know it sucks but you and your family are free now." I approached him slowly and opened my arms allowing him to decide if he wanted my comfort. He hesitated for a second but caved and I squeezed him in my arms when he gave in, trying to fill him with my scent so he could calm down.

"Well actually, that's the purpose of my visit. I was talking to my mom, and we thought the same. We figured we could reach out to Martha and tell her. Mom actually never lost contact with her, so she tried to call a few times last night and this morning but nothing. She even mind-linked with her but it didn't work. She might be too far." Kristofer's voice dipped.

"How can they mind-link if they aren't from the same pack or mates?" I pulled away from Atlas just enough for him to look at Kristofer as well.

"Mom said they had done a blood bond ritual between the four of them. It's like when you take a rogue wolf into your pack." Kristofer looked up to me and smirked. It was how I was able to communicate with the family as well since I was adopted.

"My head hurts." Atlas dug his face into my chest and took a deep breath. "So, you're saying that my mother is missing now?" Although his voice was muffled, Kristofer understood him.

Kristofer nodded apologetically just as Atlas turned his way. "The last my mother heard of her; Martha was up north in the mountains."

"North? Like where my father is?" I gasped and Kristofer's face went pale at my words.

"No, that would be impossible. There's no way your dad would know that her son is your mate." Kristofer began to fidget in his seat. "Right?"

"D-Do you think that maybe he knows that my mom was in contact with yours?" Atlas words trembled at the thought.

"Shit, I hope not." Kristofer stood up and walked to the door. "I'm going to ask my mom to try again, and I'll keep in touch."

"Wait, are you okay? How are you so calm after learning about Jude?" I finally asked.

"I may seem calm, but the shed out back will tell you differently. Now I have to repair the damage I caused since mom had a fit. I always knew his death was shady, I just never knew in what way. I'm just glad the bastard Rick got what he had coming." Kristofer squeezed his fist before he relaxed. "Alpha, Cassius." He stepped out of the room and left.

I hugged my mate in silence, allowing all the information to cement within his mind. All I wanted was for his pain and worries to go away but with every turn there was something else we had to overcome. *How is my father connected to all of this if he really does have Martha? What is his goal? Does he still want me dead?*

Atlas turned around and wiped a falling tear from my face. I hate my father. With a deep breath, I pulled myself together. *I need to be strong.*

Chapter 12

CASSIUS

Three days passed, and we still couldn't contact Martha. The radio silence left the house completely on edge and I felt at fault. While I knew I did nothing wrong, the fact that my father could be behind this made me feel guilty, nonetheless. Of course, there wasn't any real proof that my father had any involvement but something in my bones told me there might be some truth to it. We continued to do our best to track down Martha and bring her home. And while the house walked on eggshells, I kept checking in on Iris.

Iris has been locked in her room ever since she was brought back, only coming out to eat a couple of times. She kept telling me she was okay, but it was obvious that she wasn't, but I gave her space. Some guy named Finn, on the other hand, kept nagging her whenever Iris stepped out of her room, and it was clear he was annoying her. I rolled my eyes at the Finns latest attempt to comfort Iris and finished making coffee to bring over to Atlas who was busy in his study.

I kissed Atlas on top of his head as he flipped through some paperwork trying to get his affairs in order. If he hadn't thrown everything on the floor, then he wouldn't be struggling to find what he was looking for. He was so focused that he didn't even respond to my affection. His mind was lost within his inner turmoil of his mother's silence and the news of how his father died. I kept failing to pull him out of his head even if for a moment.

With much reluctance to leave him alone, I placed the coffee next to him hoping he would at least sip it. Ever since Kristofer's last visit, Atlas has been on edge. His dreams of her being in trouble or dying the way his father did were worsening. And I kept telling him that it was due to his anxiety of not finding her, but he wouldn't listen.

I walked over to the window to let in some of the cool air from outside to freshen up the room. It had become stuffy, and Atlas could use a bit of a cool breeze to clear his mind. Although, looking out the window, it didn't seem like much of a breeze was blowing. I gently touched the cold glass of the window and stared outside for a bit before opening it. It was hard to explain but the way the night sky looked cloudy and ominous, was telling of how snow might fall soon. The palm of my hand tingled as the glass began to frost into frozen fractals. I recoiled in shock, staring at the handprint on the window.

"What's wrong?" Atlas called out. I jumped to the sound of his voice, but he didn't even bother to look up from his desk.

"Nothing. Just opening the window." I wiped away the frost and quickly opened the window. Atlas continued to work, so I left him and returned home. The freaky things were now happening outside of my home, and I was convinced that something was happening to me and the magical aspect of my lineage that Dr. Michael doubted seemed more and more plausible to me. In fact, more than plausible.

Reaching my packhouse, I raced to my room to pack a bag. We had all agreed that a good idea would be to create a small search party and head north. If all went well then, we could find Martha and avoid bumping into my father or his men. To be honest, if that was the case and we had a run-in, I didn't want to face him. I didn't want to know the truth of his abandonment. It was the worst feeling to know you were not wanted, especially by those whose blood courses your veins.

***

The sun peeked slightly through the trees behind the house. The morning was rising. The sound of engines muffled in the distance grew louder as I stared at the sunrise. Atlas and a couple from his pack were ready and parking out front. In one night, I somehow turned a rescue mission for Martha into my own worst nightmare. I couldn't keep my mind off the idea of bumping into my father. He was the last person I wanted to see. I wasn't sure how I would react or if I would react at all. Yet through all of the dread the last thing I wanted was to make it about me. This was about Martha and finding her safe, not me and my daddy issues.

I wished I could go back in time and remain naive to all that my father was, but I couldn't. My breathing began to quicken with every bit of anxiety that was building within me. My nerves vibrated but this needed to be done. I need to face him, my past, and my truth. If it happened during the mission, then so be it. I couldn't let it make me unhinged. With my bag in hand, I headed out with Kristofer, leaving Cecile and his Beta, Demetrius, in charge.

***

The desolate roads were eerily quiet. No animal sounds, no wind blowing, no signs of life anywhere. It was as if life ceased to exist while we drove by. The sky was clear, and the sun was now dispersing shades of gold throughout the land. The morning chill lingered in my bones and the frosted grass beyond my window melted under the rising sun. Winter was near.

"So, when we get there your friend is going to help us find lodging?" I looked at Mavis who caught my eye in the rearview mirror.

"Yes, Luna. He moved to another pack when he found his mate. He said Martha had stayed with him a few days. We can start there".

"Okay, sounds good", I turned in my seat and faced my window. I still was not used to being called Luna.

Trees lined both sides of the road, making it feel never ending. The monotonous scenery made me sleepy with my eyes growing heavier by the second. I fell asleep a few hours into the lull of the engine. I entered a weird state of neither dream nor waking reality. It was almost as if I was in a different place, alternate to my current reality that was still very much real. I looked around and found a little old man in a rocker. It was annoying having to call out to him since he didn't hear me, but I walked closer to see what was going on.

I tapped his shoulder, and he turned around to me with his eyes completely white. It was horrifying. He stood up no longer looking like a feeble old man but a mighty one. Markings spread all over his body. His long white hair lifted in the air almost weightlessly and flowed as if underwater. "Wake up Cassius." His lips didn't move but I knew it was him speaking.

He called me without words. A pull as though we were tethered by something we couldn't see. I reached out to him, "wake up, Cassius." His voice grew louder, and I continued to reach out and when I finally touched him, he transformed into the biggest wolf I had ever seen. His silver fur was shining brightly just like Wolfie's.

"Cassius Avelious, AWAKEN!"

I jumped awake and so did Atlas. Sweat dripped down my face from whatever it was that just happened.

"Are you okay Cass?" Atlas caught his breath also having a slight sweat from his sleep.

"Yea, I just had the most bizarre dream." I sat up straight and wiped my forehead.

"So did I, it was about you." Atlas opened the window for some fresh air.

"Me? What was it about?"

"Well, at first there was this old guy in a rocker and suddenly he stood up with a bunch of tattoos. He-" I panicked listening to him describe my exact dream, so I cut him off.

"Was he telling me to wake up? Was there also a wolf?" I asked with a shaky voice.

"How did you know that?" Atlas grabbed my hand.

"Because that is the same thing I just dreamt." We stared at each other, unable to comprehend any of it. How could we have the same dream at the same time? It made no sense. I looked at my phone and it was nine hours into the drive. My body felt stiff, and I was ready for a pit stop to give my legs a good stretch. We pulled over to the side of the bleak road and stepped out to walk away the cramps in our legs and back.

"Damn, my back is so stiff," I gave a good stretch and cracked my spine with a twist. It felt good for a brief second to release all the pressure that built up from sitting in the same position for so long. Remnants of the dream linger, and I still couldn't wrap my mind around Atlas and I having the same dream.

Atlas waved his phone in the air with a disgruntled look. "I doubt you'll get reception," I called out and giggled. My mate huffed so I wrapped my arms around his waist to calm his annoyed expression. "We are too far into the middle of nowhere for that."

"Ugh, the entirety of the North is a dead zone". Atlas tucked his head into my chest as if throwing a tantrum. "Babe, I'm so tired. That dream and the long drive drained me." Atlas continued to whine in my arms, hugging me in return. "Think we will find mom?"

"Yes, don't worry. Now come on, I'll do the next driving shift." I squeezed him tight and with gentle lips I kissed the top of his head. My bond sensed how tired and scared he was. Either that or I was projecting my own fear and tiredness on him instead.

We all hopped back in the car and Atlas took the back seat to sleep while Mavis rode shotgun with me. Twenty minutes in and my mate was sound asleep again. Dead to the world.

"I worry about him", I mumbled just loud enough for Mavis to hear.

"Makes me happy to hear that from you Luna. He really needs someone like you by his side. Sometimes he gets in his own head and after his father died, he became a bit more closed off. Even though he is a great Alpha you can tell he is lonely and in a shell of sorts. He tries to mask it with cooking, but I know him well enough. I have found him so many times sitting under the tree by our home, in his office doing work, dead to the world. Unresponsive to others around him. All of those things are how he copes. That is until he met you." Mavis kept his eyes on the road but the admiration and love he had for Atlas was that of a true Beta and best friend.

"That's because it's so easy to love him. I'm just glad the goddess put him in my path. Also, I'm not your Luna yet." I chuckled.

Mavis finally turned to me, "why does it bother you that I call you Luna?"

"Because I haven't earned that title yet." I replied simply and shrugged.

"You must be joking; you have done more for our pack in these last several weeks without officially being Luna than I have seen from other actual Luna's. Don't sell yourself short.... I like you, you're definitely already Luna in my eyes." Mavis placed a hand on my shoulder and gave it a squeeze. It felt nice receiving that recognition from him. It meant more than I would ever reveal.

A low growl rumbled behind us. "If you want to keep your hand, remove it," Atlas threatened behind gritted teeth. Obviously waking from the impressively short nap he took.

"Someone's cranky. Baby need a baba?" Mavis mocked in baby talk. The laugh that escaped my throat was hearty which Atlas did not appreciate. Seeing his face in the rearview mirror after I adjusted it only made it that much funnier.

Atlas snuffed Mavis in the head prompting a hilarious cat fight between the two, despite being grown wolves. It was obvious they grew up together. They behaved more like brothers with how they bickered or teased one another. I can't say I knew what that closeness felt like though, maybe with Alex a bit up until he confessed his feelings. If anything, maybe Kristofer was closer to me since we definitely teased one another and even then, he was always so busy trying to fill his father's shoes that even our dynamic didn't last too long.

"Okay guys, enough. I'm driving and that's dangerous." I gave my best authoritative voice but failed when the whole car ensued in laughter. Even Kirk in the back was laughing hysterically and he had practically been invisible since we got in the car.

"Okay daddy, we'll stop," Atlas mocked.

I turned around wickedly, "leave that talk for the bedroom."

Everyone fell quiet when suddenly Mavis yelled, " WATCH OUT!"

I slammed my brakes which caused the van to swerve before spinning off the road and coming to a stop. My knuckles were white from my grip on the steering wheel, but I peeled my fingers away and stepped out of the car to look around. It was eerily quiet. The snow on the ground remained untouched as it had snowed not too long ago. No tracks or scents to trace. The trees barely moved, and the wind was as steady as my feet. But that was the problem. It was too calm to seem natural.

Kristofer pulled off to the side of the road as well and stepped out of his vehicle. He eyes the skid marks I left and looks around as if to find the culprit. There was nothing on the road. No signs of anything being there or running off. Nothing to show anyone was hiding or setting a trap. The hairs on my skin rose on end as I took in my surroundings. An uneasy feeling gripped me with a strong hold.

"What the hell was that?" I continued scanning the area. The wind picked up and flurries began to fall in swirls, lessening my field of view. Something was out there. Watching. I balled my fist, ready for a fight if it was an ambush.

"Looked like a witch, or ghost, or something," Mavis whispered as if too scared to say it too loud. He and Kirk stood back-to-back looking around carefully. "Would you say, like a shaman?" I reply feeling that we were already caught by whatever it was.

My wolf howls inside, *I sense them. Wolves are hiding deep in the woods. Someone was trying to warn us.* As quickly as Wolfie's words filled my mind, I knew he was right. Whoever it was knew we were coming, and we walked right into their trap.

"Guys, get in the car." I pushed Atlas towards the van.

"What's wrong?" he replied, tripping over his feet.

We all got in our vehicles, and I phoned Kristofer on speaker. "My wolf can sense them. I don't know how, but he does. He says wolves are hiding and what we saw was a warning. They knew we were coming."

Kristofer chimed in through the phone, "we have no choice but to continue".

"Yea, we just got to be vigilant", Atlas reached under his seat and pulled out bullet proof vests and handed them out. Where he got them, I could not say. However, I wouldn't be surprised if this was due to fear of the amount of hunter activities.

"Right, if Wolfie senses anything else I'll alert everyone." I hung up and began driving again.
My wolf growls.

They are angry we didn't turn around, but they made note of our presence. They can tell you are different from the others.

So maybe they are just weary? I added but I could tell Wolfies didn't believe it.

No, I think they just realized who you are. The numbers went down considerably probably to warn your father.

My father?! You sure?

It's the only thing I can think of, Wolfie didn't sound pleased, and neither am I.

Fuck, okay. Thanks, Wolfie.

I filled my lungs in a deep breath and gripped the wheel. "Wolfie just said that a few ran off. It's most likely to alert my father. They know who I am". My heart thumped hard in my chest. We were short in numbers and nowhere near friendly territory to request back-up.

The Silver Lining

"Don't worry, we expected this was a possibility. We are ready." Atlas hugged me from behind.

Warmth filled my body but it quickly faded when a pack of wolves appeared in the distance.

Shit.

Chapter 13

Several feet away from the front of the car was a group of wolves blocking our path. At least twenty of them stood in a row. They were massive in size, smaller than Cassius' wolf but still all enormous compared to the rest of us. Their fur varied in shades of either black, white, or various dark tones of gray. They were all very good-looking wolves, but it did little to take away how dangerous they seemed. It was like looking at a new tier of wolves. They were stunning to say the least but of course I will never say that out loud.

In front of the calvary of wolves was a tall man with dark caramel skin. His hair was white and long, braided off to one side with something weaved into the hair. His arms were tattooed, and his wrist was wrapped in leather bounds. He could easily stand taller than Cassius and the resemblance was uncanny. There was no doubt who he was.

***

CASSIUS

I pressed the brakes and waited for someone to make a move. The flurries subsided which allowed me a better opportunity to analyze the wolves before us. It was odd looking at this large group because I felt nothing of what I thought I would if I ever got to meet my dad or family. The man that stood tall and strong with the white hair had to most likely be my father, which left me careening into my past reliving my childhood trauma instead. I thought I would be angry or throw a fit but instead I turned into the little boy that was crying out for his mother while she was killed.

I looked over to Atlas. My poor mate was as pale as I felt. He was already anxious about the trip, but I think now he realized how much this was affecting me as well. But instead of comforting me like I so desperately wanted, Atlas just stared at me. The bond was manifesting again. Its beautiful colors circled around us trying to calm the anxiety within me. Within us. Atlas probably recognized that the man before us could be my father and didn't know how to react. He was waiting for my lead instead.

My knuckles on the steering wheel were back to going completely white as I gripped for dear life. "That's my dad. I vaguely remember him but that's definitely my dad," my voice quivered now that I said it out loud. The aura intensified, responding to my emotions. I focused on the man standing in a way to show he was ready for a fight. The stance of a warrior.

"Cass, breathe." Atlas grabbed my shoulder, and it helped calm me down a bit, but I was scared beyond belief.

"You don't understand, it's my wolf. He is being challenged". I gripped the wheel tighter. My father's Beta was challenging me and demanding I approach.

"Your father is challenging you? How do you know?" Mavis grabbed my arm. "Don't do it Luna."

"I have to and no it's his Beta. Our wolves can communicate somehow. Maybe it's because I am originally from that pack. Just… stand by in case things go south." I turned to Atlas and kissed him almost as if it was our last.

The last bits of light from our auras vanished but the strength it provided me remained. My mind resigned to what could be my inevitable fate and went blank. Our kiss was full of, I love you's and goodbyes. Something I refused to say out loud. I was grateful for the little time I had with Atlas, but this might really be it for me.

With a deep breath, I stepped out of the car and walked toward the wolves in long strides. My face was stone cold and determined because I refused to show any weakness in front of this man or anyone else behind him. As terrified as I was, I didn't know where this courage was suddenly coming from, but I desperately needed more of it. I was pretty sure the aura didn't give me *this* much strength. But this was no longer just about me but about protecting the ones I loved. An odd sense of calm washed over me pushing all my feelings aside.

Upon getting closer to the pack, some of the wolves began to fidget. The wolf standing directly next to my father stepped forward and met me halfway. His white fur, ever blinding against the sun, did nothing to mask the scar on his face. After an eternity in a standoff, I shifted into Wolfie.

I shook myself and let my fur fluff. My senses fired all at once when I stood there stealing the gaze of everyone there. Something felt different. Several of the wolves in line backed up with their heads down, as if bowing to me. They whimpered and lowered their ears in submission. Witnessing my form, they must have realized how vastly different I was to them despite their possible blood relation to me. I stand out immediately even among these pure bloods in size and color. With my silver fur I looked like something like an angel or demigod amongst them.

Although I would never flatter myself with such grandiose perceptions. Nor act as though those notions were true. My body easily towered over the other wolves including the Beta who eyed me carefully. Standing tall I howled into the cold air and bared my teeth accepting the challenge before me. Somehow, I was steady. I didn't feel shaken, and my mind was clear. My body almost moved on its own as if guided by someone else.

The Beta wolf howled in return and charged forward, attempting to pounce on me but his stiff movements were too easy to read. We snarled at each other knowing full well that I outmatched him but as a Beta, he didn't back down. He didn't seem the type to back down nor accept defeat. He clawed at me, and I swiftly dodged to the left. Each one of his attacks was as predictable as the other. But as stiff as he was, his movements were quick.

I maintained my distance. I couldn't risk getting caught and if Cassius and I learned anything from Rick, it was how determined others could be to inflict pain even if it meant dipping their claws in silver. And if they were indeed pure blood, then they could dip their claws in silver and remain unaffected. *I should end this quickly, but I need a clear opening,* I told Cassius who was trying to study the movements of the Beta as well. Just one opening was all we needed.

The searing stare of my Atlas watching me momentarily touched my mind and I could feel his wolf, Leo, worrying. I wished it didn't have to come down to a fight, but Cassius' old man didn't seem like the kind of guy to sit down and talk over tea either. I needed to thank Kristofer for all the training he put us through, or this could quickly end with a very different story.

The Beta lunged forward and managed to get on top of me. My own thoughts worked against me, and I foolishly allowed myself to get caught. Swipe after swipe, the Beta attacked. Thankfully his blows weren't as effective as he might've thought nor were his claws laced. I gave him more credit than he deserved. He nipped and tried to get a bite into my throat, but he failed.

After wiggling into position, I shoved my hind legs beneath him and tossed him off. The Beta yelped as he flew off high and landed awkwardly on his back. This was what Leo felt while against Rick. As I fought, I kept thinking about my mate and his safety. The last thing I wanted was for him to help me like Cassius tried to with Rick and possibly end up hurt. Cassius grumbled inside my mind, realizing how naive he was to think he could ignore the rules and intervene when a fight initiated between wolves.

I circled around the Beta, growling and snapping my canines. The intensity of his stare dulled the bite of the cold air around us. Like the eager fool that he was, he lunged forward again but I side stepped and caught him on the ribs leaving a nasty gash against his white fur. The wolf fell in a hard thud painted red. There was no denying that I hit him hard. I put everything into that hit. The Beta got up again and tried to bite me on my leg but just barely missed. While it wasn't deep, I still felt the sting as he barely grazed my skin.

I swiped fast and knocked him to the ground. All the strength I had mustered was in that one blow and he fell bleeding heavily from his ribs. The extra hit to his side must have aggravated his wounds as blood began to ooze from his wound. The fight was over, but I refused to kill him unnecessarily. I walked up to the injured wolf and stepped on his paw. With all my weight, I leaned forward. A whimper cried from his throat, but I quickly pounced on him, breaking his paw in place. He yelped and moved his paw closer to his body, wrapping his tail around himself.

The Beta howled in a tone filled with painful defeat and tucked his head into his body in almost a fetal position. The sound echoed within the trees and back. The wolves all moved forward at Beta's distress, making a clear line between me and him. Immediately my heart dropped. I didn't care that these wolves looked smaller than me, I still couldn't defeat them in numbers.

Sensing a sudden distress not of my own, I turned around to find my mate and the others jumping out of the vehicles. They grouped behind me, returning to me the confidence I was beginning to lose. I shifted back to Cassius and faced the father, their leader.

Unfortunately, I was now standing there naked for all to see. If it wasn't because I was so well endowed, I would have been embarrassed. It took me years to feel okay shedding my clothes in front of others. While so many wolves do it so naturally, I sometimes struggle. But I looked at my mate to find his eyes on my package and blushing. That was not something he should be doing right now but damn I loved that I made him turn that red.

Fuck he looks hot...No, no stop. Now isn't the time. Atlas' thoughts jumped into my mind, and I snickered at how hard he was trying to focus on the wolves before us. The moment didn't even feel real to begin with. My attention snapped back to the white-haired man as he cleared his throat to speak.

"I see you have trained well but are still pathetically weak. You couldn't even finish him off. My name is Honovi. I am this pack's Alpha." Honovi stepped forward without regard to his Beta.

"What do you want from me?" I spat back. After hearing his voice, something in me twitched.

"Is that any way to speak to your father?" Honovi's mouth pulled into a smirk. Everyone in his pack turned to him as if they didn't know I existed. Wouldn't surprise me if that was the case considering how ruthless he was.

"You are no father of mine. Not since you tried having me and my mother killed." The wolves around Honovi stepped away a bit. I was never able to truly confirm that it was him that sent those men, until now.

"Why would you kill her? What did she ever do to you but love you? She was your Luna. Even as she was tortured, she held hope that you would save us and look where it got her." I roared my words at my father. Pure raw emotion all in one breath. I felt hot. The anger inside me seeped out, uncontrollable, unyielding, boiling over in a rumble that was too late to tame.

Honovi laughed but as he found it all amusing, he didn't notice his pack backing away, "your mother was a whore. Luna, you say? She never meant to bear my child and yet here you are. I had to get rid of her to be a true leader. She was nothing to me but a means to an end, but you came and fucked it all up." He scoffed as if his words were just a matter of fact. *How dare he say such things about my mother?!*

"You not loving us doesn't justify hiring hunters to kill your own kind, your mate, your blood. Not to mention, you're also the buyer that wanted my head recently, aren't you?" I stepped forward with more confidence. "You think you are above everyone, don't you? We carry this pure blood in our veins as a gift not a tool for destruction, but you, what do you use it for? Fear and manipulation? Does your pack even know what really happened because it doesn't seem like they know how their Luna died?" I continued stepping forward, each step with more conviction.

My skin was crawling on fire. I could no longer think. In fact, I no longer felt like I was in control. My words, my body, everything moved of its own accord. Something in me wanted to break free and with this pain, I should let it come out. Whatever it was, I should let go and aim it all at the man that made me feel broken my whole life.

He deserved no mercy. He doesn't deserve to walk this earth while my mother's soul slept. I scanned over the wolves that have backed far away from Honovi and off to the side. The growling stopped and all the eyes were now on me in a different light. A few shifted back to their human form and got down on one knee with their palm out and a fist in the middle. A sign of respect. The only one not realizing what was happening was my father.

I continued towards Honovi, "I curse the day I cried for you. You shouldn't be allowed to be Alpha. You're unworthy of that title. Unworthy as a wolf, as a descendent of our lineage. You disgrace the blood that runs through us. Through me." My hands are engulfed in light blue flames. "You don't deserve the ground you walk on." Tattoos spread up both my arms and down my body as my hair turned as silver as my fur.

"How did you change like that? Why…why are your eyes completely black?" Honovi rambled his trembling words but quickly gained his composure. I chuckled at his momentary show of weakness. He was pathetic.

"I knew I should have finished you off. I shouldn't have left you with that sorry excuse of a woman. That pack has filled you with silly hopes and dreams. You think you can stand up to me? You're weak. You're nothing. Your physical appearance is nothing but a parlor trick." Honovi took a step back not even realizing the quiver in his voice. Obviously, he did not believe his own lies.

"Then why didn't you? Why are you backing away if I'm so weak?" The flames on my fist glowed brighter. They reacted to my words, no, to my emotions. My voice boomed over everyone. It shook the very ground we stood on.

"I couldn't prove if you were the reincarnation. At first, I thought it was your mother, it was the only reason I married her, not because we were mates. I hated the idea of a bond. Then when she became pregnant, I had to wait for you to be born. After a few years it was clear that neither of you possessed the power, I needed so I had you both killed." Honovi laughed like a mad man.

Listening to him speak about our past though it was nothing, filled me with rage. It was the fuel to the lit match I have inside.

"When she died, it confirmed my suspicion. I knew for sure she was nothing special but you somehow survived. So, I became curious. I couldn't risk killing you knowing your power might be delayed. I might have to harvest your blood for myself if that was the case. So, I will let you live. After you first shifted, I felt the power that came with it, but you somehow still didn't manifest anything after that. So, when that wretched woman protected you, I decided to find other means to get what I wanted, and I did." Honovi shrugged.

"So, all of this, is for power? Are you psychotic? We don't live in an era where that kind of power is needed. We live in peace now. We have all that we need. Our only threats are the stupid hunters which we could easily pick off." My mind slowly lost its grip on sanity and gave in to whatever wanted to take hold.

"I don't care. That power you wield right now belongs to me. Not to some child of a pathetic useless whore. I will forge the power myself no matter what." Honovi laughed.

"SHE IS NOT A WHORE!" I bellowed. My voice cracked the air beneath the pressure. The vibrations of my voice were like a whip with my words as the popper. Everything went blank. I finally looked down at my fist noticing the flames now dancing wildly around my hands. Waiting for a command.

My head panned around but I was not the one in control. I felt like a spectator in my own body and now all the wolves including our own were in human form kneeling before me. Some were in fear but most in respect including my mate. The power I felt surging through me was none I ever felt before. Not even when we shifted under a full moon. I turned to my mate and his face was pale as if he was going to be sick. This pressure I exerted exceeded that of an Alpha tone.

Honovi wobbled, struggling to stand from the pressure as well. "How can you already control it or is it just instinct? You barely just awakened." He spat on the ground trying to hold back the nausea he seemed to be feeling.

I screamed with tears burning my eyes, "what is this?" The air cracked once more. Something was happening and whatever it was had my father unable to hold a steady footing.

"You, my son, are the reincarnation of the first Shaman wolf. Every couple hundred years or so, his spirit reincarnates. That wolf will then have greater power than any other being in existence. However, that power should have been mine. Instead, I was given the ability to bend someone's will but what good is that in comparison to what you have." Honovi fell to one knee but pulled himself up again.

"You have powers?" I walked over to Honovi causing him to break a sweat in his struggle to defy the submission, but he lost and went down to his knees. All because of me.

"All of us pure blood, have powers, including your mother. She had the gift of foresight, but she would never tell me anything she saw about you, claiming your future was uncertain so she could not see. A lying bitch till the very end. I will take from you what's mine." Honovi spat at my feet.

"I fucking HATE YOU!" I exploded in anger, losing all control of my body for a moment. In a burst of power, all my senses came to life. The wind kicked up and swirled around me. I pulled back and punched Honovi with my flaming fist burning the skin off most of the right side of his face in the process. Honovi screamed but I barely heard it. The blood pumping in my ears kept me deaf to his pain.

His skin was melting off his chin and cheek, but I felt nothing. "You shall have no power. I will strip you of everything. Your wolf, your will bending, your title. EVERYTHING!" I yelled at the coward before me. My voice amplified and pierced through the flurries that now danced over everyone in its path.

The tattoos covering me glowed a pale blue and my body engulfed in flames, swirling and crackling. Chants echoed from my mind and into everyone else. The voices of the generations before us lending me their strength. The clouds above us became dark with lightning casting shadows. I formed a link with all the wolves as if I had known to do this all along. I made them rise with me and in unison, they swayed. The voices of the reincarnated bodies before me swam through the current that links our minds. Like muscle memory, I began to hop lightly on one foot and then the other.

Thunder clapped as flashes of a past I have no recollections of raced through my mind. It was almost as if I was relieving the shaman in ritual. Different visions in the different bodies I once lived in, formed before me. I could no longer tell what reality, or a vision was. The voices in our minds continued chanting loudly with the wind becoming wild in response.

My feet slid on the ground in circular patterns and then my toe stepped forward and back. I hopped again, alternating my stance, and repeated the steps again and again. Then I hopped with both feet and began footwork as if painting a masterpiece on the ground. Each pattern I created lit up like magma seeping out from the earth. It scorched into the tar and with each complete portion, a howl was heard in the distance as if the ancestors of our past were crying. The chanting grew louder. I felt the uneasiness of the wolves around me despite them swaying under my command. Most of them lost consciousness and fell from how thick the air was.

"I Shoneah, strip you of your name and title," my voice no longer sounded like my own. It was as loud as thunder and tonal with a resonance that could shake anyone to their core. I couldn't even begin to say why I referred to myself as Shoneah.

Honovi fell on his hands and knees confused. "I strip you of your power," I repeated. Honovi shouted for me to stop but as he did, his right arm shot out as if being shackled in the air above him. "I strip you of your wolf," his other arm shot out, shackled like the other.

Right behind Honovi a door manifested and opened. Out stepped two bodies, neither human nor monster. Cloaked with wolf fur, faceless with dark skin and indiscernible gender qualities. Each with a scythe, they stood next to Honovi on either side.

With my hand extended, the markings by my feet glowed brightly in red and orange hues. I stopped the dance and stood steady in the center of what I created. A geometric lattice pattern was intricately scorched beneath my feet. With a flick of my wrist, the two creatures swung their scythe and with a strike of lightning they cut through him. While Honovi remained unharmed, something began to emerge from his body in the form of smoke.

"No, don't. I need him", Honovi tried to fall over in pain, but the invisible shackles prevented him from moving. The smoke that emerged took the shape of a wolf. Honovi screamed a heart-wrenching scream filled with pain and anguish. The smoke wolf fully stood next to me bowing his head. His spirit was unscathed and free from the prison that was my father.

The door behind Honovi reopened and one of the creatures walked through and waited on the other side.

"Say goodbye to who you were and never will be again." My flames and the markings on the ground disappeared slowly. The air thinned out and those that remained conscious gasp trying to breathe in fresh air. My father continued to cry looking at his former wolf when another scream erupted from his throat as the remaining creature pressed its thumb on Honovi's forehead, burning its mark. His arms were now free but the pain from his face had him gripping his hair. The shape of a crescent moon with an x over it seared into his skin.

"You are no longer a child of the goddess, no longer a child of the Shaman wolf. You are hereby banished from this pack and any other. You will finish your days among humans, as a human, unable to reincarnate." The creature spoke in a guttural voice that dripped with tension and command. It left and the smoke wolf followed it through the door before it closed and faded away.

I walked over to the Beta who was quaking on the ground. "Where does your allegiance live?" I asked. The Beta trembled but with certainty answered, "not with him."

I smiled and placed his palm on his chest. Back to his human form, he laid there with his broken wrist.

"If you were lying, I would have known. Now let me heal you as an apology for the injury." Light radiated from my hand, covering the Beta. He gasped as the air finally expanded his lungs properly. "You are the new Alpha to this pack. Lead it wisely. I am sure you won't make the mistakes he did."

The Beta sat up looking at his healed hand and then bowed to me. I smiled at his response and walked back to my nameless father.

"Where is Martha?"

"She isn't here. It's true I had her, but I treated her as a guest. She was never privy to my intent of using her to lure you. Once I realized you were coming, I let her go saying I had urgent business, and she went on her way up further north I believe."

"How did you figure out you could use her to get to me?"

"The stupid hunters I set out to capture you reported back to me everything they saw. I soon realized you and Martha's boy were a thing. When they failed to report the last time I figured, they were dead or ran off. It was only a matter of time where either, I used her impeccable timing to lure you, or I went to get you myself." My father groaned in pain with his voice hoarse.

"The rest of you. I expect you to follow your new Alpha. Do not take your gifts for granted. Whether you decide to remain pureblooded or mate with other wolves that is your decision to make and yours alone. Just remember it doesn't make you any less of a wolf nor are you currently superior. We all were human once and all bleed red."

The sound of howls and yips warmed my heart. With that, I then turned to Atlas ready to leave when something hit the back of my neck. I lost all my strength. My body lost all its power and I returned to my original form passing out the second I reached my mate's arms.

Chapter 14

I caught Cassius before he hit the ground and checked his neck to confirm if he really was struck. A small needle was protruding from his skin at the base of the neck, just under the hairline. I pulled it out and looked around to where his father should have been, but he was gone. That bastard had one last trick up his sleeve which left us in the middle of nowhere with no clue as to what was on that needle or what the hell we had witnessed. With that, we drove to our destination in silence.

Nothing of what we saw made sense. The fact that Cassius wielded such power was terrifying. When Dr. Michael said they were born with magical abilities, I thought he meant telekinesis or something. It was all too much to take in. Mavis and Kirk sat in the front with a pale parlor reflecting the same shock that I felt.

My mate was still unconscious on my lap in the backseat with soft breaths that softened his tired features. His skin slightly glistened against the sun peeked through from between the trees as he began to whimper in a cold sweat. The amount of power he exhibited must have taken a toll on his body and with that needle taking him down, who knew what his body was fighting. With my shirt I wiped his face, *damn!* Cassius was developing a high fever, and we still had another hour drive to go.

This wasn't good. If his body was developing a fever, then he was definitely fighting something. With how he reacted last time and needing to be hospitalized, I prayed this wasn't the same case. I helped his limp body slip on a pair of pants and lowered the back windows to help cool him down. The winter cold blasted into the car as we drove as fast as we could through the winter mountains.

"Hey, reach into my bag and give me the med kit." I motioned to Mavis.

The med kit I put together should have something that could neutralize whatever was in his system. Unfortunately, without knowing what it was, I didn't want to make it worse by causing a bad reaction. I cursed the bastard for what he did but I cursed myself more for not noticing fast enough. That man and Rick deserved a special place in hell.

A small pack of charcoal pills spilled in the bag as I ruffled through it with one hand. I forgot I had put them in there. It might be the only safe thing I could give Cassius that might help him flush whatever was in his system. It was a long shot and a desperate one.

"Hey, pass me a bottle of water." I asked Mavis again.

"Sure"

"Babe, wake up please. I need you to drink this," I whispered but Cassius was out like a light.

"Fuck!" I opened his mouth and shoved the pill as far back into his mouth. Then I poured the water and closed his mouth while lifting his head. Thankfully, he swallowed but the amount of water I had poured made him choke. The water spilled from his mouth onto my pants but at least the pill was in his system. It was all that mattered.

As the winter chill seeped into his skin, his whimpering settled, and he snuggled into my stomach in comfort. Maybe he was looking for warmth and it was absolutely adorable the way he relaxed against my body as he slept more peacefully than before. The pill most likely was working, if he was acting like this. *God, I'm so in love with this man.... whoa, love?* I stroked his beautiful hair that had switched back to its dark black color. *Am I really in love already?*

The thought of love kept bouncing around my mind before turning into worry and back again. Like a ping pong of emotions. Although it wasn't long since we had met, it felt like a lifetime had already gone. A sigh slipped from my lips, and I knew then that the budding feeling in my chest wasn't the bond working its magic. It was the love that I was beginning to feel building with every moment spent by his side. *Please be okay.* I whispered and brushed his cheek with my thumb gently to not stir him from his sleep.

We finally made it deep into the mountains where Ryan lived. He was a really good friend of the family and agreed to let us stay for a few days. The large cabin nestled within a mass of trees, almost camouflaged by its surroundings. Colorful dry leaves covered everything in sight along with the light flurries that kept falling on and off. Yet even with the serene landscape and calm atmosphere, the dark ominous feel of what was still looming over us clung to our bones.

A small fire pit sat off to the side of the cabin along with some tree stumps for makeshift seating. I could see myself roasting marshmallows over a fire there. It was beautiful everywhere my eyes landed and the thought that an out of the way place like this might be nice to have with Cassius. Mavis stood next to me, pulling me from my thoughts and helped put Cassius over my shoulder.

After getting another good look, his neck swelled slightly where the needle had pricked. I gritted my teeth trying not to panic. If I ever crossed paths with Honovi again, I would make sure he didn't survive the encounter. We waited for Kristofer to get out of his vehicle with his pack after pulling up behind us.

"Hey! So good to see you guys again." Ryan opened his arms to hug Mavis in a bear hug.

"Hey buddy, how's Sacha?" Mavis pulled back.

"She is actually very much pregnant with my pup. Come in everyone and warm up." Ryan chuckled and stepped aside. Like the gentlemen he was, he shook our hands as we trailed in one by one.

"Mave hunny, how are you?" A very pregnant little redhead just like Ryan said, waddled up to Mavis and attempted to hug him. Sacha looked ready to pop.
"Hi, Sacha. I see congratulations are in order." Mavis chuckled as her tiny body waddled to a nearby chair.

Cassius

My head spun with throbbing pain relentlessly behind my eyes. There was so much pressure that it felt ready to burst any second. Nausea pricked at the back of my throat, but the waves of my fever distracted me from the bile. My body weighed a thousand pounds or at least that was how it felt and if I didn't know any better, I'd say I lost my legs. I had no feeling in my limbs. Voices came into focus and suddenly the warmth of wherever we were settled against my skin.

"Thanks…. ready." A young female voice spoke, piquing my interest. *What is she saying?* Echoes of other voices chimed in, but I couldn't tell what they were saying. Last I remembered, we were outside facing off with my father, *wait, what happened to them?*

The fever grew heavier and the sounds that were barely clear were now muffled against the throbbing in my head. I drifted away into the darkness that made every effort to claim me.

Huh? My senses carried me back from the dark abyss that momentarily held me. Atlas must be the one holding me since I felt myself sway as he walked. His lavender invaded me, pulling me the rest of the way out of the darkness. Atlas laid me down on something soft, but I couldn't put my finger on what it was. Nothing computed correctly. Atlas' smell was the only thing that registered. Something inside of me pulled me back into the darkness the moment Atlas let go but I fought it. Holding on to the shred of sanity I had left. The heat in my body rose again and the pain behind my eye intensified.

I screamed in my mind, but nothing came out physically. I couldn't move. *Did I really lose my limbs? I thought.*

"So, Ryan, do you… fevers?" That definitely was Atlas talking. *He said Ryan.* We must have reached the cabin. Pain shot from one eye to the other and it sent me into a spiral. Careening down a pit. Darkness consumed me. At least that's what it looked like, but I saw something. A small light appeared, and I could see someone. The figure looked feminine and…familiar.

Cass, baby. Is that you?

Mom?

My, you have grown so well. I'm so proud of you.

Mom! Is that really you, how? I cried holding out my arms so she could hug me but no matter what I did, I couldn't reach her. It was like chasing a ghost which in this case, might be quite literally. I missed her voice, her hugs, and how she used to play with my hair, so I fell asleep.

You can't come to where I am. Not yet. It's not your time, so I'm going to help you.

What do you mean? Mom please, just one last hug.

No son, you need to wake up. I will give you my strength so you can recover but I need you to wake up.

MOM!

Wake up Cass. WAKE UP!

I stirred awake again but unable to open my eyes still. It made no sense to have seen my mother.

What's happening to me?

"Is this…were telling… about?" A male voice asked. His words fell in and out of my ears in incoherent fragments, *Ryan maybe.*

A growl escaped Atlas' throat. "H..s... mate", Atlas spoke but I barely understood him.

"Oh, my apologies Alph-" I slipped into my mind again. This heat was eating me alive, but I did my best to snap out of it. Everything was a bit difficult to do, even breathing but then...darkness.

Crows cawed in the distance and the sound of water rushed nearby. A wolf called out in the distance. I ran towards it, allowing my feet to guide me. Eventually the path opened up into a clearing. A field of dried wheat laid flat on the ground pressed tightly onto one another. In the center was a circular space free of wheat and lined with stones. Another howl broke out, pulling my attention up to the sky and I saw a wolf in the face of the moon. Or I thought I did. When I blinked again, it was gone.

A loud bark echoed in my ear, sending my skin crawling in freight. As I turned to see who the wolf was, it was gone. Nothing stood there but as quickly as it had caught my attention, I turned back to the circle to find a wolf in its center. He sat there with glowing blue eyes. His fur was pure silver and flowed softly to the gentle breeze. I walked up to it, effectively entering the circle it stood in.

"......... he can be happy."

I barely made out Atlas' words as my mind grasped reality again. My heart panged at his words, either that or I was having a heart attack. Hopefully it was the former. A soft hand wiped away the hair from my face. "Dan… fe… get wose," Atlas sounded far away and jumbled but then his hand stiffened, "What?" He shouted and this time I heard it clearly.

"Nothing," Ryan and some other male replied.

"This is all-" A woman's voice joined us as I slipped into another spiral of darkness cutting off her words.

The darkness embraced me again and this time I was face to face with the wolf. He howled as he walked around me. He nudged me with his snout as he circled me. Inspecting me. I didn't feel anything threatening but I didn't understand either. *Who are you?* I asked but he just continued circling me.

He howled again and he shifted into his human form. His body was covered with the same markings I had. Blue flames enveloped him the same way mine had. It then dawned on me how terrifying I must have looked to everyone else. He extended his hand to me still doused in the flames, but I accepted it without hesitation, "my name is Acktoo, the first shifter to reincarnate as Shoneah". Howls broke out all around us.

One by one other wolves appeared in the circle and shifted into their human forms. With each human shift they placed a hand on my body, all turning blue from their flames. All of them shared the same markings and white long hair. As the last person placed their hand on me a sudden pressure fell, and all their flames flowed off of them and into me. With each person losing their flame, they disappeared until I was left with the initial person. He shifted back to his wolf and licked my face. With a small yip he vanished.

It's not time yet. Wake Up!

"...all I have.." She handed something to Atlas, at least I thought that was what she did. After a moment of rustling, I felt his lips. He gently lifted my chin, transferring the medicine into my mouth and helped me swallow. Atlas wiped my lips with something and covered me well with what could be a blanket. My mind was foggy.

"WHAT?!" Atlas yelled, almost making me flinch. If my body didn't feel like it weighed a ton, I would have jumped out of my skin. All I heard were the exasperated sighs and a few of them walking away.

As I laid there with my mate stroking my hair, grogginess from the medication took hold.

Atlas

It's been a few hours since arriving. Everyone sat in the dining room entertaining themselves and waiting for Ryan to finish making dinner. I transferred Cassius to a bed in one of the rooms so he could sleep comfortably but every time I felt him move, I ran to check on him. I was worse than my mother at this point, but it couldn't be helped. I was worried. I've already cleaned up after him twice because he kept throwing up in his sleep and I would go into a panic making sure he didn't choke on his sickness. Even with a bucket next to his bed, he missed it every time.

The area on his neck was red and slightly swollen. It was a relief seeing the size go down compared to how it was before. His breathing had been labored for a while because of it. I slipped in the bed next to him in defeat to my tendencies. If I was going to keep checking on him, I might as well stay next to him. I honestly felt better this way anyways and got comfortable on my side facing him which prompted his unconscious body to turn towards me as I drifted away content.

I drifted into a dream and found myself running in the dark. Through the shadows my mom called out to me. She was trying to tell me she was okay, but I couldn't see her. I ran and ran but there was nothing but darkness that surrounded me. With a last-ditch effort to find my mother, I called out to her but as I screamed all I heard was-

"Babe? Where are we?"

The sound of Cassius' voice jerked me awake. Tears threatening my eyes spilled the second I blinked. The relief that Cassius was finally awake and the lingering fear of chasing a shadow in my dream dredged up a well of emotion that had been teetering on the edge of overspill. Tears welled in my eyes as my mate looked at me tired with heavy bloodshot eyes. My arms flew open, and I hugged him with all the strength I had left in me. I didn't realize how long I was holding my breath until I heard him speak. It was the sweetest sound.

"This is Ryan's home. Do you remember anything?" I pulled away and kissed his forehead, taking note that his fever broke, and his sweaty skin tasted salty as a result.

"I remember yelling at my father, and I was in and out, but everything's jumbled inside my head." Cassius sighed.

"Here, take another charcoal pill. Just in case." I handed him some water and waited for him to drink enough water to wash it down.

"I feel like I fought a bull," he closed his eyes, wincing at the pain in his neck. He touched the swollen area as he laid back down and slipped back into another tired sleep. Honestly, I didn't mind. Now that he woke up I felt better knowing that he was out of immediate danger. I could trust that he was going to wake up again. My eyes fell and I let his breathing lull me into a deep sleep. Hopefully, a sweet dream.

CASSIUS

I, Shoneah, strip you of your name and title.
> *Your mother was a whore!*
I strip you of your power.
> *Stop, don't…the power you wield should be mine.*
I strip you of your wolf.
> *Nooo, I need him…I should have finished you OFF!*

My eyes darted open. My breathing erratic from the dream but as I listened to the quiet of the room my heart steadied. We were in Ryan's cabin. I took in the darkness and the sound of Atlas soundly sleeping next to me holding onto my hand. His nearness gave me a level of calm that drove away the echoes of what happened from my mind. With a deep inhale, I breathe in his scent. *So cute. I can't possibly love him more than this.*

I had come to realize my deep love for him quickly. But with everything that happened, I just couldn't find the right time to say it. Although, I want to tell him when the time is right. I rubbed my head to massage the pain behind my eye. The remnants of the headache that plagued me earlier.

My mind was a tornado with all that occurred. It was hard to recall what happened while I was with my father, but I remembered bits and pieces after we arrived at the cabin. Rather, I remembered the dreams I've had since being here.

Are you awake?

Wolfie? Yea I'm up.

Things have changed, you're stronger now Cass.

Can you tell me what happened, Wolfie?

Sure.

This was something I did not expect. How could everything take such a dramatic turn? *This is making my head spin,* I mumbled taking a deep breath slowly trying to process everything Wolfie told me.

As softly as possible so Atlas wouldn't wake, I rolled off the bed and left the room. With how dark and quiet it was in the cabin I could only assume it was already pretty late. The only sounds that filled the still walls were the hoots of the owls and the wind that howled against the windowpane.

I passed the living room trying to find the kitchen and I ended up spotting Kristofer sleeping on the sofa. A smile slapped my face at the sight of his huge body hanging half off one end. If I had my phone, I would have taken a picture to tease him with it later, but I would have to risk going back into the room and waking Atlas. While it would have been funny, I dropped the idea and entered the kitchen. It was a rather updated kitchen to my surprise which for some reason made me hungry.

The last time I ate was the morning we got ready to make our way here. Without having greeted Ryan or his wife, I felt weird if I just started whipping up something to eat so instead, I made my way to the sink and to fill a glass with tap water. The cool liquid filled me with chills as it slid down my throat quenching my parched body. Quickly, I filled a second glass and downed it as if I had just discovered water for the first time. Satisfied, I rinsed the cup and placed it in the rack before walking back to the room.

Atlas jolted up from the bed when I entered from the creak I made on the floor in the entryway. He looked around confused before his eyes landed on mine and I sensed the relief wash over me. However, that relief wasn't my own but his coming through our bond seeing that I was safe.

Walking into the room I closed the door and perched myself on the bed with one knee. Atlas hugged my waist with sleep-hooded eyes, sighing against my skin. It was then that I noticed I was shirtless. *My tattoos are gone!* I thought as I stared at my bare torso.

"Hey, sleepy head," Atlas whispered on my stomach, squeezing me tighter.

"Hello there, my Alpha". Atlas glanced up at me and even in the dark I could see his eyes flare gold.

"You know what those words do to me," Atlas licked my stomach slowly with his eyes locked onto mine.

"And why do you think I say it," I bent over and kissed my mate, pushing him back on the bed. "I'm taking you tonight," a smile formed against my lips, but his moan of approval made my body hum.

Atlas' kneeled on the bed before me with his hands roaming my body. They frantically touched every inch of

194

my exposed skin before they circled to the small of my back. He moaned and dug deep with his nails into my skin as he pulled me towards him. Atlas pressed my hips against his to find his hard length which sent jolts from my groin up my body. Another moan escaped his lips but as sexy as he sounded, I couldn't focus. Flashes began to emerge of what happened.

I closed my eyes to chase away the images but instead I saw myself fighting. The blood from the Beta I injured splattered across my lids and the way I broke his wrist echoed in the trenches of my mind. His screams orchestrated into jolts that synapsed across my brain.

"What's wrong?" Atlas touched my face, pulling me from the visions. His face filled with worry.

"I…" I shook my head as if to put aside his worries, but another flash played out of me morphing into blue flames and the tattoos. The room around me shifted. The wrath of my rage and anger rang loud in my ears. The creatures and the mark burning on my father's face played like a reel. "I'm sorry, I can't," I get up from the bed and leave the room. My chest was tightening up and the longer I stayed the heavier and tighter my chest became.

"Cass wait…" Atlas came after me but as I passed Kristofer who woke up from my harsh steps. He stopped Atlas and let me walk out the front door. Kristofer was always quick to notice the mood I was in and made sure that I had my space.

"Let him go," was the only thing I heard Kristofer say right before the door closed.

I walked up to the van and sat inside. My head filled with images of everything Wolfie told me and matched it with what actually happened. It was suffocating. The things my father said and the spite in his words all crashed down on me tenfold each time it replayed in my mind. *How can he be so cruel? How could my mother ever love a man like that?* Tears streamed down my face as I curled up in the backseat.

"I was never wanted or loved," I whispered to myself. I thought I was strong enough to endure facing him, but I was wrong. Nothing about me was strong. The very second I was faced with his words, I broke into the millions of pieces I had just put together. That wasn't me that faced him. In fact, I didn't know who or what that was because the real me was still that scared little boy that hopelessly waited for his daddy to save him.

My heart broke unbearably and in the hollow of the van my cries became the company I kept. In violent waves my cries crashed within the confines of the van. Like the little boy that cried for his momma, I cried decades worth of tears. With my pain fastening me against the seat, I lulled myself to sleep with a face full of tears.

***

A knock on the car window woke me up from the stiff position I laid in. The weather almost had me like a corpse in the van with how cold it was. Atlas stared through the window with swollen eyes, and I knew he cried just as much as I did. I opened the door for him, and he stepped inside to sit next to me.

"I'm sorry. I didn't mean to pressure you into anything. I thought that maybe I could distract your mind a bit." Atlas' voice trembled.

"No, it's my fault. I instigated it to begin with. I thought I was fine but then I started to remember what happened and it was too much." I sighed and threw my head back on the headrest.

"Not coming to get you was the hardest thing I have ever done. Kristofer told me to give you space but I felt it all. Your pain, your cries, your… thoughts." Atlas whispered the last word as he moved closer towards me.

"Babe, you are not weak, and you are very much loved. Not just by me but by everyone. You are an amazing person and not because of your powers but because of your heart. Without knowing your lineage, you jumped in and saved my sister twice. You fought off hunters and faced your father."

"Then why do I feel this way?" It was hard to look him in the eyes because I knew I would cry again.

"The fact that you don't see it shows how great you are. You're selfless. A righteous person would boast of these qualities like your father, while you lay blind to it all and then kick yourself for not being better and I love you more because of it."

I jerked my head up at his words. *He loves me? Did I hear that right?*

"Cassius please don't ever sell yourself short. As my Luna, I won't allow you to think any less of yourself than what I think of you. So, if I say you are incredible then that is your standard. Got it?!"

I nodded, feeling a bit better but not because of his words. The sincerity and affection I felt through the bond soothed my pain better than any words could.

"Thank you for the medicine by the way. But you could have woken me up though."

Atlas' eyes grew wide, "you were awake?!"
I chuckled, "sort of but I appreciate your efforts." A single tear rolled off my cheek. My emotions were everywhere and controlling the waves in my heart seemed impossible.

"Come on, let's go back inside and eat something. Sacha is making breakfast." Atlas opened the door and gave me his hand. I grasped it knowing his hand would always be there when needed.

Chapter 15

ATLAS

As the morning progressed Cassius showed signs of mental stress. He zones out every few minutes. His facial expression would flood in a range of emotions. And when a fork fell onto the floor, Cassius jumped as though he had seen a ghost. With his stomach full of breakfast, he quietly excused himself from the table. It made my stomach sour seeing how listless he was.

He walked over to the room we slept in and got lost in his own thoughts. It was hard to watch because I felt everything so clearly as if it were my own. He had no control over his emotions, and they leaked into me whenever he slipped into a distressed state. A wave of nausea rolled over me with a great sense of hate filling the pit of my stomach. Cassius hated himself and the man that claimed to be his father.

I helped clean up the kitchen and then made some tea hoping it would help calm Cassius down a bit. The things I was feeling were hitting too close to home and I knew better than anyone where those types of thoughts lead.

Everyone made sure to give him space but was also unsure of how to approach him. They tiptoed around what to say. Kristofer tried to talk to him now and then, but Cassius ended up throwing a pillow or yelling to be left alone. It was hard to watch but I wasn't sure what to do. What if I tried to comfort him again and I made it worse like before?

My purple and gold aura emanated from me wanting me to find my mate so I could comfort him. It must have responded to how I felt. I walked over with the hot chai tea I made and knocked on the door despite it being open. Cassius sniffled a bit but continued to quietly sob on the edge of the bed. He didn't yell or throw pillows but instead sat in silence.

I approached him slowly and tapped his shoulder. "NO!" Cassius screamed and knocked the tea out of my hand. The cup shattered on the floor snapping my mate out of the furious daze he was in. His face fell in horror at the mess he made and the way my skin turned red from the burn.

"Oh my god, babe! I'm so sorry. I didn't mean to. I was… it's…just…" Cassius dropped to his knees to help pick up the broken pieces as he sobbed once more.

I sighed. "It's okay. It's my fault for startling you." I took the pieces from his hand. "Let me do it so you don't cut yourself. Want me to run you a bath instead?"

Cassius stared at me doe eyed and nodded, "will you take one with me?" His voice cracked slightly with tears streaming steadily down his cheeks.

"Sure," I replied, smiling at him trying my best to not show the worry in my heart.

***

After an emotional tug of war, it was finally time for bed. After crying for hours on and off he was exhausted and numb. Patience was all any of us could really give him. I tucked him into bed and waited for him to fall asleep before I closed my eyes.

Cassius

I woke up just before sunrise. The cabin was quiet with everyone still asleep. The birds outside had yet to begin chirping and the wind was barely a knock against the sides of the cabin. Atlas lightly snoring rolled over to one side with all the covers wrapped around him. It was cute but we were going to need separate blankets if I didn't want him to steal it in the middle of the night. A smile tugged my lips. I couldn't thank him enough for dealing with me these last twenty-four hours. My mind had become a battlefield that I couldn't navigate through.

Yet, he patiently took care of me every step of the way. I could only move forward however hard or slow that may be. But I hoped that whatever took over my body would be there for me if I needed that strength.

I took a deep breath and rubbed the sleep from my eyes. It might take time to find my strength, but I couldn't have everyone wait for me when we still had Martha to find. I got up from the bed and looked out the window. The moon was really low in the sky, but I still spotted it between the trees.

"Moon goddess, if you're listening, please hear my prayer. Help me clear my mind and fight my demons. Allow me the strength to help my mate find his mother safe and sound. Also thank you for matching me with the most wonderful man, I only ask that you help me be everything he wants until we are too old to remember our names. Moon goddess, am I deserving of this gift? Am I really worthy? If so, please guide me-"

"You are more than worthy."

I yelp at the sound of Atlas' voice cutting me off. I didn't even notice he followed me outside.

"Sorry, did I wake you?" I walked over to the bed.

"I woke up the second you left the bed. Babe you truly are a beautiful heart, you know that? You are definitely everything I want and need. How could you not think you are worthy?" Atlas smiled.

"Really? You really think so?"

"Wait, what was your name again?" Atlas never missed a beat to tease me. I slapped him on his arm and chuckled. "I deserved that," Atlas giggled and pulled me into his arms. "Stay in bed a bit more."

"Hey, um…would you like to try again?"

"Try what again?" Atlas asked while fixing the blanket he held over us after succeeding in getting me back in bed.

"…sex," I replied.

We laid there in silence for a bit. Now that I was a bit calmer, I wanted comfort. I wanted to feel close to him. I needed the connection and so did my wolf.

"Are you sure?" Atlas whispered.

"Yes, Alpha. I'm sure."

Atlas growled, making me giggle. He must truly love it when I called him that.

"Shh baby you can't be loud here," I licked his lips.

"I don't care," Atlas breathed into my lips. This was what I needed. The bond was already working its magic, allowing my mind to slip away from the emotional coaster it was on. It was just me and my mate entangled in our need for one another. Atlas pulled off his shirt and returned to kissing me while I removed his pants and underwear. My fingers fumbled with his button and zipper too anxious to get them undone. I broke away from his lush lips and grabbed his thighs to pull him up into a straddle position.

He smiled a wicked grin as he whined his hips against my length. If there was doubt that I wanted this then my erection would have told him otherwise. I wiggled my body down a bit, so he sat on my chest. With my lips ready to feel his flesh, I grabbed his cock between my lonely fingers and lifted my head so I could run my tongue up his length, flicking the tip. He shuttered with a gasp that was loud enough for others to hear.

My fingers cupped and massaged his balls while sucking the tip of his crown before taking him in completely. Because I was laying down, I couldn't take him in like I wanted but Atlas must have thought the same. He lifted his hips and tilted them so I could go down deep before coming back for air. I spit onto his cock and released his balls to grab the base of his shaft. Atlas groaned with a fierce look in his eyes. His hips slowly rocked into my fist, finding his own pleasure in my grip. Going down on him again I synced my mouth going up and down with the rotation of my hand on his shaft.

Moans slipped through his fingers in a failed attempt to cover his mouth. It was sexy to watch him lose his composure. I watched Atlas as I worked on unraveling him further. Our eyes locked and seeing his pleasure build made me drip. "Babe, wait, I'ma cum," Atlas closed his eyes and threw his head back.

I go faster.

"Babe," a strained whisper pleaded.

I didn't stop.

"I'm coming," he breathed between his teeth. I deep throated him until he unloaded into me. Atlas squeezed my face with his thighs enjoying his release. I pushed him off and got on top of him and made him watch as I then poured his cum onto my hand.

"What are you doing?" Atlas asked between breaths.

"Using your cum as lube." I smeared his love on his hole and slid in a finger. Atlas' breath caught in his throat with the intrusion of my finger. He bit his lip and grabbed his legs behind his knees giving me the most magnificent view with full access. He moaned, finally relaxing against my finger so I could enter another. This was perfect. I was so out of it that I needed to hold the reins again and this gave me what I needed to feel that control.

"I'm putting in another," I whispered. Atlas nodded and eventually rocked his hips against me. Echoes of his wet hole ricocheted in the room. The naughtiest sound to ever touch my ears.

"Babe, I want more," Atlas whispered in a raspy voice filled with horny desire.

I slid a third finger. His hole was soft and tight asking to be fucked. Atlas was a moaning mess beneath me, and my dick was twitching with each whisper that left his lips. I pulled down my pants and placed my dick at his entrance. My mate rocked his hips against it, searching for it. His face told me he wanted it, and it made me leak with lust. My Alpha was submitting to me and the way this moment felt had me in a high I would never forget.

"Why is my Alpha so impatient?" I teased him, pushing in the swollen tip slightly.

"I want you," he whimpered. This was dangerous. If I wasn't careful, I would end up losing it and ramming it inside him. My mind could easily become addicted to this type of dominance in bed.

"Want me? I can't give it to you if my Alpha doesn't ask properly." I pushed my hips slowly against him. He growled at me. He was desperate and I loved it.

"Shove your cock in my ass, now!" Atlas demanded barely able to contain himself, letting his Alpha tone slip.

Of course, I complied, and I slid my length into him slowly. As much as he and I wanted it, I also knew I was bigger than average and didn't want him to hurt. Atlas gasped at how much I filled him. A tear rolled down one eye. I stopped once I was all the way in, "you okay babe?" I wiped the tear from his eye and kissed the other.

"It hurts a little but I'm okay now. Keep going." He cupped my face and kissed me.

"Good but use that tone on me again and I won't be so gentle next time." I pulled out halfway and went back in with a bit more force. With each thrust I picked up my pace using every ounce of will power to not orgasm from the warmth around my cock. My mate pulled me down and assaulted my mouth with his tongue. He turned into a starving puppy, and I couldn't help but want to feed him everything.

I pounded away as if his life depended on it and my cock was the cure. The sensation that coursed up my length was exhilarating and wild. With each thrust I pushed my memories aside where they can't control me or take over. Atlas bit his lip clutching the sheets beside his head. I've never been on top because I never thought I'd enjoy it this much or maybe I didn't have the right partner. But this made me wish I'd done it a lot sooner. The way his body ate my cock was almost therapeutic. Thrust after thrust, moans escaped our entwining lips. It wasn't enough, I wanted more of him. I broke away gasping for air.

My head landed on cloud nine. The warmth of his body that clung around me sent me further into an abyss of ecstasy that I never knew I wanted. His moans and whimpers tickled my ears as his hole tightened, sucking me back in with each attempt that I made to pull out. My wolf howled. He was enjoying it as much as I. Euphoria draped over me. I pulled out, turned him around, and bent Atlas over. His round ass perked up for me searching for what filled him mere seconds ago. Full palm, I slapped his ass and rammed my dick back in his tight hole. Atlas screamed before I could shove his face into the mattress. His muffled cries spurred me on as I grabbed his arms and leaned back to hammer away. My hips slammed against his ass, clapping our sex.

The sound carried around the cabin, but I didn't care about the ramifications later on. I'll let the whole world know this beautiful man was mine if I had to. Atlas screamed his pleasure, announcing his rise to climax. Our bodies raved in the idea that he was the one who pulled me out of my mind, gave me the pleasure I desired, and fulfilled my every wish. I moaned over and over as he tightened harder around me. My hips moved in circles trying to find his spot. "Ah! right there!" Atlas almost yelled.

I let go of his arms to pick up my speed. Gripping his waist, I brought him up to me with impossible speed. I couldn't get over this feeling. The sensation. My body was climbing in an orgasm I knew would take me out. Waves of pleasure bounced through me and back again. I couldn't think. The depths of my mind were firing in every direction, overloaded with pleasure.

Atlas sucked me in harder into his body and each time it confirmed how much he was mine. Lifting Atlas so his back was against my chest, I slammed into him catching my breath as I ground my hips into the innermost part of him. I trailed my hand up his chest and grabbed his neck, turning his face toward me.

I kissed him, biting his lip and sucking it until it swelled nice and plump. With my free hand I reached down and jerked him off still using my cock to massage his prostate. "Fuck," he cursed into my lips with a gravelly strained voice. I pulled out slowly and slammed into his wet hole in long slow strokes, choking him against my body.

Atlas squirmed against me, melting into a puddle while I jerked him off in rhythm to his quickening breaths, "FUCK CASS," Atlas screamed his orgasm. Ribbons of his release flew onto the bed as I pumped my own into him. We stayed there, connected and in the moment. Our chest rose and fell in unison, our hearts banged violently against our chest, with sweat glistening on our bodies. I was officially addicted to the drug that was Atlas

We plopped down onto the bed after our bodies came down enough to move and kissed, still unable to let go of one another. A giggle erupted between us when we finally parted our lips.

"We are going to get an ear full later," Atlas said with a smile, kissing my nose.

"Oh well," I replied, as we laughed in each other's arms. Content.

Chapter 16

KRISTOFER

After sleeping on the couch for so long, my back was as stiff as ever. Half my body hung off it and I couldn't find a position to keep myself from falling off. So, there I slept in a planking position while trying to sike myself into thinking I was comfortable. After a few nights sleeping that way, I was definitely going to ask for a blanket or pillows to sleep on the floor at least. For the life of me I couldn't figure out why I didn't think of that after the first night. If that wasn't bad enough already, I woke up to a live porn session at the crack of dawn and haven't gone back to sleep since. *Oh, speak of the fucking devils.*

"So, you guys finally got the nerve to show your faces?" I crossed my legs as I finished my coffee on the rocker in the living room. Even while sipping the strong Colombian coffee, my sleepiness remained unrelenting.

"Sorry about that," Cassius blushed and looked down to the floor avoiding making eye contact with me.

"Sorry? That's all you have to say? How about you horndogs take a seat right now!" I placed my mug down on the coffee table and waited for the love birds to sit down before I unleashed my sleep deprived wrath.

"Do you guys have any idea how loud you both were? And to top it all off, this isn't your home. Not only that, you're being rude to my poor ears. For fuck's sake, I didn't want to hear that shit. All your oohs and ahhs. What the hell man, these walls are as thin as paper. I don't know who clapped whose cheeks, although I have an idea, but I'm positive that crap echoed even outside. I'm sure you caused an avalanche somewhere." I took a deep breath to calm down.

"Jeez, we weren't that loud," Atlas mumbled under his breath.

"You're kidding, right? I clearly heard you telling your Luna 'Fuck me daddy' one too many times." Mavis walked into the room laughing at the high pitch voice I used to mock Atlas.

"I…I DID NOT!" Atlas jumped up from his seat, red as a tomato and quickly regretted it when his sore back ached.

"Okay, okay. Let's stop talking about it. Thinking about Cassius' gyrating hips is making me queasy," I mocked and grabbed my mug for another dose of caffeine.

CASSIUS

Waking up to a scolding by Kristofer was something I expected. We weren't exactly quiet, and he slept only a few feet from the door on a sofa made for toddlers. There was no way in hell that sofa was supposed to be for adults. With embarrassed faces, we followed him to the kitchen where the rest of the house was laughing at us, mocking the things they heard us say. Seriously, they were like high schoolers who just discovered sex.

Ignoring their ridiculous attempt at complete embarrassment, which they achieved, I made something to eat. We were famished from our extracurricular bedroom activities and a good meal was in order. Thankfully, I found the dinner they saved last night. I popped it in the microwave and split it with Atlas, almost spilling it on the counter.

"My goddess, this is good. Either that or it's my hunger talking." I shoved more food in my mouth, almost choking.

Atlas laughed and grabbed a napkin, "can you not eat like a pig." He wiped my mouth, and I blew him a kiss as a thank you. His cheeks reddened and a low growl built in his throat.

"You guys make me sick, you know that". Mavis took a seat at the table with us and rolled his eyes in jest.

"Shut up. You and Dona are the same or did you forget how many times I've caught the both of you." Atlas snapped.

"You shut up, we are talking about you, not me. Besides, how are we the same?" Mavis threw a scrunched-up napkin at Atlas chuckling.

"In love..." My mate said without hesitation and blushed at an alarming rate. I blushed as well, shoving more food in my mouth too scared to say something stupid. *Damn he said it again. He just keeps throwing that word around.*

After a few awkward silent moments Mavis spoke first, "so, Luna, what happened the other day with the change and all?"

"Well from what Wolfie told me, my soul is that of the great shaman wolf. Even though I am still me, I also carry all of the shamans' memories and abilities from every time he reincarnated but it's also not that simple. It's almost like we are two halves of the same soul and all this time his half had been dormant. However, now that we face danger, the other half of my soul has awakened. It's like I feel complete for the first time in my life." I tried to put it into words but, I myself had a hard time understanding. Mavis and Atlas just looked at me bewildered.

"Now that I am fully awakened, I can wield magic and all the other gifts the Shaman has to offer. Although I have no idea how, it explains a lot of the weird things that've been happening to me lately. So far, whenever the soul of a Shaman becomes whole, it usually means that something is coming. Be it war, conflict, or even the need for unification among wolves or all magical creatures." I finished off my plate and stared at the table. *What if my father isn't the only thing we should be worrying about?*

"You got all of that from your wolf?" Atlas' eyes seemed ready to pop out his head.

"I know it's a lot. My body shut down as a defense mechanism while it adjusted to having my soul at full capacity. The time I spent yesterday was partly me slowly finding all this out. I kept having flashes of memory of my father but also of my past lives as a Shaman." They nod their heads still looking confused.

"Wait, what weird things?" Mavis furrowed his brows only just registering what I said earlier.

"I'd randomly catch things levitating around me or something suddenly would set on fire. At one point, I froze a window, but I couldn't figure out how or why or if I was simply going mad?" Mavis and Atlas gasped.

"So, if that's the case shouldn't the threat be over? Despite him disappearing in the end, you technically stripped your father. He should be harmless now, right?" Mavis leaned back, crossing his arms. His tattooed arms had caught my attention from the beginning because I always wanted one but now, I guess I could compete with my own. Although mine came and went which I guess could also be a perk.

"I don't…. know." I stood up from the table annoyed that it seemed to be a never-ending problem. This was supposed to be a simple mission to find Martha and bring her home but instead, I faced my father, unleashed my soul, and was faced with something that could potentially be beyond my control. The weight of my father and newfound powers settled on me again.

I left the table and locked myself in the bathroom. Finishing the conversation no longer seems to hold my interest. I leaned on the sink and stared at the man in the mirror. My face was haggard with dark circles and fine lines. The whole experience aged me or at least it felt that way. But fortunately, the area the needle hit finally healed. Atlas was smart enough to give me charcoal pills which helped to draw out the toxins quicker.

I sighed and stripped my clothes so I could melt under the hot water of a shower. If I was going to have powers, then I needed to practice and gain control. I knew I could produce fire, ice, and possibly have telekinetic powers but I wondered if I also had the powers I saw in my visions? The shower steamed the bathroom, and it stirred me with anticipation to wash the stress building in my shoulders away. While stepping in the shower, I flicked off the light to bathe in the dark. The hot water pelted against my skin massaging my worries. It was heavenly.

A knock softly played on the door before it opened slowly, "Cass?"

"Yea?" I whispered just above the drone of the water. Atlas closed the door and stood in front of the curtain. I could tell he was there but with the light off, I couldn't see his shadow.

"I'm sorry I upset you."

"You didn't upset me, Atlas. I'm just worried and scared about everything. We came here for Martha and now I'm some kind of great shaman monster freak?!" I sighed into the water hitting my face.

"I know it must be scary, but you are not a monster or a freak. You have all of us here to help you figure it out. You don't have to do this alone. We are your family and that will never change." Atlas opened the curtain, but I still saw nothing although my eyes were slowly adjusting.

"I know. I just can't shake the feeling that my father isn't done. I don't think a man with that much hubris would back down so easily. Even with my powers, he still scares me. I didn't feel powerful with him before me. I feel like a child with nuclear codes and no idea how to read the manual." A tear rolled down my face in the cover of the dark.

214

The Silver Lining

"We can train so that you can have better control. We will figure it out. You don't need to face him alone if he comes back or anyone else that comes along later." Atlas caressed my face, pouring into me his sweet calming scent. Small colorful globes of light danced around us. Purple, gold, silver, and blue swirled, entwining along our bodies. Seeing it in the dark made them seem like glow sticks in a rave. It was then that I saw glimpses of Atlas' face.

"Thank you." I took a deep breath enjoying the comfort of our auras. Atlas closed the curtain so I could finish my shower while he sat on the toilet making light conversation while waiting for me.

Everything would surely be alright as long as I had everyone with me.

****

After lunch, Atlas and I sat in the kitchen talking about ways to help me develop my powers. I turned to the sound of Sacha walking into the kitchen on the phone. The sound of her feet was distinct since it gave away how she waddled when she walked. I chuckled at the sight of her as she waddled into view just as I predicted. Her pregnant belly was no joke.

She sat at the table with a grunt and hung up the phone. "Ugh, gotta be kidding me!" She slammed a hand on the table making us flinch.

"What's wrong?" Ryan ran into the kitchen out of breath with a fear-stricken face.

"Nothing, you dork. I just sat down and now I gotta pee." Sacha rocked herself up and out of the chair waddling as quickly as she could out of the kitchen. We all did our best to not laugh but I was sure she could hear us trying to stifle our snickering.

"What's so funny?" Kristofer walked into the kitchen with one of the other men and grabbed an apple from the counter.

Ryan waved away the matter, "so I reached out to an acquaintance of mine in town. I had put out some feelers on Martha when you guys first arrived. Still nothing though. Hopefully, we'll have something soon." Atlas slumped his shoulders in response. "Don't worry Alpha, we will find your mother."

We all agreed and decided to help Ryan around the house to prepare for the baby. It was the least we could do for putting us up for the time being. A couple days went by like this and no word was sent out from the feelers. Because of it, Atlas had been biting his nails in worry.

"Babe?" I tapped Atlas on the shoulder. He jumped half out of his skin. "Are you okay?"

"Sorry, I just...what if.... ugh… I'm scared. What if we can't find mom or they confuse her for someone else or what if we find her but she's..." Atlas choked on a cry threatening his throat. I didn't blame him for thinking that way. I would have too had it been Cecile.

"Stop thinking that way. No need to worry about something that hasn't happened. She is safe and we will find her. Stay positive." I kissed his head and hugged him until he was satisfied.

***

Sitting in the living room practicing how to use my new abilities, I flinched when Atlas tapped my shoulders. The fire ball I was trying to control in my hands then flew out and hit the curtain. "Oh shit! Quick get something." I shouted to Atlas as he ran to the kitchen and grabbed the fire extinguisher. I almost exhaled in relief when Ryan walked in the front door to the spectacle.

He was returning from town with a few essentials. A cold breeze came in with him, but he quickly closed the door. The weather was definitely cold. It was almost Thanksgiving, and the weather was just about right for snow.

"What the hell happened?" Ryan stared at the black curtain and then at me and Atlas holding the extinguisher frozen in the act.

"He did it!" Atlas pointed at me.

"Traitor!" I gasped.

"You're buying me another one." Ryan walked away to the kitchen with the things he bought.

"Way to sell me out." I shoved Atlas playfully.

"I don't know what you're talking about." Atlas crossed his arms with a smug look.

"Uh huh. Let's go outside before I burn the cabin down." I walked out the door without giving my mate a chance to respond. "I think I figured out how to make the fire come out. So far, it's all about envisioning what it is that I want." I opened my hand and created the ball of fire. "Now I want to see if I can shoot the fire like I did earlier but intentionally this time."

"Oh, okay. What if you think of the fire as a projectile, like a bullet or an arrow?" Atlas motioned, releasing an imaginary arrow with his hands.

"Hmmm okay, let's try." I put out the fire and formed a finger gun. I focused and a small flame formed on the tip of my finger.

"Oh, that's good. Now try to shoot it." Atlas jumped excitedly next to me.

I focused on the fire pit that was off to the side of the house. I tried my best to picture the flame flying out of my hand, but it didn't work. Instead, the flame died off.

"Well, that was a failure. Let's try an arrow." I took a deep breath and motioned as if I were drawing an arrow on a bow. With my eyes closed I began to feel the tension build in my hands as if I were truly holding an arrow in place.

"Whoa, how are you doing that?" Atlas asked in awe.

"Shh, I need to focus." I muttered as I tried to picture the arrow between my fingers, the tension of the bow, and the strength at which I pulled. It was difficult to do but as I opened my eyes, I saw a flaming arrow.

Immediately, I let go, shocked from succeeding. The arrow flew far between the trees and hit the mailbox at the entrance of the property. The arrow must have traveled over fifty feet.

"Holy crap, you did it." Atlas hugged me while laughing at the way the mailbox split in half.

"What was that sound?" Ryan stuck his head out the window with the burnt curtain.

"Nothing!" I quickly responded but it was too late.

"What the hell did you do to my mailbox?" Ryan threw his hands in the air annoyed. I turned to Atlas and laughed. This was going to be interesting but at this rate, I didn't think the cabin would survive.

Chapter 17

The next couple of days I spent it trying to speed up how quickly I could draw the arrow and how effectively I could aim. The training was draining but definitely paying off. Unfortunately, a few trees, a part of the fence, the shed out back, and the new mailbox all have suffered the wrath of my misdirected arrows. Ryan gave up after the shed burnt down. Now he just sighed and added it to the list of repairs he would make the pack do after this was over.

"So, I finally got some news," Ryan put down the bags of salt he carried in from what was supposed to be a shed outback. "Martha was spotted a town over. I had them tell her to meet us tomorrow morning at the town square."

"Really? Finally, something good. That means she's okay. I'll go tell Atlas." It was exactly what Atlas needed at the moment. Even with all his help and support in helping me learn my abilities, I knew he was hiding his pain. He was worried sick that he would leave here without his mother and return to Iris empty handed. It was a worry he didn't even need to express for me to know it was exactly what was on his mind.

I ran to the den where Atlas and some of the guys were having a drink. "Hey, we found Martha." The words spilled out of my mouth the moment I laid eyes on Atlas. Everyone in the room fell silent. "We're going to meet her tomorrow morning."

"Why not now? They sure it's her?" Atlas finished his beer as if ready to go.

"Yes, it's her. She was spotted in the next town over. Ryan sent one of his men to deliver the message of where to meet. The weather is too crazy to go now." I walked over to my mate and kissed him on the forehead. "Don't worry, at least we know she is safe now." I smiled at my Alpha in hopes that it would instill some calm into him. Kristofer walked in behind me shortly after having heard.

"Then we must prepare for tomorrow in case there's an ambush." Kristofer pat Atlas on the shoulder. "We came this far, and you have this mutt as your mate. We got this. Go get some rest. Tomorrow you finally see your mother." Kristofer left the room as Atlas put down his drink.

"Actually, I want you to try something, let's go try a few arrows and hit the sack after. Come on mutt." Atlas chuckled at my hurt expression from the use of the word mutt. I hated that word. It's what we used to call a rowdy child or teen. I was most definitely none of those things although to Kristofer it didn't matter how old I got. I followed Atlas sensing the worry behind his steps

"Say that again and I'll have you saying something else later," I snapped in an attempt to distract his mind. The room snickered in chaos causing Atlas to turn bright red. With nothing to say in return, he stomped out of the room. Everyone broke out in laughter, unable to ignore the small tantrum of embarrassment.

"Only our Luna can put him in place." Mavis raised his glass to me. "To Luna Cassius."

"To Luna Cassius," they all cheered in unison. I did a small curtsey prompting more laughter and left the room to find my pouting mate.

"Okay you big baby, teach me what it is you want me to try." I pat Atlas on the back and followed him outside.

"Well, I was thinking, if you can control conjuring up flame arrows, why not trick flame arrows?!" Atlas smiled; a bit too cheesy if you asked me.

"Okay buddy, you might have had one too many." I chuckled.

"Oh, shut up, you know very well I'm not even tipsy. I'm serious here. If you can mask your arrows or do something that can trick the opponent, it might increase your success rate. I saw it in a movie once."

"Really, babe? Okay, let's say I humor you; how do you propose I do that?" I crossed my arms with a smirk.

"Well, try and see if you can make the arrow invisible!" Atlas starred in waiting and all I could do was take it seriously.

"So, you want me to conjure up an arrow just to make it invisible?"

"Well, when you say it like that, it sounds stupid but yes. It could be like a surprise attack. Something he literally won't see coming." Atlas stepped aside so I could give it a go.

I extended my arms like I had so many times before and drew a blue flaming arrow. With a deep breath, I tried to make it conceal itself but instead the arrows went out. I could tell by the loss of tension in my fingers. So, I tried again but all I accomplished was putting out the arrow again and again.

"This isn't going to work." I drop my hands tired.

"Okay try just one more time but instead of trying to make it disappear, think of it as camouflage. As if you're masking it," Atlas was having way too much fun with my powers.

"Fine but if it doesn't work, we are done. I'm tired." I lifted my arms again and drew an arrow.

I had done it so much that it was almost instant. I concentrated on the flame arrow and imagined it refracting light, causing it to seem like it disappeared when it hasn't. Although the thought was clear in my mind, nothing was happening. I pulled the bow tighter and let go, focusing all my energy on the arrow in mid-air when suddenly it vanished. Well, it was more accurate to say the flames were clear now.

"Holy shi-" I barely finished my sentence as the arrow exploded, revealing how far off the mark I was. My lack of focus made the arrow turn towards the water well instead of staying in a straight line.

"Was that an explosion?" Both Ryan and Kristofer ran outside. Ryan was shirtless with anime pajama pants and Kristofer was in his boxers and a tee shirt. They must have jumped out of bed from the sound.

"Sorry, everything is okay though," Atlas called out. Ryan gave me the finger when he spotted the water well's damage.

"Okay let's practice a few more times." I turned to Atlas excited at my new ability but terrified that Ryan would murder me in my sleep.

After a couple of hours and many failed attempts, I called it quits and headed inside. I couldn't seem to get the arrow to stay in a straight line with every shot. Some went up, others down into the ground, or off to the side hitting a couple of bushes. Very few stayed straight and because of this, I lost my temper a few times and Atlas left me on my own. He didn't like to argue.

Entering our room, I found Atlas packing his bag upset when he clearly had enough time to cool down. Maybe he was more annoyed than mad. "Babe?" I called out and Atlas shot daggers at me.

"What?"

"Is my Alpha mad at me?" I closed our door and got on my knees.

"Don't try to butter me up." Atlas stopped what he was doing watching me kneel on the floor.

"I'm sorry about the mean things I said outside. Isn't my Alpha going to reward me for learning a new trick?" I know this was shameless of me, but he loved it. Deep down he loved me being submissive. Atlas walked over to me and stood with his arms crossed.

"What kind of reward were you expecting?" Atlas tapped his foot. I leaned forward to rub my face on his crotch and looked up with my best puppy eyes. "I see." He responded but I could tell even with his indulging me in my play, he was still upset.

I undid his pants and pulled out his semi erection. It was nice to know that even when upset, he could still get turned on by me. Opening my mouth to take him in, I stuck out my tongue and waited.

"What's wrong, want me to feed you as well?" Atlas asked in exasperation. I nodded my head and whimpered while I scooted closer to my mate's legs. My mate's erection stiffened at full mast. "Guess I have no choice since you're suddenly obedient." He grabbed his member and placed it on my tongue. Rubbing it in circles to get it wet, he painted my lips with it before shoving it in my mouth. I moaned against his shaft.

"Is my puppy enjoying his meal?" Atlas grabbed my hair guiding my movements. With how he held my hair, I knew he wasn't as upset anymore. I moaned but it wasn't enough. He pulled back my head making a string of saliva and pre cum stretch from his tip to my lips.

"Speak! I asked you a question." Atlas commanded.

I want nothing more than to fully submit to the man before me. The way he took control. The way he asserted his dominance. It was something that made me twitch in anticipation. I hated that I lost my temper earlier. I knew all he did was try to help. And it wasn't his fault that I kept failing.

Seeing him now, taking over, displaying pure dominance, my pants were ready to explode. I would argue with him more if this was what I got in return.

"Yes Alpha, I am enjoying my meal. Please feed me more." I whispered against his hard cock. My body felt hot, and I could smell the arousal off him. Atlas shoved his dripping rod into my mouth once more. Slamming the back of my throat. I was in heaven. Over and over, he thrusted into my mouth. He quickly whipped it out and slapped me with his hard dick before shoving it back in.

"Fuck," Atlas groaned. He continued to pick up speed. I was so hard; I could release without even touching myself.

"I'm gonna cum little pup," Atlas pulled out of my mouth and pumped everything on my face. His hot cum covered my eyes, nose, and mouth. I was sure some landed on my hair as well. "My, my. Looks like you made a mess with your food." He teased as his erection still lingered prompting him to rub it on my lips.

"Hey, do you thi-", The door opened, and Mavis walked in on me on my knees covered in my mate's thick release and his dick on my lips. "Sorry," Mavis closed the door quickly.

"Will I be punished again later?" I licked his erection.

"You naughty, naughty pup. Clean yourself up. I guess I'll have to finish punishing you another time." Atlas handed me a tissue to wipe my face, never breaking eye contact. Standing up, I pulled my mate close and pressed my hard bulge against his manhood wanting his attention.

"Don't make me wait too long Alpha." I grabbed his ass and squeezed it before I walked out of the room and to the bathroom. *I want him inside me so bad.*

My pants tightened further at the thought.

I passed Mavis who leaned against the wall in the hallway on my way to the bathroom with a cheesy grin from ear to ear. The look on his face as he spotted what was in my hair shouted everything he was thinking, and I couldn't help but laugh to myself. *Best walk of shame ever.*

Chapter 18

CASSIUS

It was the next day and finally time to meet Martha. Everyone was on pins and needles but no one more than Atlas. He was the first one to get in the car and yelled at everyone to hurry up only to sit impatiently for forty-five minutes as we drove further north. Atlas fingered his phone aggressively, typing away with Iris. A chime here and there was all you heard in the quiet of the car. The silence was heavy but none of us wanted to admit how scared we all were.

We were meeting up with her after waiting for so long. Atlas had suffered at home and had nightmares which must have stemmed from his own inner demons and need for his mother's guidance. I fiddled with the steering wheel trying to find a way to comfort him, but he seemed so on edge, I was afraid that if I touched him, he would scream. Unlike the encounter with my father, this would hopefully be pleasant and very much welcomed. I was also curious to see who was the woman that not only stole Cecile's heart but also escaped my father unknowingly.

At this point she seemed like a crafty ninja, or this woman must have had a lucky streak to her. I think I'd also remember her, but I wasn't sure. If Martha was the same woman that used to hang out with Cecile, then it's possible I knew her around when I first joined the pack.

Thirty minutes into the drive the tree line thickened. A bit of frost was evident on the needles of the trees we passed by. The sun was just above the horizon casting gold, pink, and purple hues into the morning sky. This morning's weather was the perfect recipe for snow and today would surely be the day it came down heavy. Although Ryan was already well prepared and had the salt laid out around the house.

As werewolves, our bodies were naturally warmer than humans, but we could still get very cold in our human forms. Enough that we would need to bundle up and today was definitely one of those days. The road continued winding up the mountain but just as we reached the peak of the road it leveled out and a town came into view. It was a small and quaint town nestled at the base of the mountains surrounding it.

Atlas

"Well, I guess we're here," Cassius drove into the quiet town and followed the GPS to the town square. My nerves were shot. It all still felt like it was unreal, and I was still at home dreaming. *What if it's not her?* I thought but the question was chased away by our arrival. We parked and waited by a gazebo anxious and now noticeably cold. Only a few of us came so we didn't stand out too much. Even in human form all our bodies were tall and well built. We could easily be confused for bad intentions with us huddled together in the middle of a town at the break of dawn.

Mavis, Cassius, Kristofer, and I chatted away to kill time and stay warm, but my mind wasn't really present. My eyes kept scanning the area for my mother or anyone that would resemble her. Not many people were out and about, which was a blessing. It'll make spotting her easier and make us less likely to be approached. It was so early in the morning that nothing was open and getting a hot coffee was out of the question. The streetlamps flicked off as the sun rose fully behind the clouds that accumulated quickly in the sky.

"Look up guys." Mavis stuck out his tongue like a child in wonder. Flurries made their way down in the crisp air to announce winter's official arrival. We all looked up in unison at the cloudy sky and took in the little flakes melting against our frozen noses and red cheeks. It was a nice momentary distraction from the anxiety in our hearts. The quiet and calm that tended to accompany the snow was always one of my favorite things about this weather.

"Atty?" A gentle voice called out in our direction. We all turned to the familiar sound. Well familiar to most of us at least.

"Mom?" I questioned the woman walking towards us in a winter coat with a faux fur hood hiding her face. My heart raced and I wanted to run to her, but my feet were frozen to the ground. Is it her? I couldn't smell her, and she was too far away. If only the wind blew my way to carry her scent to me. She laughed and removed the hood. I suddenly grew warm from the sight. She looked beautiful.

I gasped at how rosy her cheeks were and how healthy she seemed. Since father's death, she hadn't looked so lively. Like a child leaving his first day of school, I ran to her like the child I was inside and lifted her in the air. In one fell swoop I spun her around in a hug.

I could breathe now. My mother was safe and sound. Mom could come home, and I could share with her my happiness. Our family could be whole again, free from the dark shadows that haunted us every day of our lives.

"Atty put me down, I'm too old for that. This isn't a hallmark reunion, you know," Mom chuckled. She never failed to make a joke in any situation. I put her down, but I didn't let go and instead cried on her shoulder. The stress of everything was finally gone and I no longer needed to be strong.

Forget being an Alpha for a moment, I just wanted to be her son. I couldn't bear the thought that I would have lost both my parents. So, feeling her in my arm broke the dam inside me, and without control, the tears fell filled with sorrow and relief. She hugged me back, crooning as though I was still her little pup. And I was sure in her eyes I still was.

After a moment allowed to us by the others, I pulled away from my mother and wiped the tears from my frozen cheeks.

"Hi Martha, it's very good to see you're doing well." Mavis hugged his former Luna.

"And I you, my child," Martha pulled back and spotted Kristofer. "My goodness, is that you Kristofer?" She squeezed him next into a hug and he groaned. Either he wasn't much of a hugger, or she made him uncomfortable.

"Yes, hello Martha."

Finally, she turned to Cassius and gave him a once over. Unlike the others, he rarely ever got to see her as he grew up. "You must be Cassius." A smile crossed his lips and he nodded with excitement. "You look just as Cecile described. Last time I saw you, you were barely a teenager. I wouldn't have recognized you now." She pulled him into a hug as well which I didn't think he expected. He blushed at the foreign affection but welcomed it all the same.

I interlocked my arm with my mother as she let go of my partner, "let's go mom, we have a lot of catching up to do."

Mom agreed and as we walked to the car, I thought back to everything that led up to this moment and I suddenly remembered the little fact about my mother being a swinger. *How did I not realize this growing up?* It was hard to see my mom as a wolf with a wild sexual private life and for it to turn into a crime of passion that extended over to me and my sister. My parents and Kristofer's would probably still have been together if Rick hadn't intervened.

I sighed into the cold visible in the air as smoke formed from my lips. The snow stuck to the ground and already made a nice blanket in the quiet morning throughout the town. Little by little as we walked to the car, the lights of the town stores turned on and opened for business. More people were bustling about and the small-town feel, boomed to life. Green and white striped canopies opened up on the store fronts while trucks pulled in with morning deliveries. The smell of baked goods wafted in the air reminding me of how hungry I was.

In my excitement to see my mom, I didn't grab anything to eat before leaving. There was no way I would be able to stomach anything with my nerves bundled up. Like the gentlemen that I was, I opened the door for my mother and helped her into the van. Cassius took the wheel while Mavis sat up front in the passenger seat. I stepped aside and let Kristofer into the back row before I sat next to my mother.

On the way back to Ryan's cabin we were all distracted swapping stories and laughing at each other's antics. We shared with mom the things she missed and the trouble with hunters recently increasing in our area. The things about Cassius' father and Rick were more of a conversation better left for when we got to the cabin. For now, light-hearted chatter was a nice way to enjoy the ride without any awkward silences trying to avoid the obvious questions we all wanted to ask.

Now that I thought about it, why didn't she keep us updated? She clearly was in contact with Cecile up until recently. *Was she satisfied with whatever Cecile reported to her?*

"Mom, how come you never called to check in with us?" I turned to her unsure how to feel. The van fell silent as I officially made it awkward.

"I have my reasons. I can explain better another time." Mom grabbed my hand and rubbed my fingers with her thumb.

We pulled into Ryan's driveway and luckily, we didn't have to sit too long in the silence that followed her response. The weather was picking up, mimicking the annoyance building inside me. I couldn't accept her answer.

"Does it have to do with Rick?" My mom flinched at my words.

"How… do you know? Did he hurt you or Iris? IS EVERYTHING OKAY? CECILE?" Mom began to shake.

"Mom! It's okay, relax. While he did try to harm me and Iris, we got him first. Cecile is fine." I pulled her into a hug. "It's okay now."

"What do you mean you got him first?" Mom mumbled between sobs.

Everyone stepped out of the van and left me alone with mom. She continued to sob in my arms as I rubbed her back.

"Rick…is…he's dead." I stuttered. Mom stopped sobbing and pulled away slowly.

"Dead?" She repeated after me in a whisper. There was a twinkle of relief in her eyes.

"Yes, that son of bitch had it coming. I will not hesitate to snap his neck again if I could. There's so much I need to tell you but for now, I want you to come home, mom."

"Are you sure you and Iris are okay?" Martha wiped her face.

"Yes, as I said, I have a lot to tell you. Cecile told me everything between you. I'm not upset but there's more to the story which led to Rick's fate." I hugged my mother. I truly missed her warmth.

"You don't hate me?"

The Silver Lining

"No, I could never."

We stepped out of the van and met everyone inside.

Cassius

We hopped out of the car making the snow crunch under our shoes. The snowfall seemed to look like it would build up fast. The weather had become relentless. Ryan opened the door and ushered us in. I looked back at the van and watched Atlas hug his mother again. Every bone in my body was happy that they had a moment to themselves.

I went in with everyone else and waited for Atlas and Martha to come inside after their private talk.

"Hi Martha, good to see you again," Sacha waddled into the living room as Martha stepped into the cabin shaking off the snow from her coat.

"Oh crap, I left my phone in the car," I announced when I couldn't find it in my back pocket. I hurried back out and opened the driver's side door to check if it fell between the cushion or seat. Silence fell within a second. The wind stood calm, the birds had fled, and with the van turned off, a deafening silence filled my ears. Slowly, I reached over and grab my phone from the cup holder forgetting I had placed it there while driving.

Under the seat, I knew we had a gun with silver bullets that I accidentally found when I was adjusting my seat for the drive. I tried not to make any sudden movements and grabbed the gun as discreetly as possible. Not one sound broke the silence which told me that any animal within my radius must have felt threatened and fled. Someone was definitely around and lurking. A crunch in the snow echoed. I looked around in the direction of the sound but with the echo bouncing between the space of the trees, I couldn't be too sure which direction the sound was coming from.

He's hiding to your nine. I sense him. Wolfie warned.

Are you sure?

Yes, be careful. And that was all the confirmation I needed to know I might be in danger.

I gently closed the car door and walked in the direction the person was hiding. The deafening silence had me on edge, so much so that I didn't notice, or rather, failed to notice the presence of a wolf.

I don't feel them as strongly anymore. Masking themselves maybe? Wolfie whispered in my mind as if anyone other than me would hear if he didn't.

I held my breath in wait. Wolfie was right. Whoever it was, could enjoy playing games with me. I scanned the snow for prints but all I saw were my own that trailed behind me. My heart was most likely the loudest sound between the crunching of snow beneath my unsteady feet.

"Stop being a coward and show yourself," I whispered loud enough for any wolf within distance to hear. I backed up towards the van slowly. The eyes I suddenly felt stalking me were definitely in front of me. The sinking feeling in my stomach told me to run inside, this danger could very well be my father and I don't think I could face him again so quickly. As a presence to my left approached, I turned around afraid of who I might find.

"AH!" I jumped out of my skin when Kristofer emerged from around the van. "What the hell, you scared me, man." I locked the van, hesitating on going inside. My gut was never wrong with things like this. Someone other than Kristofer was watching.

"Are you okay? You seem spooked." Kristofer looked around and landed to my left. Exactly where I thought the wolf would be. It had to be a wolf to be able to hide so well. Unfortunately, not well enough to go unnoticed.

"You sense it too, right? Someone is out there watching us right now." Kristofer grabbed me and we headed inside. I asked the others if they felt anything off, but no one did. To be honest, neither did I. It was only after I went to the van that I felt someone was there. Still, Atlas put one of his men on guard by the back of the house trusting my and Kristofers instincts.

"I think we should scout," Kristofer suggested.

"I think so too. Take Mavis with you and one of ours. Call out if things get nasty." I looked back at everyone staring at me as if I were an alien.

"Who made YOU Alpha?" One of our men scoffed. While Atlas and Kristofer smirked, which meant they didn't care I was taking charge, Doug felt annoyed by my instructions. Mavis clicked his tongue and answered in my stead.

"He may not be your Alpha, but he is my Luna. Which in turn puts him at a higher ranking than you. So, either way, show some respect." Mavis gave Doug a smirk with a bit of murderous eyes that neither said I am kidding, or I am serious. It was the most unsettling expression I had seen him give.

"Yea, what he said," Kristofer chortled.

Doug flicked his eyes between the two before landing on me. "My apologies, Luna."

I waved it off unbothered by the whole thing and sent them on their way. I didn't want to start any trouble and what I said was more out of concern for everyone's safety. I wasn't trying to overstep. Then again, Doug was the only one that thought I did. But this isn't the time to fight amongst us.

"Well now that we are settled in, I feel I need to tell you all something I discovered." Martha accepted the cup of coffee that Sacha offered her as she spoke. "After meeting Honovi, Cassius' father, I discovered the truth behind his reason for killing his mate and attacking Cassius. Even though my initial intent was to hire him to get rid of Rick, I found out something much more valuable."

"His intent was to use their blood to gain power, right?" Atlas questioned Martha.

"Yes, how did you know?"

"We already had a run in with him. But please continue mom," Atlas answered.

"Did you just say you wanted my father to get rid of Rick?"

"Well, he already proved to be ruthless so I figured he could get the job done without the council knowing." Martha hummed in thought and continued.

"Well, maybe it wasn't such a thought-out plan. Anyways, he attempted a ritual after he was told that your mother died. A vial of blood was collected from her and given to him but due to inaccurately reciting the incantation and his mate not being the true incarnate, the spell backfired. He ended up growing weaker and losing his mind in the process. All these years it took him to gain his strength to try again." Martha sipped her coffee allowing its elixir to warm her cheeks. "He truly is a madman."

"How did you find this out?" I scooted closer to where she sat.

"Well, that man was keeping track of everything in a journal. He has everything in there. How to cast the spell, the ritual circle, the time of year, the calculation for his body mass, everything you can think of he has written down. Makes sense considering he was losing his mind; he couldn't trust it."

It was a terrifying thought and it made me feel all the more thankful for having the ability to stop him. Mavis, Kristofer, and Doug walked in shaking their heads with no luck in finding the potential spy.

"Well, don't worry. I took care of him. My father doesn't technically pose a threat anymore." I smiled at her, and the others agreed.

"Is he dead? That's the only way he won't pose a threat. As long as he has that book, he is a dangerous man. He can still perform it." Martha finished her coffee and set down the mug. "He intends to kill you by any means necessary. Now that he is no longer Alpha, he has nothing else to lose." The worry filled the lines of her face. She truly believes my father would stop at nothing and after feeling that odd presence earlier, maybe she had a point.

My brows furrowed forming a thin line on my forehead at her, questioning how she knew that Honovi could still perform the ritual and that he was hellbent on killing me. "I have someone who is the child of a dear friend that lives with that pack. They keep me posted."

"Wait so you're telling me, that man is still-" My wolf inside jumped on alert. I stood up immediately listening with my eyes closed. "He's here."

Chapter 19

CASSIUS

I could sense them approaching.

"What's wrong Luna?" Mavis rushed over along with Atlas. One on each side of me.

"Luna?" Martha's voice squeaked.

"Shhhhh," I listened and counted. With my abilities I could feel the presence of the wolves within their host of those around me, but I couldn't detect them accurately just yet. "We are surrounded. Roughly 8 wolves and one broken wolf. Or maybe he is human, I can't tell."

"What? How do you know, I don't sense anything?" Kristofer stepped over to a window and peeked out.

"I can feel them somehow. It wasn't like before when they were masking themselves. It's almost as if they want me to know they are coming. Everyone, on guard. Ryan, get Sacha upstairs and keep her safe. Everyone else, let's go outside so we don't destroy the cabin in the process." This time the words left my lips in a command filled with fear but determination.

Ryan grabbed Sacha, helping her upstairs along with Martha.

Something inside of me itched. My senses were firing in all directions as the intruders approached. We stepped outside and lined up on the side of the cabin where I knew the wolves were approaching. The snow had picked up again while we were inside and was now getting heavier. The ground was already a thick blanket at least a half inch deep.

The white of the snow was slightly blinding so I closed my eyes to listen instead. Growls grew in the distance. Their presence roared clearer now as they closed their distance. Everyone shifted into their wolves but me and Atlas. If I were to try everything I practiced in the last few days, then I needed to remain in my human form. I tried to sniff the air, but the wind worked against me. They must have planned it that way so they could hide their approach.

As they closed in, I confirmed we were outnumbered but not by much. This could actually be the best-case scenario for us. Atlas grabbed my arm as he caught in the distance, the group coming into view. That nameless bastard was the one I confused for a human. I should have known right away it was my father. He approached us with a smug look about his burnt face. It made my blood curled just seeing his stupid mug. *I should have killed him when I had the chance,* I relate to Wolfie who was growling inside me.

"Didn't I embarrass you enough?" I bared my canines at him. The wolves stopped advancing. If they were smart then they would leave but if they were following my father, then that answered my question. It wouldn't surprise me if those fools were loyal to my father regardless of his status. He must have promised them power if he succeeded. Power, he knew very well, couldn't be shared.

I slowly took steps forward towards them, watching their every move. Atlas was to my right along with Mavis' and Paul's wolves while Kristofer', Kirk's, and Doug's wolves were to my left.

"Oh no, you got it all wrong. I'm here to take what's mine!" The nameless man shouted, and the wolves all attacked as if on command. One of them came towards me but I tossed him aside, but I lost my footing in doing so and fell to my knees. He jumped on me again but with his massive size, I couldn't hold him off as well in my human form. The size difference was too great to manage. I grabbed the wolf's throat and squeezed while emitting the fire I learned to command from my hands.

He yelped and jumped off me before falling to the ground in pain. The wolf had patches of hand shaped burns on its throat with its skin exposed and bleeding raw. That wolf did well to distract me because another wolf's teeth were tearing into my arm. The enormous white wolf with gray spots tried to yank my arm off but I punched his nose dead on, over and over to make him let go of his hold. I screamed in pain but continued punching the wolf until I heard the crack of the snout breaking against my fist.

Blood dripped down my fist. He let go of my arm and shifted back to his human form. His face was a bloody mess as crimson poured from his face. My arm on the other hand was mangled and I could barely move my fingers because of it.

Cass! Atlas' wolf, Leo, called out to me through our link as he snapped the neck of the one I burnt earlier. At some point Atlas must have shifted to fight.

"Look out!" I yelled back at Leo who was being charged by another wolf. He quickly turned around and snapped his teeth at the wolf charging him.

I ran over to my mate and kicked the wolf, but I only hurt my arm further when I fell to the floor. It was the only thing I could do in my human form without giving away my secret weapon, but the increasing snow was making my balance harder to keep. Leo, thankfully, acted quickly and swiped at the wolf's neck in an attempt to finish him off.

In complete chaos, every wolf was fighting for their lives. I survey the grounds and make notes of those who are down for the count. The man with the broken nose was unconscious in a pool of his own blood, Kirk seemed badly hurt and was propped up against the cabin with a torn-up leg trying to heal. So far, we were one for one.

Kristofer's wolf, Zeus, snapped the neck of the wolf he fought but the heavy panting told me he was exhausted. But that was two of the eight wolves down. It was now their six against mine with Kirk out of commission healing.

My arm was slowly healing on its own and I could move my fingers without pain. The muscles had reattached, but my flesh was still exposed. The cold sliced through my arm which made the pain of healing that much worse. I winced but the pain I felt was nothing compared to the fire I had inside to protect everyone.

Honovi laughed while watching the fight. He leaned against a tree enjoying the sight of blood soaking the snow like a cherry snow cone on a summer day.

"Luna!" Kirk ran to me and pushed me out the way as the guy with the nose I broke tried to stab me with a broken hefty branch. I stumbled to the side while Kirk fought him off, both in human forms. He must have healed enough to dart off the ground the way he did, either that or he was pushing through his injuries for my sake. I have to remember to thank him later for what he did.

I turned my attention back to my father who had his eyes locked on me. Seething inside, it took a great deal to keep control of myself. But before I could do anything, two wolves jumped between me and my father. I looked back and three wolves were fighting my men, one was missing. The two before me were stopping any advance I made. Something was wrong.

Zeus and Kirk's wolf joined me as they finished off two of the three wolves they had. The sound of a wolf whimpering as he flew against a tree echoed as the rest of my wolves finished him off. Now it was just us, against two wolves, the one missing, and my father.

The two wolves split and while one attacked Kristofer and Kirk, the other lunged towards me.

"Fuck!" I yelled as I fell to the ground. No matter how I tried, it was hard to fight a wolf in human form. With all my strength, I tried to fling the wolf off of me, but he managed to bite my shoulder. I screamed in pain in a way that shook the air around us all. The wolf then quickly let go of me and ran to the nameless bastard that was my father. I watched as the wolf drooled my blood out of its mouth and into a bowl my father held.

"Thank you for your cooperation", and in one swift move he snapped the wolf's neck. That sick bastard offed one of his own without batting an eye. My father drank my blood without letting a single drop fall from his lips. I tried to attack him to prevent whatever he was doing from happening. But I stopped. I was too late. His chest glowed and he ripped his shirt open. He had what I thought were ritual markings on his chest ready to go. He mumbled a few words over and over like a chant meant to channel something greater. I heard the last wolf was still fighting Kristofer and Kirk, but it didn't register completely. It was background noise to what I was witnessing.

My father screamed in pain. Whatever he said triggered the markings on his skin. His body contorted and black markings spread across his torso and limbs oozing a reddish glow. The smell of cooked flesh spread in the air as the marks seared into his skin.

The power coming off him hit everyone at once. The incantation worked. My wolf barked inside me trying to calm my beating heart, but I was scared. I couldn't move a muscle. The strength he exuded was like my own. His strength surpassed anything I had ever felt. The pressure was strong, and it forced Kirk, Paul, and Mavis' wolves to pass out. Only Zeus and Leo were conscious as Alphas but even then, they were struggling to stay on their feet.

Don't be intimidated. We are still stronger. He doesn't even have his wolf. Wolfie tried to calm my nerves.

How is he this strong then? What is he now?

Still a nameless asshole with a reflection of your powers. Do not back down. We all have your back, Cass.

Okay. I replied to my wolf, but I was terrified I would fail.

All I knew was that I could not let that bastard continue to hunger for power.

I lit my blue flames and faced the maniacal man laughing at his red and black flames.

"Finally, the power I deserve. Now to clean up the trash." He looked at me and then my arm, taking note that I had enough time to fully heal.

My instincts twitched as I caught from the corner of my eye an arm swinging at me with its black flames at incredible speed. Like a whip extending from his hands, I barely dodged before he came in with an uppercut. I didn't even see when he closed the distance between us. His speed was nothing to laugh at. He clipped me under my chin and sent me flying back on the ground.

Light flashed behind my eyes. The pain radiating from the blow had my vision seeing spots. He came at me again just as relentlessly as the snow that was building to a foot and kicked me. That one kick sent me flying into the burnt shed. I landed on a pile of salt bags and thankfully not on the tools instead.

I stumbled out of the shed huffing and puffing. The fight was draining me, and I was unsure if I had enough strength to fight my father. But by instinct, I fully engulfed myself in my blue flames. It helped me regain some of the strength I had lost. Over to my left, Kristofer was in his human form ready to pass out and fell on one knee. Now that both my father and I were in our flamed forms, our strength was too much for the Alpha's to handle. Atlas looked pale and moments from throwing up as he used a tree to lean on. I ran to my father trying to mimic the same speed he hit me with.

I closed the gap between us and hit him twice on the ribs, but he hardly stumbled from it. Each connected blow landed with reasonable force, but nothing came of it. I then swiped him from under and brought him down onto his back. I foolishly hesitated too long relishing in my success of bringing him down that he grabbed my leg and tossed me against a tree. My ribs cracked on impact. Undeniable pain shot through my body as I fell to the ground. I coughed up blood and groaned when the cough itself hurt just as bad.

"Not so tough now, my son." Honovi called out. That bastard dared to call me his son while he beat me to death. Or at least tried.

"Why couldn't you have been the one to die?" I jumped up and my flames ignited brighter. As it filled every pore of my body, I felt it healing me from the inside. "Why hasn't the council punished you for what you did all those years ago?" I spat in anger.

"The council? You still trust those fools?" He laughed as if he heard the funniest thing in the world and walked up to me. "Even now you are as naive as the child I threw away." More wolves showed up but stayed hidden within the trees ready to join the fight if needed. I ignored the growing danger. Ignored the possibility of them aiding my father and guaranteeing our demise.

I screamed all my hurt and frustration. Closing in on him I punched his face, his ribs, his chest, and anywhere else I could land a hit. With a barrage of attacks, I cried my anger forcing my flames to intensify each time. I felt like a ticking time bomb.

You need to control your emotions, Cass. He is playing mind games with you and you're letting him.

Shaman Acktoo? I asked as his familiar voice popped into my head.

Remember who you are!

One of the voices of the reincarnated versions of the shaman rang in my head. Quickly, I retreated several feet back. I needed time to calm down. Acktoo was right and I needed to regain control. With a wave of his hands, my father sent a quick blast of his flames at me. It clipped my arm and burned my skin. I howled in response. I wasn't able to dodge it quickly enough. The difference in his power from before and now was significant and I was a fool to take him lightly. I lost all confidence to win. I was scared.

Remember who you are!

The voice echoed again in my mind and snapped me out of my self-deprecation. Atlas called out my name and I turned to find him in his human form down on both knees. He was wobbling but holding on. His strength poured into me and with a deep breath I tackled my father to the ground. My mind went blank as I engulfed my body in the most intense flames I could manage.

He screamed as his skin burned under me. My body heated up further, intensifying the heat of my blue flames. The fire was negating his red and black ones, burning his flesh in return.

Another wolf came rushing in from the side at full speed and knocked me off. He didn't care that he was caught on fire. All that mattered to him was my father gaining his power. The power he promised to share. It made me wonder again how smart they were if they hadn't yet realized the lies my father told them. He must have been the wolf that was missing earlier. But before I got my chance to take him out, he disappeared again.

Honovi covered himself in his own flames again, protecting his body from further damage and ridding himself of my blue fire. I watched his skin heal the same way mine did.

Cassius, I need you to listen. The voice reappeared.

Acktoo?

Yes, I can't speak for long, just listen. Raise your hands as if holding a bow like you practiced. Breathe really slowly and steadily. Upon exhale release as if the arrow is truly between your fingers.

I know that already.

Do it now! Concentrate!

I jumped at the strength of the Shamans voice in my head. It commanded in a way I had yet to learn to do. Swiftly, I dodged a few blows, but a fist caught me right on my chin. My skin sizzled as his fire burned my skin. Punch for punch we burned each other, weak to the other's flame. I knew nothing of how to use my powers except for what I practiced. All I could do was draw it out and sustain it but that trick I just learned was still unstable.

Just do it. I will guide you. It's my power you are using. I will guide you, but hurry.

I pushed my father back as hard as I could and ran away to create distance between us.

"You coward, why are you running?"

I took a deep slow breath and raised my arms as I was told. I still didn't understand how I was talking to the spirit of Acktoo but I listened to his voice and let him guide me. I looked my father dead in the eye as he walked towards me and hissed out my breath slowly. My father laughed, clearly not understanding what I was doing.

In the lapse of judgment Honovi was giving me, he provided a clear shot to his demise. With a steady hand the flaming arrow appeared. My father stopped and fell silent, unsure of what to expect. He was a little over thirty feet away and just within my range. I released my fingers. A blue and red arrow flew at lightning speed. The air crackled at the sound of the arrow slicing through the falling snow. It never did that before. The snow was heavy and the wind strong, but nothing seemed to phase the arrow. Then it disappeared or at least it seemed that way. In the small moment it vanished, I burst into laughter because I actually expected something different.

"What the hell was that? You actually had me worried for a second." He tossed his head back laughing.

Then stopped himself short when the cracking sound appeared once more as the arrow reformed just a couple feet from him piercing his chest. He stared down in shock. His face morphed between horror and pain with his voice caught in his throat while his mouth hung wide trying to speak. The arrow burrowed into his chest slowly, twisting as it went in deeper. The ritual markings burned away red, branding his skin as his flames disappeared. He finally screamed. A tonal scream from the depths of his soul as he became the embodiment of pain.

"Cassius…" He tried to speak finally while clutching his chest.

"You have no right to speak my name."

"My…. son…I-"

Listening to him call me his son for what was his last time, I felt nothing. I was no longer afraid. No longer that abandoned child. And no longer in shackles from his torment in my mind.

"I am not your son, I have no father," I spat at him. I was free.

His body burned to ash until there was nothing left. The flames had reached a temperature so intense that it reduced him in mere minutes into the nothingness he was. The wolves that were hiding stepped out from behind the trees whimpering and lowering their heads to me. Acknowledging defeat. They came here to fight and instead were now witnesses to the death of their leader. I could never fathom how anyone could follow a man such as my father. But I assumed, where there was one, there were many.

"You all will be tried and punished by the council. If you dare run, I will find you and punish you myself. Understand?" My voice echoed in what was now a blizzard. They yelped in understanding, cowering under the tones of my voice.

A scream ripped through the cabin walls. Not even the howling of the blizzard snow could drown out the horrifying scream.

252

The Silver Lining

Atlas managed to get up and steady himself as I put out my flames. He ordered Mavis to watch over the wolves as I ran inside and up the stairs to find Ryan fighting the same wolf from earlier. Everything in the home was a mess. The walls were scratched, picture frames were shattered, and everything they had on the dresser was thrown on the floor.

While Martha protected Sacha who bled from her belly, Atlas ran inside to his mother's side. Atlas and Martha helped walk Sacha to the corner of the room furthest from the wolf and sat her in the chair. Ryan shifted and flipped the wolf on its back which gave me enough time to grab the intruder by the neck. Despite his size, I transformed only my arm and gripped the wolf with ease.

"Wrong move," I snarled and snapped his neck, dropping his limp body to the floor. "What happened?" I turned to help Ryan who shifted back and was limping to the bed.

"That son of a bitch snuck up on us and swiped her stomach." Ryan groaned, gripping his leg which was already beginning to swell around the ankle.

"She's going into labor!" Martha shouted.

The room fell silent to the screams of labor.

Chapter 20

Screams bounced off the walls in the cabin. The very sound pierced through me like the arrows I shot from my bow. Sacha was in active labor and with the blizzard outside, going to their pack house was not an option. I had heard countless women go into labor back home, but this time felt different. Maybe it was because of the fight we just had with my father or maybe it was the unforgiving weather, but I was on edge and scared that her labor would be one more thing to add to the series of bad events.

I prayed to the goddess that wasn't the case. Martha being with us now was definitely reassuring because had it just been us men. There was no knowing how efficient we could all be in this situation. None of us have helped with labor before.

Martha helped Sacha to the bathroom and ran her a hot shower. She had explained to Ryan that running hot water on the lower back could ease the pain of contractions. Maybe it was the same as putting a hot patch on sore muscles. One time I tried helping during a delivery of one of our pack members or at least I tried. I passed out when I saw the head coming out. I ended up just being another patient in the infirmary. By the time I woke up, the mother was already holding her baby girl.

I chuckled at the memory. I was glad I was not a woman. Carrying a child for months to then go into labor sounded harder than the training we do as wolves.

While Cecile continued helping Sacha, the other men rounded up the wolves outside that were dead or wounded. The wind let up enough for us to collect the bodies. The few that were still breathing were tied up to keep them from doing further harm. Ryan locked them all in one of the empty guest rooms and put a wolf on guard. Kristofer and Paul loaded the dead wolves in the back of the van and drove off deep into the woods to bury them. After a few hours, they returned to the dull screams turned groans as Sacha sat in a tub of water using her breathing techniques to work through the labor.

Atlas went pale and looked ready to throw up. He didn't not do well with seeing women in pain and the screaming visibly took a toll on him. He ended up in the kitchen making food for everyone as a way to distract himself. It was always his way to self-soothe I was learning. It was kind of like how Kristofer liked to make hot chocolate using his secret recipe when he needed some comforting.

Martha pulled me from my thoughts as she instructed Ryan on what to do and took her place to help his wife with labor. This part of the process seemed so intimate. Now that the dust was somewhat settling, I left them to focus on their pup coming into this cruel cold world filled with wolves that will love him. Although I won't admit it out loud, I was mostly leaving so I didn't pass out again.

The smell of food lured me to the kitchen to find my handsome man cooking, "what are you making?" I snuck up behind Atlas and kissed his neck. He moaned in delight when my lips hovered where I had just kissed him.

"Fried rice and stir-fried steak with peppers," Atlas proudly announced. He removed the wok from the heat and turned around placing his arms around my waist. His strong arms pulled me close while his tender lips nipped at mine.

"Feeling better?" I whispered against his lips.

"Yes," he kissed me gently, but I noticed the blush in his cheeks.

Too weak to his kisses, I leaned into him further. Our soft passionate kiss turned hot and heavy. It almost felt as if the weight of today was finally melting away and I could finally breathe. His hand slid up underneath my shirt while the other grabbed my ass. I almost moaned to the heat of his body on mine. "Babe," I breathed into his lips. That was all Atlas needed. I could smell his arousal climbing just as quickly as my own. Without even looking, I knew our aura was dancing around us. It was intoxicating and made me want to drip in anticipation as his erection firmly pressed against mine. He kissed me harder this time. Our tongues battling each other. *I want him.*

"Something you want to tell me Atlas?" Martha's voice cut through our passion like a knife.

We turned to find that Martha stood at the entrance of the kitchen with her arms crossed. Her presence sucked our lust and auras out of the room like a vacuum. From the look on her face, it was obvious she could not only smell our desire but got a glimpse of our auras as well.

"Mom!" Atlas pushed me to one side causing me to fall over our entwined legs. He wiped his lips and looked down at me apologetically. I would have felt hurt if it wasn't so hilarious to see the pure panic on a grown man's face.

"First, Mavis calls him Luna and now you're practically eating his face. And was that your aura?" Martha didn't actually sound mad. It sounded more like she was annoyed that she was the only one in the dark.

"Mom, Cassius is my mate and soulmate." Atlas helped me up and stood by my side, locking his fingers in mine. "Mavis and the others call him Luna, but we haven't had our ceremony yet".

"Boy, you better sit down and tell me everything." Martha pulled out a chair and got comfortable. Atlas nodded but before he could begin, he turned to the stove to finish making the steak before placing the food on the table for everyone to eat. He called out for the fellas to come and eat.

This wasn't how he wanted to tell her. He wanted a nice quiet dinner with the three of us where we could talk without interruptions. Unfortunately, life had a way of changing plans.

While the kitchen filled with hungry mouths, Atlas, Martha, and I all stepped into the living room. We each sat in silence for a bit before Atlas began the story.

"Mom, before I tell you how Cass and I came to be. I promised I would tell you the whole story about Rick." Atlas took a deep breath, and I got up to leave to give them privacy. "No, stay. I want you to hear it as well." Atlas grabbed my arm and pulled me back down.

"Are you sure?" I trembled because I didn't want to see him reliving his pain. He gave me a half smile and I sat back down next to him.

"So, after father died, I had a hard time processing everything. I was a young teen wolf and all I wanted to do was drown in my pain. I had drunk a few bottles and was beginning to feel the effects of the alcohol. It felt so good to drown my sorrows and I was feeling nice for the first time in a long time. However, I didn't stop. I had another bottle of rum but halfway down that bottle, Rick found me sitting behind the barn." Atlas' hands were shaking. So, I slid my hand into his to help him steady. He gave me a squeeze and continued.

"We spoke a bit about dad and how great he was but then the conversation turned, and I somehow felt the courage to confess to him how I was gay. I had already come to terms with my sexuality, but I never told anyone about it. I was scared of being thrown away but after dad died and having so many bottles in my system, I thought if I told Rick who was also like a father, that it would be okay. But it wasn't…" Atlas began to cry.

His tears streamed steadily down his cheeks as he looked down at the floor. His body was hunched over as he rested his elbows on his knees letting the droplets fall by his feet. Martha's lips trembled as she stood up and sat on the other side of Atlas and rubbed his back. "Take your time son, take your time." She whispered.

"I confessed to that asshole my only secret and he thought he could fix it by…. he…he chugged the rest of his whiskey and pinned me down. He reeked of disgust and touched me calling me all sorts of names. I was so drunk that I had no strength to push him away and with him being so much older, his strength was already superior to begin with. I cried and screamed but no one heard me, no one came to help. He forced himself into me. He raped me, mom. I still remember the pain, how it felt when he tore into me, how his disgusting hands roamed my body while his lips seared against my skin." Atlas broke down again, heaving with his cries. Martha and I hugged him desperately, trying to comfort him.

Everything I imagined, all of which I thought was a possibility became amplified with his words. His story was much worse, much crueler and more disturbing than anything I could conjure up in my mind. Atlas continued to cry in our arms as my own tears fell on his shoulders. "It's okay babe, you don't need to finish the story. You don't need to relive it anymore. Let me take your pain away."

Atlas sniffled and took a deep breath, "I have too. It's the only true way to heal. It will be the last time I tell the story, but I need mom to know." Martha looked at me with soft eyes glossy with tears. We pulled away from Atlas so he could continue.

"When he was done with me, I could smell my own blood and I knew I was injured pretty badly. He looked down on me and laughed at what he did and threatened to do the same to Iris if I told anyone. Thinking back now, he probably did it because of his jealousy over dad and Jude being in love and the guilt over killing them both. But when Cass and I realized we were mates, Rick caught on quickly and used it as an excuse to go after Iris. Fortunately, he didn't do anything to her, but he did manage to kidnap her. When he approached me about it, I lost it and we fought. Mavis showed up and killed him after I had received a nasty blow. And if it wasn't for Cass always being there for me and Iris, I don't know how things would have ended. He alone saved Iris twice. Once from hunters and another after discovering where Rick hid her."

"You know. I always wondered how Mavis knew to find us there," I interrupted.

"Well, he said, he followed Rick. Since I had already put Mavis on alert about him and told him my story, he had been keeping an eye and followed him into the woods."

"Oh," I mumble.

"I really need to thank that boy. He is such a good Beta to you," Martha smiled.

"Yea he really is. So, Cass and I ended up realizing something as mates. We are apparently also soul mates. It's what you also saw earlier. When our moods are heightened, our auras seem to manifest. We don't know how to control it too well but when it does manifest, everything feels different. Depending on the situation, it either calms us down, riles us up, or heals us in a sense." Atlas looked at me with a smile and my heart squeezed.

Martha wiped her face as tears fell steadily. She apologized over and over, feeling guilty for never having realized it about Rick but he assured her it was okay. They hugged for a long time until they both stopped crying. They needed this bonding time. They needed to start healing old wounds.

"Thank you, Cassius. Thank you for being there for my boy and my daughter. I owe you a lifetime of gratitude." Martha got up and hugged me a little too tight, but I accepted it happily.

"Martha, I will do it again in a heartbeat."

She pulled away and Kristofer entered the room.

"Here you go, I saved you a plate." Kristofer handed Martha some food.

We all sat in silence looking at one another. Kristofer and his timing did wonders. "What?" Kristofer asked with a cheek full of food. I rolled my eyes and leaned my head on Atlas.

"So, tell me Kris, have you found a mate yet?" Martha took a fork full and hummed her approval. Kristofer on the other hand choked on some peppers he just took a bite of. I burst out laughing and he shot me an evil look.

"I-I did, actually." Kristofer stuttered but it caught me by surprise. I wasn't expecting him to admit it. Not with how he acted when he first found out. Martha and Atlas both almost suffered whiplash at his words. Not that I blamed them if they did.

"Who?" Atlas asked. I snickered anticipating his reaction to the answer. This should be interesting considering Martha just found out about me and her son. Kristofer squirmed in his seat.

"You know don't you," Atlas punched my arm.

"Yes, but it's not my place to say. Kristofer will announce wh-"

"It's Iris!" My words fell short at Kristofer's outburst. It was probably his nerves which I found even more hilarious.

"WHAT?" Atlas' face shifted from overprotective brother to disgust and back.

"That's wonderful, both my babies found their mates. Oh, I can't wait for my grandbabies since Atlas can't give me any." Martha nodded her head my way with a smirk.

"Hey... that's not nice. We can always use a surrogate." I protested defensively and chuckled.

"Well, she doesn't know that I know yet. At least I don't think so. I haven't said anything. Although I plan to when we get back." Kristofer rubbed the back of his neck.

"Damn right you will," Martha egged on. "But after hearing everything that's happened, I can understand the hesitation."

A scream pulled us from our conversation followed by Ryan yelling for Martha. She put down her food and ran upstairs. Soon a baby's cry in Sacha's place filled the cabin and my heart jumped in delight.

"You want pups?" Atlas grabbed my attention from my momentary bliss. I could see his eyes excited over the thought and I kissed his nose.

"Yes. I'd love one or two of you running around." I kissed his lips. My heart was ready. I was finally going to tell this man those three little words when we got home. It'll be perfect.

The Silver Lining

Kristofer cleared his throat reminding us he was still there which was good since I was about ready to straddle my mate. Atlas stuck out his tongue at Kristofer who actually did it back which provoked an eye roll from me. One moment he was an Alpha and the next he was a child.

A knock pounded on the door making Kristofer sniff the air. No one was expecting a guest, especially not in this weather. His eyes grew wide as if recognizing the scent. He jumped up and opened the door, stumbling over his feet.

"Good evening councilmen." They all nodded to one another. "What brings you here?"

"We were called and are here to pick up the wolves but before we do I need to see for myself what occurred." The tall man in a dark black cloak walked in. His eyes were dark as coal which only stood out due to his baldness and no brows. If I had anything to do with it, I'd say he was an alien instead of a wolf.

"I assure you; I am not an alien." The councilman sighed but he wasn't directing his words at me.

I turned to Atlas, "you think so too?" We both chuckled before the councilman approached me.

"You had the same thought?" He looked at me, annoyed and closed his eyes, "interesting I can't hear your thoughts. That's never happened before."

"You can hear thoughts?" I asked bewildered.

"Yes, as a councilman, it is a power we are given during initiation so we may judge an accuser without the lies of the mouth. A bit of focus and wolves are an open book." The bald man answered rather smugly.

him. He closed his eyes again and placed his forehead against mine. Atlas growled but I could tell Kristofer was making him back down. My mind then became cloudy. It was uncomfortable with the slight intrusion in my mind, so I fought it.

"Why can't I see your mind?" he grunted. I shrugged again. Now he was clearly angry, but he closed his eyes once again and repeated the process. "Relax and let me in. Give me permission." I closed my eyes and relaxed like he suggested. I cleared my mind the best I could and felt him placing his thumbs on my temples. Instantly, my head jerked back. My eyes shot open, and they glazed over white. Or at least that was what I thought happened.

I saw every memory the councilman was seeing. They played in my mind like a reel. One by one he sifted through my memories and found the one with me fighting my father. Satisfied, he let me go and my vision returned. "What the hell? That was some freaky shit." I tried to shake off the feeling.

"I saw all I needed. Give Martha my regards." The councilman stepped back out and more came in. Without a word they went to the den and escorted the rogue wolves out of the cabin. The one that had sifted my memories stopped looking at me. "There's something odd about you." He sneered but then left along with the others.

We bid farewell and noticed the blizzard had stopped. I didn't even try to comprehend what the man did but my wolf told me he blocked the fact that I was the reincarnation. Which made sense. Basically, I instinctively only showed a vision crafted for the councilman to hide the truth of my power. It was a defense mechanism to protect the soul. I thought it was odd that the memory I saw wasn't what actually happened but close enough to the truth. The sound of snowmobiles roared in the distance pulling me from my thoughts. *How did we not hear that before?*

A baby's cry filled the cabin again. Ryan ran down the stairs in joyful tears. "It's a girl". We all went to congratulate him when Sacha started screaming again. He ran upstairs in a panic. A few moments later another cry rang slightly different from the first. Ryan ran back down, "it's a boy!" Everyone hesitated for a minute, half expecting another scream. When none came, we all attacked Ryan in hugs.

Neither of them knew they were having twins. It would be the first set of twins in the family. So much joy to end such a crazy day. I sat with Atlas in the kitchen making ourselves a sandwich since no one left any food for us. It was baffling that no one thought to at least feed the chef, but I guess this was their way of getting back at us for having loud sex the other day. I chuckled to myself. Everything was finally coming to an end. Peace was settling in.

***

It has been a week, and we were back home. Martha was back home with us, and she couldn't seem to stop crying every time she saw her daughter, Iris.

I slipped away to the back porch to make sure everything was ready. Thankfully it only lightly snowed here compared to up north by Ryan's home. The backyard looked serene because of it with the light powder of snow covering the ground. The winter wonderland added a perfect touch to my set up.

My hands clammed up and I was thoroughly a bundle of nerves. *Breathe, you got this.* The mantra was on repeat in my mind. I whipped out my phone and texted my Alpha that I needed his help with something out back. Within two minutes he arrived, and I stood in my best shirt and pants before him. Unfortunately, I didn't own fancy clothes so my best chinos I bought a while back that barely fit were the next best thing and a black tee that I tucked in.

The porch was covered in white peach petals that took me forever to pluck. A small table was set with dinner and candles danced to soft music that filled the night with soft classics. Fairy lights decorated the walls and ceiling, twinkling like fireflies in the night.

"What's all this?" Atlas eyed everything once more.

I pull Atlas over to me. "May I kiss you?" My mate smiled and I gently placed my lips on his. We swayed side to side letting the music move our feet. Atlas moaned into my lips and pulled away to dip his head on to my chest. I lifted his chin, so he looked up to me and I placed one more kiss on his lips. Looking right into his beautiful honey eyes had me puddled inside.

"I love you, Atlas. I love you so much that I thought you felt it. I only recently realized I never really said those words and how important it is that you knew with certainty. I don't ever want there to be any doubt about what I feel. However, that is one mistake I will never make again. I am never letting go of the man who stood by me as I faced my demons. The man that bandaged my wounds. The man that would do anything for his pack and those he loves. You are My Alpha, no one else's." I pulled away and dropped to one knee.

Atlas blinked in shock, releasing the tear he was holding back. I pulled out the ring that Martha gave me. It was one of my mothers. Her inside person managed to get it to her along with other things while we were at Ryan's. My father may have said he didn't love her, but he still kept a lot of her things stored away.

"Alpha Atlas, my love, my world. Will you take my mother's ring and take this fool of a wolf to be your Luna, your mate, your companion?" I could barely contain my heart that pounded profusely against my chest.

"I don't see a fool. Only an extraordinary silver wolf...yes!"

I slipped the ring onto a chain and put it over my mate's head. The ring was too small for his manly fingers so the chain would have to suffice. I kissed him with more heat than ever before. Unable to contain my happiness

"Cass?" He whispered against my lips. "I love you too", his words burned into me a desire too big to control. I growled in approval and slammed my mate against the wall of the house. I thought it was safe to say, this would be another dinner served cold.

Chapter 21

CASSIUS

I scrubbed a pot from dinner thinking back to how last night went perfectly. A smile curved at my lips as I rinsed the sink down before rolling down my sleeves.

"Hey, I could have done that." Iris walked in with her hair in a messy bun, an old shirt with holes, shorts and a broomstick.

"Oh, stop it. You have been cleaning like a mad woman all morning." I leaned on the counter crossing my arms.

"Yea well it keeps me from my thoughts. Atlas cooks and I clean." Iris shrugged and reached for the dustpan.

"What's wrong, talk to me?" I walked over to block the doorway, noticing how heavy the circles were under her eyes.

"Nothing," she mumbled.

"No, what's wrong? You're basically my sister now. You can talk to me not as your Luna but as your brother."

Iris slumped her shoulders and her lips began to quiver. Her big hazel eyes looked up at me teary and sad.

The Silver Lining

It was the first time I saw her like that. "Remember when Rick took me?" My ears perked up not expecting to hear the name on her tongue.

"He didn't just strip me and tie me up. He tried to rape me." Her words were shaky, but she continued. "I fought really hard and thankfully he gave up. Instead, he laughed and said he was going to go after Atlas and give him another go since he was easier than I was. He left me there feeling violated and terrified. I could still feel his disgusting hands on my body touching and grabbing. His breath on my neck and his nasty stench of whiskey. Yet, right along with that disturbing feeling lingering on my body, his words keep replaying in my mind. I realized he abused Atlas and that made me all the more broken."

I hugged her immediately and gave her a good squeeze, "I am so sorry sis. I hate that you had to go through that. I hate that he was such an asshole. I won't ever let another man treat you that way again. I'll cut off his dick before that happens.… Your brother, he is strong. He did all he could to protect you from the same fate. He loves you dearly." I rubbed her back while she sobbed quietly. That filthy man managed to touch both of them, and it pained me to know such truth.

"I'm never drinking whiskey again. The smell alone makes me want to vomit," she pulled back, and I wiped away her tears. "You're the first person I've told. Thank you for listening. Hopefully there won't be any future dicks being chopped." She chuckled but I could tell she was just being brave.

"Well, what are brothers for, hm? I also think you should have a one-on-one with Atlas." I pinched her nose and she giggled.

"I'm happy you're our Luna and between you and me I like you better."

"Do you, now?" Atlas came up behind her nudging her shoulder as she laughed. She obviously knew he was there. Atlas walked around me and kissed my neck. "What are you and my fiancée talking about?

"Nothing, just sibling stuff." Iris winked at me and walked away but the panic of possibly being caught was clear in how tight she made a fist.

Atlas oblivious to it all, trailed kisses down my neck. "So, when can we plan our wedding?" His hands roamed freely down my front and cupped my package massaging me to life.

"Well, I'd like a spring wedding." I perked my butt and rubbed it against my mate.

He groans aching for more, "Really? Not a winter one? Well either way babe, there's a big problem." I turned around in question. He smirked and looked down. I followed the gesture and discovered the massive problem he was referring to.

I grinned and grasped it firmly, "you mean this big problem?" I jerk him watching his face fill with pleasure rocking his hips into my hand.

"Hey gu-" Kristofer popped into the kitchen before turning on his heel and stepping out again. He stood off to the side just outside the kitchen entrance. "Why every time I see you guys, your hands are on each other's dicks." He tried sounding annoyed, but he was holding back his laughter for sure.

"Come in, my hands are dick free now." I called out and Atlas laughed at the blush on Kristofer's face as he entered the kitchen.

"So, what's up", I asked, hopping onto the counter.

"Obviously you!" Kristofer bellowed in laughter at his own joke but continued, "So my mom was thin-" Kristofer swayed a bit and steadied himself on the breakfast bar, eyes growing wide.

"Hey Cass, where is the laundry bag with all-" Iris walked into the kitchen and stopped as if hitting a wall. Kristofer turned around slowly. They both stared at one another before Kristofer reached to touch her face. Her eyes closed and she leaned her head into his hand that caressed her cheek. She hummed lingering in his caress then took a deep breath. Her face went red, and her eyes shot open. With eyes full of tears, Iris pulled away and ran out of the kitchen.

"Iris wait", Kristofer was about to go after her when I jumped off the counter and grabbed his arm in her defense.

"Leave her. She just needs time." Kristofer slumped and faced us.

"Mom wants to have dinner with Martha but since their mind link doesn't work anymore, she asked me to ask you if you can repair their link with your shaman stuff." Kristofer says all in one breath without looking up from the floor.

"Um sure, I can try. I'll head over in a few. Let's take Martha with us".

"No, mom wants to surprise her with the mind-link. We need to try it without using blood. She still really loves her. I honestly still find it weird, but I haven't seen her this excited in a long time." Kristofer sighed as if the world was on his shoulders but finally faced me. "I'ma go for a run. I'll meet you at the house." He undressed in front of us and shifted before running out of the house.

I folded the clothes and clutched them against my chest looking in the direction he went. "Babe, do you know why she ran?" Atlas asked almost as if he already knew the answer.

Knowing what I knew now, it must have been difficult for her to find her mate so soon. She was still traumatized. She most likely wasn't ready to have another man touch her intimately. And rightfully so.

A very carefree hand groped my butt. "Alpha, you don't learn, do you?" I faced my mate and licked his lips to distract him from probing questions. Atlas lifted me over his shoulder and ran up to our room. *Oh shit, what did I just activate?* He tossed me onto the bed. I had no idea how I managed to hold on to the clothes. Atlas growled in a deep throated tone. I shivered.

One by one, I tossed the clothes to the floor and seductively opened my legs sliding my hands up my thighs. I rested one hand on my crotch and the other continued up and under my shirt exposing one nipple.

"What are you doing touching what's mine?" Atlas stepped closer to the bed, but I put out my hand telling him to stop.

"Alpha, just watch." I locked my eyes with Atlas and unzipped my pants. My hardening bulge made its appearance. With eager fingers, I grabbed it and massaged myself, moaning as I do. My other hand found my mouth and I sucked on two fingers flicking my tongue between them. Then I pinched my nipple with my wet fingers, teasing myself as I masturbated. Atlas growled loud and deep.

"Mmm, like what you see Alpha?" I teased, now releasing my hard erection from my briefs.

"Yes Luna, you're being very naughty." Atlas pulled down his pants, boxers, and stroked his member.

"What you called me?" My voice was husky. I groaned in need of something more.

"Luna?" my mate smirked with his eyes glowing brighter in desire. He had never called me Luna. It. Is. Fucking. Hot. I removed my briefs still not allowing him to touch me and spat in my hand to continue jerking off as I lifted one leg and inserted a finger in my hole.

My mate twitched. He was clearly holding back because I told him to, but his body screamed to hold me.

"Mmm, Alpha," I moaned, feeling my hole twitch around my fingers. "Still like what you see?" I inserted another finger releasing another moan in the process.

"Luna, you are playing with fire." He began to jerk himself faster. My orgasm on the edge and I was ready for something much harder and bigger inside me.

"Master, I'm ready for your cock." Atlas froze at my words. I pulled out my fingers and got up on my knees. I've been wanting to role play like this for a while.

"What's wrong, master?" I pulled him by his shirt closer to me.

I licked his member. "Master, do you not want your little whore anymore?" Atlas' eyes turned full wolf. He gripped my hair and shoved his length down my throat. I choked on the massive thing and gagged a little before he threw me back on the bed.

"My little whore huh. Are you wanting to get punished for being naughty all by yourself." Atlas climbed the bed tossing his shirt. He shoved his fingers in my mouth, and I sucked on them. A switch flipped inside him. He opened my legs and shoved his now wet fingers. Pumping quickly, I was ready to come but he stopped. "You can only cum by your master's cock, got it?"

I nodded with a grin ear to ear. "Fuck me, master," I wiggled underneath him.

"Bad, bad little Luna." He lifted both my legs off the bed and bent them towards me forcing my ass to go up in the air for him. I had never been in a position like this before. It was as submissive as it got. My mouth dropped when Atlas went down and began to lick my hole. His arms wrapped around my waist, holding me firmly against his face.

"Don't do that master, I'm dirty," Atlas didn't move. My words fell on deaf ears. He was completely lost to his carnal desires. I had never seen him like this. I moaned loudly to the sensations I never felt before. Whatever he did was on another level of kinky. The way his tongue swirled made me drip on to my stomach some pre cum. The sucking and biting of my cheeks had me on fire. I gasped but then his tongue slid into my hole.

"Oh my god!"

All I wanted to do was divert Atlas' attention away from his sister but instead I activated a kink I didn't know he had. Roleplay must be his thing. He thrusted his tongue repeatedly and slapped my ass. I screamed in pleasure. He reached down and started jerking me off, face deep in my ass. I could not look away. Our eyes lock on one another as he devours me. It was the most intense thing I had ever experienced. "Master, I'm close". A loud slurp sound echoed. My ass was dripping with his saliva.

"Cum for me Luna" Atlas jerked me harder while slamming my ass with his tongue.

"I'm cumming", I released myself all over my chest and unfortunately on my own face as well. Atlas dropped my legs and slid in his massive member already dripping in anticipation. "Ah, master." I cried out. "Wait, I just came."

Atlas bent over and licked a bit of the cum off my face, "salty," he whispered.

I still couldn't believe this man was my mate. The way he drove me over the edge was like no other. He kissed me and I could slightly taste myself on his tongue, but I didn't care. I loved his lips on mine. I wanted every inch of him.

"Now scream for me Luna", Atlas choked me with one hand and grabbed my hips with the other. He rammed me hard. Pounding me with every inch of his thick length. I screamed his name louder than I should have but I think I might have secretly wanted this. I couldn't get enough. "Shit, this tight hole of yours is sucking me in."

"Master!" I screamed against his grip on my neck. Even though he was choking me he was still careful not to hurt me.

He fucked me harder. "mmm", he groaned. "Fuck Luna, I'm gonna fill tight that ass right now". He choked me a little tighter, "LUNA!" Hot liquid poured into me. His body twitched with each pump. Atlas dropped on top of me.

Sex with this man rocked my world.

"Let's go shower and head over to Cecile." I looked up to my sexy Alpha and pouted. "What's wrong?" Atlas kissed my cheek.

"Some stupid Alpha rammed me so hard that my legs are weak." Pup eye mode activated. Atlas chuckled and carried me into his arms with ease.

"I love you Atlas," I kissed his neck.

My Alpha.

The End

Acknowledgements

Where do I begin? This story was a long time in the making, and it went through changes that I never expected it to take. What started out as a way to kill time turned into a story that unraveled itself through my fingers. It was created through hard work and the eagle eyes of individuals that helped shape it into what it has become today. I am so very proud to say the least.

I would like to thank my husband for his endless support of my writing and the barrage of questions I would throw his way when I would hit a roadblock or can't think of a word that's on the tip of my tongue. He is my biggest supporter, and his strength pushes me to keep going even when I feel that I cannot.

Lastly, I would also like to thank a friend that helped critique my work to bring out the best in my character. He was tough but honest with his advice and through that, I was able to grow as a writer. Thanks, Simon.

Nothing Stays Buried

Book 2
(Early-Stage Preview)

Chapter 1

Kristofer

Is this what I have been reduced to? The night is quiet and cold, even colder than most, I'd dare say, but I enjoy weather like this. It's in these quiet moments that I can gather my thoughts and truly organize my feelings. Although I didn't always seek solitude in the comfort of cold weather, it is a result of learning to compart-mentalize after my father died, a feeling I wish to never experience again. But I guess it's better than falling apart knowing my mother needs me to be strong right now. If not for me then at least for the pack. Coping with my father's death is still the hardest thing I ever did, even as an Alpha. Yet, the time to cry in mourning is shorter for me than it is for most.

As a leader, I must hold it together for everyone and show them that even in a time of grief, I can still be strong for them. I can mourn because it is only normal to do so, but I must quickly recover as well. So, I have a library of sorts in my mind where I sort out my thoughts into books and shelve them in their respective genres. Now and then, when I am alone, I find that book and open it to its bookmark so I can pick up my emotions where I last left off.

I pull out my favorite gray sweater and zip it up using the worn-out, faded zipper that tends to snag on the stressed fabric. The material is worn down by the wrist from excessive use and a couple of small holes grace the lining of the sweater which I am sure is due to the ancient washer we have. Our washing machine has been known to destroy a shirt or two.

A small stitch comes undone on the hem of the left sleeve and unwinds a bit more as I tug the cuff. I yank on the thread and break it off but because of its character, it's the most comfortable sweater I own. I have had it for years now and it simply has personality and holds memories that I am not ready to let go of. The only time I can wear it is during this time of year, when the temperature drops to where the bite from the chilly wind is enough to add on an extra layer of clothing. Even with winter upon us, as a breed of werewolves, we don't need much to keep us warm. Well, at least for most of us, that seems to be the case.

Normally, wolves naturally have warmer bodies than humans, and when we shift, our thick fur keeps us toasty against the cold. Yet, as we evolve and interbreed with humans, some wolves are born without the ability to regulate their bodies to the same degree that most can. But even with the ability to keep warm, now and then an extra layer is needed—like tonight. And while I have a lot of muscle, I still need my trusty sweater.

Content with my attire, I step out of my room into the silence of the lived-in walls I call home. The house is empty at the moment and yet I feel suffocated within it. With every step I take, the walls cave in on me and it hurries my steps. I distract my mind, reminding myself where everyone is. Alex is hanging out with Demetrius doing some training, Cassius is with his new mate, Atlas, and my mother is…well…she is out. That's everyone that lives in the house at the moment, though I do suspect that sometime soon Cassius will move in with his mate as the new Luna and Alex will move out the moment he finds his mate. It's almost like I would end up getting the empty nest feeling even though they are not my children. But might as well be considering that I look over them as the Alpha of the pack.

My mind slips back to the idea of my mother and the fact that she is now dating Martha. I try to shake off the uncomfortable feeling that never seems to roll off my shoulders at the thought, but it's pointless. As grown as I am, I just can't seem to let go of the idea or rather what it represents, which is my father being officially gone and out of her memory and our lives.

I step outside into the clear night with an inhalation of the calm breeze in hopes that it will settle my wandering mind. As if on autopilot, my feet take me around back to the old swing I built as a kid in the backyard. Just looking at it, the tension previously building in my shoulder dissipates. The swing aged well for something built on a whim and withstanding the weather of time. The long sun-bleached ropes are still intact and sturdy while the wooden plank, although not the original, sits strong with little stress on the grains of the wood.

My father helped me put it together on a random Saturday morning and every memory of us filters through my fingers as I run my calloused hands over the aged, lacquered wood. The cold pricks at my skin from the ice that settled between the cracks, sending chills through my bones. It reminds me of the day we had to replace it because Cassius and I both stood on it at the same time trying to prove the quality of my handy work. That day the seat broke in half and Cassius twisted his ankle. My father taught me a lesson in the form of running laps around the property that I remember well to this day. My muscles gave out that day. Yet, it is my favorite place to be when I want to think or be alone.

Out of all the things that have come and gone in my life, this swing is the only thing that remains the same. The constant to the forever revolving door that is my life. It's become my safe haven of sorts. While I did also try to go to my mother with my thoughts, I realized it isn't fair to burden her with her new kindling romance or rather rekindling romance. And honestly, it's okay. The guilt I would feel if I sabotaged their relationship is far worse than the fog clouding me. I can't wrap my mind around her and Martha being an item. To no fault of their own. How could I explain that it's simply hard seeing someone other than my father by her side, without making her feel bad about it?

I rest my weight on the old slab as it screams from the weight it hasn't held in a long time. Either that or I have put on a few pounds, and it is testing the limits of the rope's strength. The half breath in my throat holds as the final creak releases from the wood and I can safely relax into the seat. I look up at the stars admiring the clear sky, twinkling as if in morse code, revealing the events of its past. The child in me hides behind the tears at the thought of my late father. There is so much that he is missing out on.

With wet eyes blurring my vision, I trace in the air the constellations above me with my finger. I have them all memorized after doing the same thing for so long. Spotting the constellation at this point comes easy to me.

With another deep breath I blink away the threatening tears on the brink of escape and focus again on the stars. I search for my father's favorite in a futile effort because it only appears in the summer. I always liked pointing out the Lupus constellation to him because my father would then tell me stories of the great wolf. It is the first one he showed me and now I believe the stories he told me were of the Sham-an.

The late November wind blows hard against me, rocking the swing in place as I spot the stars directly above me, Orion's belt. Always the easiest one to distinguish among the others.

A howl hoots in the distance, pulling my attention to the left of the trees surrounding me. The moon hangs above them almost completely in its phase. In two nights, it will be a full moon, and it thrills me to no end knowing it is almost time for our monthly run. I want to feel the escape. I want to let go and let my wolf, Zeus, take over. Running with my pack and bonding with them freely is a feeling like no other. It'll give me the clarity I need during this confusing time. Not that I couldn't just shift now as I am but it's a different feeling during a full moon.

Shifting under the powers of the moon means relinquishing control to the goddess. And the confusion in my heart is not only about my mother but…Iris. Something that I need the guidance of the moon goddess to help me understand. With my eyes closed in thought, I take one last deep breath and exhale slowly the exhaust my mind is drowning in. Using the weight of my body, I begin to swing, letting my feet dangle and kick the higher I go.

Another gust of wind aids my momentum and sends a slight chill down the small patch of bare skin exposed on my lower back between my lifted shirt and my pants. It is a clear reminder that next week is thanksgiving and we are inching closer to Christmas. Both our packs, Alpha Atlas' and mine, want to have dinner together but I don't know if I am ready to be around my mate when she clearly and blatantly rejects me.

I know I should have said something when we first met but I let the shock of it all get the best of me. Not only did the situation she was in shock me, but I was also shocked that my mate lived so close to me, and I never knew. Now too much time is filling the space between us, and I am left wondering if I should end the bond. How can I live thirty years and finally find my mate, only to have her run away from me? It was just my luck to find and lose my partner at the same time.

I suck my teeth at the thought. I should have said something. Iris might have reacted differently… or maybe not, I don't know, but it hurts, nevertheless. It sucks being rejected to my face without being given a chance. Now, as it is, I will never get the opportunity to try and love her because she is opposed to having love exist in the first place. At least that's how it seems.

The fear of how her brows wear scrunched up and the tears-stained cheeks haunt my thoughts every time I think of her. Her quivering lips and heaving chest made her seem like she was simply waiting for her inevitable end. No one should ever have to experience that kind of feeling. She went through an ordeal I cannot fathom, but the bond certainly helps with healing, right? I am sure that if I have the opportunity, I can help her work through her trauma.

A tear finally breaks free from me and slowly rolls down my stubble and down my neck. I hate that I feel this way because honestly, even listening to myself I know I sound like a prick. I am putting my own broken heart before her traumatic experience. Another gust of wind kicks up and this time it slices through my sweater, allowing me to feel the bite of the cold a bit harsher.

If only the cold could numb me just enough to think with my head and not my aching heart. I just don't want to hurt like this anymore. The fact the I never allowed myself to grieve my father's death properly is now taking its toll. For so long, the responsibilities of the pack did well to push his memory aside but watching my mother find love while my own ends before it starts is digging up wounds, I forgot I had. I know if I give up Iris, then this pain wouldn't last long but I want a fighting chance. I just need to convince her to give me and us a chance. If not, the bond will eventually die and although that thought terrifies me, it is what it is.

"UGH!"

I kick the air causing my swing to twist a little. The creaking of the swing echoes into the night scaring off a few squirrels in the process. The thing about a mate bond is that it only really gives you a suggestion as to who could be your perfect match. It's like a spiritual cupid if you will. It amplifies the ability to see the redeeming qualities of both parties and to cut down the time it would normally take on your own. I guess it was made that way to help preserve the species. The faster we find love the faster we want to reproduce.

The mate bond doesn't force you to love either, it just makes it easier to do so. Of course, if you truly don't like the person for whatever reason, then a mutual rejection between both parties would erase the bond completely. Unfortunately, if only one person rejects it, then it becomes agonizing until the bond fades on its own or the other gives in. But I won't give Iris that satisfaction unless she gives me a reason to let her go.

"I wish I could see you", I whisper into the wind almost expecting it to grant me my wish.

I can still smell Iris. Her scent is like warm brownies freshly baked out of the oven and roasted marshmallows. It's captivating. Who knew I would develop a serious sweet tooth after meeting her. I groan at the pang in my chest. Iris is beautiful with curves that accentuate her small waist and thighs that are strong enough to crack my head if I dare put my face between them. Her adorable messy hair she keeps in a top bun and the almost too small worn-out clothes she wore when I last saw her, stir something inside me. The shorts are a treat to see her in because it gives me a perfect view of her deliciously rounded bottom. At least one conversation would have been nice with her, my mind momentarily laments again, and I shift uncomfortably in my seat with how tight my briefs are becoming at the image I conjured up.

If I must pick a feature, I'd say her hazel eyes are probably the most heavenly of them all. I couldn't look away from them the moment they caught me. They suck me right in and I don't mind it at all. My wolf, Zeus, whines inside as my thoughts reel inside like a movie at a drive through. Zeus wants to see her again and meet her wolf. Trust me Zeus, I want to see her too. I remind him.

The swing comes to a full stop. The wind, now gentle and wispy, picks up a few leaves and whisks them away before me in a small twirl. I smile at how carefree it all seems and wish I could be as such. Carefree without all this confusion in my heart. Uncomplicated. Un-phased. Instead, witnessing the whimsical nature only makes my heart heavier than before.

Tires rolling on gravel reach my ears followed by doors slamming shut and giggles. Martha and my mother are back from their date, and it sours my mood further. I guess it's good they arrive now to break up my thoughts because I was depressing myself further. What I thought would be a moment of clearing my mind on the swing, ends up being a session of self-deprecation and pity. This needs to stop because it is only doing more harm than good. For the first time, the swing failed to tame this old man.

I hop off the swing and drag my feet around to the front of the house only to find my mother's tongue down

Martha's throat. My mother's hands are cupping Martha face as she slides her arms around my mother's waist and pulls her in close to her body. I truly do not know how to feel whenever I see the intimacy between the two. They are moving too fast despite how natural it seems for them.

I barely find out about her and my father's escapades with Atlas' parents and here she is flaunting it…. everywhere…all the time. For all to see. It may have been a while for her but it's fresh for me. I clench my fist, anger cracking at my knuckles. I don't want to watch them necking but I won't dare say anything either. Stomping right by them, I slam the front door behind me as I make my way into the house. The seesaw of emotions weighing on either side of me between Iris and my mother teeters violently. My chest tightens. How can my mother not care about father's memory? I know my mother said that they were all together at one point, but things have changed.

Everything I remember, all I know, is her and my dad. Just them. No one else. No third or fourth person. Now, I have to accept that it was four of them this whole time. It's one thing to hear my mom talk about it but to see it, to see her with Martha so eager and intimate, shakes me. It's now real and it feels like a betrayal to my father's memory. I continue stomping up to my room not caring how loud I am in the process and throw myself in bed.

Tantrum much? Zeus echoes in my mind.

Shut up! I mentally retaliate. I know how I am acting or mentally sound, but I don't care.

∗∗∗

Tossing in my bed, I wipe the sweat from my brow. The sheets tangle around my legs as I continue to find a new position because everything is uncomfortable. I feel like someone knocked down all the books from my mental library and I must carefully pick each one up and put them back where they belong. All I want is Iris and fuck everything else. I want my chance at a happy ending too. Even though I thought I was fine without it and bragged to Cassius about remaining alone, I realized that I simply did not want to admit the truth. But I want it. And I want her.

I punch my pillow over and over to fluff it out. Angry, frustrated with myself, sad, confused, and... the loneliness I am feeling, I direct it at my poor pillow, "When is it my turn to be happy?" I whisper into the quiet of my room before I drift to sleep.

＊

The morning sun shining into the room is melting the top half of my face. With the window being directly behind my bed, the open curtains allow the sun to shower me with warmth. During the summer it is especially annoying if I forget to turn on the air conditioner. I end up cooking for myself in the mornings. The sounds of people talking and laughing downstairs carry into my room and chase away the silence.

My chest vibrates in a deep growl matching the eye roll I learned from the little wolf that visits now and then with her parents. I stretch in my bed and try to release the tightness in my muscles along with the sleep that is lingering in my body. For the first time, my bed feels un-comfortable, but I can't stay in this slump hiding in my covers like a moody teenager that didn't get his way. Although, I'd much rather do that right now than face people.

My heavy feet touch the cold wooden floor and stand firm as I will my body to go to the bathroom. The reflection in the mirror mocks me with a face that is haggard. The wrinkles on my face are more prominent along with the dryness of my lips and the dull complexion that complements the dark circles. I stick out my tongue at the unrecognizable version of me and undress for my shower. The water starts cold at first and my toes lift away from the tub as the water pools towards my feet. Little by little the steam begins to build as the water turns hot.

With one foot first, I step into the shower and allow my skin to adjust to the temperature before I submerge my body completely. Each drop washes away my sleep which sits crusted on my eye's lids and embedded in my bones. It is exactly what I need to change my mood and recharge my mind.

Lathering up, I scrub myself with my blue loofah and work through every inch of my skin. From my head to my toes, I work every inch of me, finding every nook and cranny of my aching body. I melt and relax just a bit more with each scrub and rinse away the residual of last night.

Drying off with the gray towel I recently bought, I do a little shimmy with it on my back before tying it off around my waist. Drop-lets of water make a trail as I leave the bathroom and walk over to my closet with my wet hair. The walk-in is neatly lined on the right with my shirts on the bottom row and suits at the top. To my left I have wooden shelves with my jeans, sweats, and shorts folded neatly on one row while the other shelves have a few of my dress shoes, sneakers, and work boots. Towards the back of the closet, I have a cabinet that encloses my neatly folded ties and arranged accessories.

For today, I want to keep my attire casual and pull out a light gray short-sleeve tee and a light pair of jeans. I roll up the hem of the sleeves a little and throw on a black belt. The shirt remains partially tucked in front and I finish off the look with black combat boots.

I make my way downstairs and of course, Martha and my mother are chatting away and eating sandwiches. I guess she slept over, I think to myself and sigh at how much my thoughts are annoying me.

"Good afternoon son."

"Good mor-afternoon mom...Martha," I furrow my brows but add Martha's name to my greeting to avoid the glare I will no doubt receive if I ignore Martha's presence.

I mumble to myself how tired I already am without looking at them but instead looking at the clock on the wall as it ticks onto the hour and confirms, it is indeed the afternoon. Guess I slept longer than I intended to and there is much to do for the day. Although, I can't say much of it will get done if I don't clear my mind. One of them says something to me but the question barely filters into my ears, and I grunt in response.

Tantrums again? Zeus snickers at me from the back of my mind.

Mind your business, I snap but Zeus laughs, infuriating me even more.

"Have you spoken to Iris yet?" Just the sound of her name is enough to take the edge off my building mood, but I grunt in response to the voice that said it. "What did she say?" Martha insists. I slam the fridge shut causing both to jump in their seat. The contents of the refrigerator rattle and I am sure something inside fell.

"She ran away!" I shout, truly not intending to. I leave the kitchen and grab my keys from the tray by the door. I will find my breakfast elsewhere because being at home is not it. My anger once again rears its ugly head, and I am the only one to blame. My emotions are nowhere near being under control and the last thing I want is to let it out on anyone. I see easily I am allowing myself to be triggered and I hate it.

The only thing I can do is remove myself from the situation and drive away. I look in the rear-view mirror as I slam my door closed, spotting my mom by the house entrance. The pain in my chest grows tighter at the sight of my mother crying and Martha hugging her from behind. It is not that I said anything insulting but I also never lash out like that toward my mother. I throw the vehicle into drive and watch as they grow smaller behind me. There's no doubt that I want to be happy for my mom, I do, but I need to get myself straight before I can see her with someone else that isn't my father.

It's selfish, I realize that, but I can't help how I feel. It is what it is and this whole thing with Iris just has me on edge. Both situations are playing off each other and I feel like I will fall no matter which side tips over. If I hadn't met Iris yet, then maybe my mom's situation wouldn't be as tough to deal with but when is life ever that easy?

Moments later, I pull into a diner and order the breakfast special with a large coffee. Emphasis on large. The diner is small and near the outskirts of town. Its food is better than most and the place is family owned. The vibes are always welcoming, and it is what drew me in since day one. The furniture is old, and the leather seats are cracking from age. The tabletops are a bit newer, and the floors were recently re-done but it still doesn't take away from the feel the place gives off. Even with the few remodeled touches, the history is still well-established. The hanging pictures of family, past celebrity signatures, and the old clock that stopped working ages ago add to the homey vibes that you can feel in your soul. It is like visiting grandma's house on a Sunday morning.

"Coming right up, big guy," Jodi taps my shoulder with her notepad and walks away after I rattled off my usual order. She is one of the more mature ladies who works the morning shift. She is the sister of the owner's son's wife. The eldest son now runs the place since his father is too old to work. Being in his late eighties, the owner only comes around to hanging out by the bar from time to time. Unfortunately, his arthritis ended up becoming too painful for him to keep up with the demands of the diner.

Off Jodi goes humming the same tune that seems to stay resident in her mind. The longest earworm I ever heard. I hum the same tune to myself with a smile. After hearing the tune so much, I learned her song and made a habit of sitting at the same table. It is another one of my safe havens when I want to get away from it all. Because of this, Jodi has watched me grow up and knows just about everything short of me not being human. I doubt she would mind and sometimes I think she knows but I wouldn't dare be the first to say it out loud unless I had to.

My food arrives and Jodi sits across from me locking her wrinkled fingers together, "so what's troubling you son." I look at her and ponder for a bit. I can't tell her about mate bonds, so, I guess my mother, it is.

"My mom is dating again, and I can't accept it. Even though dad died a while ago, I still can't accept someone else with my mother. It almost feels like she is betraying his memory. The woman is a good person and treats my mom well but...." I stuff food into my mouth before I end up saying too much and out myself as a wolf.

"Is she happy?" Jodi simply asks.

I stop chewing and look her in the eye. The answer is there, and she knows but still waits for me to respond, "Yes, it seems so."

"Listen son, I understand how you feel but you need to see it from her perspective. She is probably lonely. She won't have many years left compared to you. I remember clearly when you first came here after your father passed away. I remember how distraught and alone you felt. Imagine your mother. She was hurting because she lost her husband and the father of her children. She isn't betraying your father's memory. I'm sure he would want her happy after all this time, especially if the lady is treating her right. Wouldn't you want a warm bed after being cold for so long?" Jodi's name is called out by one of the cooks to pick up an order for another table.

Jodi gets up and offers me a smile before tending to her other tables. She is right. Who wouldn't want a warm bed. Look at me now, for example. I have been alone for thirty years basically and after one sniff of Iris, she is all I crave. I can't imagine how it is for my mother who has already had Martha in her arms only to lose her and find her again. They aren't even mates and yet they love each other as if they were. Jodi returns to her seat.

"Listen to me Kristofer. You are a good kid, but you are al-so a grown man and the head of the household. Think long and hard about why you are reacting like this and truly ask yourself if it is your mother, you are angry about, or something else. There is something you are not telling me and that's okay but do not give Cecile the cold shoulder out of selfishness. You hear me?" Jodi lifts her brow waiting for a response while pointing her finger at me.

"Yes, ma'am." I reply.

"Good, now eat up." Jodi stands up again and gives my shoulder a squeeze imbuing comfort and a warning to do better.

It is true that mom grieved long enough and deserves to be happy. I need to accept that aside from being my mother she is her own person. Maybe I'm just projecting my own anger on her since I can't be with Iris. Seeing her happiness while I can't have my own could very well be the trigger. Yet knowing the truth of my feelings doesn't make it easier to control. This just makes me feel more like a prick.

My plate is practically clean as I mindlessly eat while lost in my thoughts. Finishing my breakfast with the

The Silver Lining

last gulp of coffee, I leave a tip for Jodi tucked under the mug. She waves goodbye and I return her warm smile. She must think I am such a mama's boy, but her deductive skills are impressive. Back in the truck, I sit to let the vehicle warm up before I make my way back home.

Authors Other Works

1. Color Me, Sugar- Now Available

2. Nothing Stays Buried (Lunar River Series Book 2)

3. Safe Word Lobo (Lunar River Series book 3) - Coming soon

For the latest news and updates, follow the authors social media at:
Instagram: @_LCONCEPCION
Threads @_LCONCEPCION